TWO COMPLETE ACTION WESTERNS AT A FRACTION OF THE PRICE!

TRAIL TO HIGH PINE

The grass and timbers were dry and water scarce. The High Pine country of Montana was like a tinderbox.

Dab Jones rode to the crest of the hill and watched a thin column of smoke burst into red flames as the farmhouse turned into an inferno. He raced down the valley and looked beyond the next crest and saw another thin column of smoke...

Suddenly he was knocked out of the saddle and just before blacked out he thought—range war!

WEST OF THE BARBWIRE

Guns and tough riders lurked everywhere on the Sagebrush range, and Ric Nelson's flock of Eastern sodbusters was in bad trouble. As the lawyer who had deeded their new land to them, Nelson had to get them there safely. But cattle baron Pete Brookhaven wanted their range and would spill blood to get it.

Nelson had no choice. He had to lead his wagons into Sagebrush territory—and into the gunsights of deadly killers...

**BY THE TWO-TIME
SPUR AWARD WINNER
LEE FLOREN**

Other *Leisure Books* by Lee Floren:

Triple Western

RENEGADE RIFLES/BUCKSKIN CHALLENGE/GUN QUICK

Double Westerns

**NORTH TO POWDER RIVER/THE GRINGO
SADDLES NORTH/GAMBLER WITH A GUN
GAMBLER'S GUNS/BOOTHILL BRAND
WYOMING GUN LAW/FIGHTING RAMROD**

LEE FLOREN
TRAIL TO HIGH PINE/WEST OF THE BARBWIRE

LEISURE BOOKS   NEW YORK CITY

A LEISURE BOOK®

November 1991

Published by

Dorchester Publishing Co., Inc.
276 Fifth Avenue
New York, NY 10001

TRAIL TO HIGH PINE Copyright ©MCMLVI by Arcadia House
WEST OF THE BARBWIRE Copyright ©MCMLXVII by Lee Floren

All rights reserved. No part of this book may be reproduced or transmitted in any form or by any electronic or mechanical means, including photocopying, recording or by any information storage and retrieval system, without the written permission of the Publisher, except where permitted by law.

The name "Leisure Books" and the stylized "L" with design are trademarks of Dorchester Publishing Co., Inc.

Printed in the United States of America.

TRAIL TO HIGH PINE

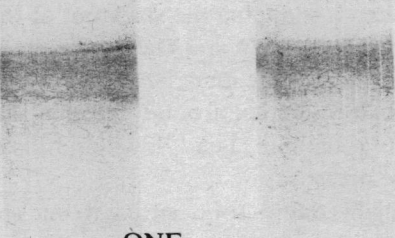

ONE

Young Dabney Jones was mad. So, for that matter, was the bogged-down cow, there in the bog hole. Dab swung into saddle, and he was muddy and wet and cold. He had waded out, catch-rope in hand, and he had stood knee-deep in the slimy ooze, while he had worked the lasso through the mud under the cow's belly. Then he had brought the noose up on the nighside of the critter and had made his tie around the cow's barrel. Now, swinging up on his big buckskin gelding, Dab was ready to pull the cow out of the mud.

Blue mud clung to Dab's levis. The water, being spring-fed, had been cold. Before wading into the bog he had taken off his boots and socks. Now he rode barefooted on his oxbow stirrups. His pants legs dripped dirty water. He took his dallies around the flat horn of the Miles City saddle and grinned angrily back at the cow who lay deep in the mud shaking her long wicked horns.

"Time you left the bog, bossy," he said. "Come on, pony; hit the end of this twine . . ."

With the free end of the catch-rope Dab Jones slapped the buckskin across his broad rump, and the big horse lunged ahead, snapping the slack out of the lasso. He was wise to this chore. He and Dab had pulled more than one ornery cow out of the mud. The rope lost its slack, the cow bawled as it tightened around her, and then the buckskin was pulling her free, head down and his saddle creaking under the pressure.

Holding his dallies solid, sitting to one side of his saddle, Dab watched the cow leave the bog, sliding on her side in the ooze. She was mad and she would want to fight, he figured; she had tried to hook him with her horns while he had worked at putting the rope around her. Her calf was in the brush, watching the antics of his irate mother; he bawled to the cow but the cow, busy fighting to gain her feet, did not bawl back.

The buckskin dragged her to dry ground and Dab reined in, saying, "Good work, Buck," and the cow, head down, charged him. The buckskin, although tired, was still nimble; he jumped to one side and the cow went on past him, head down. She hit the end of the rope and this threw her. But as she rolled over, the rope broke at the knot, there on her backbone. This freed her and she started toward her calf, mud and water dripping off her belly.

Dab said, "So long, bossy."

He started to coil his broken catch-rope. He had expected the rope to break any time now; it was old and he used it only as a bog-rope. He took his eyes off the cow . . . and there he made a mistake.

The next thing he knew, something travelling about a hundred miles an hour—or so it seemed—slammed into the buckskin from the rear, making the big horse lunge ahead, almost throwing Dab Jones, for he had been sitting loose in the saddle. Dab realized then that the cow, her fight not gone, had pivoted and had smashed into the buckskin, head down.

The buckskin jumped and the cow went past him, the power gone from her lungs. Dab glanced down at the horse's rump and saw that the horns had not cut him—one horn, in sliding past him, had hooked loose some hair, but had not cut the skin. Then, without warning, the buckskin stumbled over a rock and went rolling end over end. Dabney Jones hit the dust belly down.

He skidded, tearing his shirt. Behind him the buckskin scrambled to his feet, saddle empty, stirrups swinging. Dab got to his feet, and then the cow, seeing him unprotected, rushed him, head down.

What had been a simple job had suddenly turned into a dangerous task. Dab Jones silently cursed his luck. He was not thinking too clearly today, for yesterday he and his Mexican partner, squat Gordo Alvarez, had celebrated too much and too unwisely down in the nearest cowtown, Beaverton, Montana.

Because of this celebration, both Dab and Gordo had been put in the calaboose, and Dab's uncle, frosty old Jim Jones, had had to bail out his nephew and his nephew's best friend.

Old Jim had come down the cell aisle, mad as a wet hen, and all five-foot-four inches of the old cowman had expressed belligerency and anger when he had stationed himself in front of the cell holding Dab and Gordo Alvarez.

"So you two finally got throwed in the jug, huh?" the

cowman had asked, his voice heavy with anger.

"Sure looks that way," Dab had said.

"We are een here," the Mexican had said.

Then Jim Jones had exploded.

After he got through swearing he got to the meat of the discussion. "Ain't I got enough trouble, you stupid ox, without havin' to bail you out? Here you are in the county clink, you an' this fat Mexican side-kick of yours! Dab, you got to help me, not hinder me, son. Them nesters is crowdin' in an' takin' our grass an' our water—we should be fightin' them, not scrapping with John Barleycorn! I'm needed every minute out to the ranch, and here about midnight last night this scissorbill sheriff Pat O'Mahoney rides out, big as life an' twice as full of gall, an' he informs me you two is incarcerated in this jug!"

"You feel that way about us and I'd just as soon you never went our bail," Dab Jones had said, his own temper starting to bubble.

Gordo Alvarez had sighed, had walked over and sat on the cot, and had said, his voice heavy, "Well, I think like Dab does, *tambien, Tio* Jeem." Jim Jones did not see one dark eye come down and wink at Dab. "We stay here the rest of our lives, no, Dab?"

"Sure," Dab had said.

Old Jim had gone off on a tangent again, and for a moment he was speechless with rage. Finally words spurted out of him.

"You'll stay in jail—like heck you will, you two devils! I need every hand on my payroll out the ranch; you'd do me no good settin' here an' playin' cards at the county's expense." Dawn had washed in the small window and had shown the old cowman's wrinkled, weather-stained face. Dab watched his uncle turn and speak to the sheriff who had come in from his office. "Lawman, how much bail is needed to get these two devils out of your hoosegrow?"

Sheriff Pat O'Mahoney had shifted his cud of eating tobacco and had scowled. He had heard old Jim call him a *scissorbill*, and in his opinion the office of sheriff demanded respect.

"I ain't the justice of the peace, Jim."

"What do you mean by that, Sheriff?"

The cud had sought the other side of the lawman's mouth, prodded there by the man's tongue.

"They got to stand preliminary trial in front of the j.p., Jim Jones. I can't jes' turn the two loose. They got a charge against them."

"What is this charge?"

"They broke up some furniture in the Saddle Back Saloon—"

The lawman never got to finish his sentence. A wild snort from the arrogant old cowman had cut him short.

"Furniture! In the Saddle Back! Lord almighty, that *is* a joke, O'Mahoney! They ain't no furniture in thet dump!"

"They busted up five chairs. They wrecked two card tables."

Jim Jones said, "That ain't furniture—that's jes' ol' junk. But I'll see the owner and pay for it. What else did the two do?"

Dab Jones had listened, hands on the bars. Gordo had remained seated on the steel cot, head in his hands.

Gordo's head was not too steady. Neither, for that matter, was the head of Dabney Jones.

Dab didn't remember wrecking the furniture in the Saddle Back. He had a dim, hazy recollection of riding his bronc through some building, but right now he did not know which building it had been.

"Well, they got on their cayuses and started to ride through the Mercantile. Dab spurred his bronc into the store, but the Mexican only got the head of his horse inside the door, and the clerk hit the horse with a hunk of lead pipe between the ears and knocked him out, jammin' him in the door."

"Jammin' who? The hoss or Gordo?"

"Both of them."

"No wonder my leg she hurt me," Gordo said. "I must have skinned him on the door. Did you get my horse out of the door, Mr. Lawmans?"

The sheriff and a wrecking crew had had to tear out part of the doorway in the store to free the horse, which got wedged against the jamb. This had pretty much wrecked the door, the sheriff related. Dab had ridden out the back and had intended to ride back in the front door but, with Gordo and his bronc piled up in the doorway, that had been impossible.

Old Jim had said, "I'll see Charlie and settle for the damage done to the Merc. I'll settle things in the Saddle Back, too. Then I'll look up the j.p. and get you two wild young ones outa this steel corral."

"I'm happy here," Dab had said. "Except my head . . . it aches."

"I like it here," Gordo said.

"You two'll git outa there and go to work," the cowman had said, and had stumped away, back as straight as a lodgepole pine tree.

Dab had looked at Gordo. "Unc was mad," he had said.

The Mexican had assumed a look of stunned disbelief.

"Why he mad? We no do nothings."

"Nothing at all," Dab had said.

Dab leaped to his right; the cow thundered past him. His head ached as if a Sioux buck were in it beating his tomtom. Dab was only twenty. Gordo was twenty-five, or so he figured; he couldn't count too high, Dab knew. Dab Jones had been on his uncle's Double J outfit for a little over a year. And it seemed to him that his Uncle Jim rode him with long spurs every time he got a chance.

"He will get us out," Gordo said. "He is the man of influence around this town—the old cowmans type—"

"I don't want no favours from that ol' billy goat," Dab had growled. "He rides me with long spurs every time he gets a chance."

"That ees because he likes you."

Dab had glared at the fat Mexican. "Likes me? You must be chewin' loco weed or smokin' marijuana. A man doesn't mistreat somebody he likes."

But Gordo had only shrugged.

"Jeem is all right," the Mexican had said. "That is just his way, Dabney boy. These farmers—these sodbusters—they got him with his back to the wall. He has worked hard—year after year—to make his ranch a big one, like it is at last. He whipped the Sioux and the Blackfoots and he hung the cow-thieves and he fought with his fist and his gun . . . and now the pum'kin rollers, they build the fence and plough up the sod, and his cattle, if this keeps on, they have no grass, *no es verdad*?"

"That's right," Dab had said soberly. "And it is too bad, too. You know, they must put croton oil in that licker at the Saddle Back. Otherwise, I'd never feel like this, just because of gettin' drunk."

Within an hour, old Jim Jones stomped back, a paper in his hand. The sheriff read this and unlocked the cell and said, "No more free meals for you buckos," and Gordo Alvarez and Dab Jones were free men, standing beside Jim Jones in the cell aisle.

"Almost mortgaged my soul to get you two out," the old cowman had grunted.

"You ain't got no soul," Dab had muttered.

Jim had stared at him, eyes sharp. "My ears ain't what they used to be . . . What did you say, nephew?"

"I said, *Thanks, Unc*."

"Oh."

So they mounted their horses and rode out of Beaverton, the cowtown that was the county seat and the trading-post and post-office for this gigantic area of northern Montana.

They rode for a mile or so without speaking, only the hoofs of their horses making any noise.

Finally Gordo said, "I wonder if the head on my horse she aches, too? He got hit with the lead pipe and knocked cold."

"I got some information for you two," Jim Jones had

Trail to High Pine 13

growled.

Dab had not looked at his uncle. But he had winced openly, and Jim Jones had seen this, and anger had spread across his leathery face.

The old cowman had clipped his words. "I should fire you both."

"Why don't you?" Dab had asked. "I'd rather get fired than lectured, Jim. Give us both our walkin' papers."

"Fire you, heck! Both of you is workin' for the Double J. And what is more, you're goin' to work for me until I take the starch and fire out of both you, my nephew mostly."

"You wouldn't like me meek and submissive," Dab said.

"Forgit such talk. Some day you'll own this outfit, Dab boy. Here is your punishment, so stop talkin' an' lissen."

Dab had looked at Gordo. "Bet we have to stand in the corner of the bunkhouse when we get home?"

"No, we get the mouth washed with soap, I think."

"Can that talk, too." Jim Jones was all authority. "You two ride the bog holes for two months or until snow comes, whichever date comes sooner. You'll ride the bog holes, stay in a line camp, and not get to town once until two months is gone, or snow flies."

"Terrible," Dab had said.

"He is the monster," Gordo had said.

Old Jim had tugged on his jaw and had glared at his nephew. "I'm thinkin' of your old pappy, Dab, my good brother. He sent you out to me to make a man outa you, and I'll make a man outa you or kill you in the attempt . . . You two hole up out on Wine Crick . . . in the line camp there. You're not free yet, you know. You're out on bail until the fall term of court, and if you step outa bounds one step, I can put you back into jail, savvy?"

"Good idea," Dab said. "Then we couldn't have you lecturin' us all the time. Maybe your lawyer can get the charges dismissed. You can take our wages for the next two months and apply them against the damages we did. If they ain't enough to cover it, take the third month's wages."

"That's not a new idea to me," his uncle had said. "I figgered on doing just that, Dabney."

"Gracias," Gordo had murmured.

Dab had loped away then, with Gordo following.

Riding the bog holes was the worst job on the Double J, not to mention the dirtiest—both figuratively and literally. Cowpunchers hated pulling cows and bulls and steers and calves out of the bog holes. A couple of times riders had drawn their wages and had ridden off the big ranch before agreeing to ride bog holes. And now Dab and his partner were stuck with the job for two months or until snow came. It was September. Well, a sudden early fall snowstorm might shorten their sentence, at that.

Possible, but not probable, Dab figured. Because of the drought water was scarce, and the waterholes back in the hills were for the most part dry. Therefore cattle came to the valley for water and promptly waded out too far in their haste to drink, and then got bogged down, as this ringy cow had been when Dab had found her a half-hour before, only her back and head above the slimy blue ooze.

Riding bog and pulling cows out of bog—well, it was a job without end, and with no thanks, either. A man was always muddy and wet from wading out into the cattails and other rushes to put a rope around an ornery critter that had waded out too far and got stuck in the mud.

Old Jim had sure given them the short end of the stick, Dab reasoned as the cow whirled and charged him again. The cow was really enjoying herself. She had a man on foot, not in a saddle; the man was barefooted and the ground was strewn with sharp stones. Dab did the only thing he could do—he threw himself on the ground, belly down. The cow could not hook him, for she could not get her horns low enough. She sailed over him and kicked as she cleared him, but he kept his head down; he had been expecting the kick. She had rammed her snout into him, though.

The force of her charge made her slow to turn, and this gave Dab his chance. He ran as fast as he could, bare feet hitting rocks, and he slammed himself into the saddle on the buckskin just as the cow successfully completed the turn, and came roaring in again.

Dab grabbed his lasso, doubled it and rode in, whamming down savagely at the cow with the hard-twist rope. Just at this moment, much to Dab Jones' surprise another rope came into play, but this was not being used as a quirt to beat the mad cow. This rope came in like a noose. The loop missed the cow's horns, for the roper used a loop far too big; the cow jumped into the noose and it settled around her, one leg in the loop, the remainder of the noose around her barrel.

Gordo had been riding the foothills, and Dab at first figured his Mexican partner had seen him and the cow going around and around and had ridden in to rope the cow and throw her. But common sense quickly told him that his sidekick would never be guilty of using a loop that big. Only a green hand at roping would ever let go of a length of rope like that.

Dab glanced up. The rider rode a pinto—a gaudy bay and grey horse. At this moment, the cow hit the end of the rope—she slammed into it with all her weight, and she was not a small cow, either.

After that, there was a wild mix-up of cow, thrown horse, and thrown rider. For the cow hit at a tangent that caught the pinto off-balance. The cow went tail over tin cup and the pinto went to his knees. The latigo strap on the saddle snapped and the cow lurched to her feet to run away, dragging the rope and the saddle, leaving the pinto with only the bridle, and with the saddle blanket lying on a clump of greasewood.

The pinto scrambled to his feet. The rider hung to the saddle for a few feet, then lost his grip on the horn, and then the rider was sitting there in the dust, without his horse. And the cow went roaring over a hill, dragging the saddle behind her.

TWO

Dab rode over to where the stranger sat on the ground and then, for the first time, he saw the rider was not a man—the rider was a young woman. He dismounted and stood looking down at her, and she glared up at him. He judged her to be about eighteen or thereabouts.

She had lost her hat, of course. Dust and sticks and dirt were in her blonde hair. Her blue man's shirt was torn. She wore a split buckskin riding skirt so she could ride a man's saddle instead of a side-saddle.

Her blue eyes were leaping with fire. "You stupid Double J jackass," she stormed. "You sure are a bum cowboy!"

Dab kept on smiling, wondering all the time who she was. He asked innocently, "Why cuss me out, Miss?"

One hand went up and tried to restore her hair into some semblance of order.

"If it hadn't been for you, I'd never have roped that crazy cow, and if I hadn't roped the cow, I'd not be here on the ground—my horse over there and my saddle going over the hill!"

"The thing that puzzles me," confessed Dab Jones, "is how you got here in the first place. I never seen you until you roped the cow."

"I was out for a ride on Patches. I came over the hill and that cow was killing you, so I roped her. What kind of a cowboy are you, anyway—letting an old cow get the best of you like that?"

Dab Jones was starting to get angry. She was making fun of his riding and his ability as a cowhand, and that was too much.

"You ain't much to harp about me bein' a bum cowboy, Miss. If you was so good at ropin', you'd not have used a loop you could have caught a barn in."

"Don't make fun of my roping, you grinning ape! I've only been riding and roping a couple of months!" She squinted up at him suddenly, her blue eyes still icy. "Seems as though I recognize you. . . . Ain't you the nephew of Jim Jones, and ain't your handle Dabney Jones?"

"Can't help it if I got thet name when I was hatched, Miss. Are you a nester, ma'am?"

"Yes, I'm a nester—as you call us farmers—and what do you aim to do about it, please?" Her voice dripped sarcasm.

Dab shrugged. She sure was frosty chicken. He liked them when they could and would talk back.

"What is your name, ma'am?" he asked.

"Lincoln. Martha Lincoln." Some of the anger was leaving her pretty eyes. "And don't laugh, Dab Jones. Sure, I know just what you're going to say next."

"And what is that, smarty?"

Trail to High Pine

"I've heard it a hundred times, I'll bet. Martha's last name was not Lincoln—it was Washington. Don't you know your history? Blah, blah, blah. . . ."

Dab Jones smiled. "That was the way my history book read," he had to admit. "Of course, I didn't ride herd over the book until it ended—teacher booted me out for not shavin' in the fifth grade—so maybe before it ended Martha did change her name to Lincoln, at that. But that Martha would be lots older than you, Miss Lincoln."

She tried to stand, then sank down with a grimace, a gasp of pain breaking from her lips.

"Oh, my ankle."

Dab said, "Is it broken—which one?"

She sat there and looked at the hill over which her saddle, rope and the Double J cow had disappeared.

"How am I going to get my outfit back?"

"I'll get the cow and saddle for you, Miss Lincoln." Dab was serious now; maybe her ankle was broken. "Let me help you to your feet. Your ankle might be just sprained and it might be hurt worse, too."

He got her arm around his shoulder and she hobbled a few paces, favouring her left foot, and then she sat on a rock. He looked at her face. Blood had drained away under the push of pain and sweat was on her forehead.

"I got to take off my boot—my left boot."

Dab said, "We'll cut the stitching, Miss Lincoln."

"No, I can't. We might cut the leather and it can't be sewed up again, and these are my only boots—"

"I'll buy you another pair. I'm the cause of you gettin' hurt."

"I don't want a cowman's money! I won't take a cent from old Jim Jones, after the way he has treated us farmers."

"It'll be out of my money, not my uncle's. But regardless of whose money it is, that boot should leave your foot. If your ankle swells fast, we'll have to cut the boot to ribbons—then it will be a total loss. I'll cut slow and only split the stitches on the side, and then you can have it sewed again by the cobbler down in Beaverton."

"All right. But be careful."

Dab got the flash-blade on his jackknife and slowly and carefully slit the seam, being careful to cut only the threads and not the leather.

"You sure helped me when you busted thet ringy cow," Dab lied.

"Somebody should have roped you like that yesterday down in Beaverton," she said. "Then you wouldn't have got as drunk as you did nor have done as much damage as you did."

"You heard about our party?"

"Party? Oh, sure. If one of us nesters did that we'd get thrown in jail and the sheriff would throw away the key!"

Dab grinned. By this time he had the boot free. Her ankle was beginning to swell very rapidly.

"Me an' Gordo sure had fun," he said.

"If that is your definition of fun, I want none of it."

"Nobody invited you, did they?"

"I was in town for supplies. You hollered and whooped so much the whole town rocked, I do believe."

"You can't scold me like this, Miss Lincoln. We ain't

married, you know."

"No, and we won't ever be, either."

Dab was gingerly feeling her ankle to see if it had any broken bones, and when he looked up his eyes were imploring.

"Old Jim really bawled me out this morning. He put me an' Gordo to riding this bog section until snow came or two months went by—and judging from the pain in my head, I don't care if two months ever go by or if snow ever comes. I am a sick, sick man."

Her blue eyes were on him. They were serious for a moment and then laughter ran across them, making them girlish and even prettier.

"Man alive, what a grand and glorious punishment. If you could only have seen yourself yesterday— Here, you, let go of my ankle. That hurts me."

Dab dropped her ankle and stood up. "Don't reckon no bones are busted," he said.

"Thanks, Doctor Jones."

Dab shook his head. "A cynical woman," he told the world.

He looked at Martha Lincoln.

She was bent over using her thumb as a prod to test the puffing around her ankle. Her pinto was trying to crop the short salt-grass but getting nowhere, because of the bit in his mouth.

Dab's buckskin had settled down for a nap, with one hip higher than the other as he dozed in the forenoon sun.

"I don't think it is broken," Martha said finally.

"Too purty to be busted."

She looked up at him with a slanting glance. "You're a great one," she said. She even smiled a little.

"You sure got a purty smile," Dab said.

"Oh, go on with such talk. Help me to my feet?"

"Sure."

She hobbled a short distance, testing her ankle. "I guess I only sprained it. I sure hit the ground hard. When I was a little girl I turned my ankle bad once. Sliding into third base, I believe."

"Where do you live?"

"About four miles east of here, close to Wishbone Springs."

Dab had a sudden thought. Old Jim Jones had cussed out some nesters and in particular he had talked about the farmers that had settled on Wishbone Springs, and now Dab knew they were the Lincolns. Dab didn't know just what to say or think. Old Jim was getting in bad with the farmers, and Dab figured the old cowman couldn't hold his range against the encroachments of the grangers. He was not too old, but he figured the farmers represented progress and he figured progress was something nobody—not even a cattle king—could hold back. But he had not told his uncle this. Had he mentioned this fact to Old Jim the old cowman would have busted a cinch, latigo strap and all.

"Two riders are coming," Martha said.

Dab turned and looked at the two men who had ridden over the opposite hill, the hill over which Martha's horse had not gone. Dab recognized one as Deputy Sheriff Miles Turner and the other was Will Martin, the land locator. Martin's job was to locate farmers on their homesteads.

He put his attention first on Deputy Sheriff Mike Turner. A squat and dark-complexioned man, this deputy sheriff. He was about fifty, Dab guessed. Turner filled his long-forked Miles City saddle and he wore a black stiff-brimmed Stetson that somehow seemed to fit his hawkish, dark face. Dab swung his gaze over to Land Locator Will Martin. He saw a thin man who wore a neat blue suit with the well-creased pants legs crammed into the tops of short justin boots, black and highly polished. Now Martin's dull eyes took in the situation and a thin smile came to his lips.

"Is this Double J man bothering you, Miss Lincoln?" the land locator asked silkily.

"Keep out of my affairs, Mr. Martin." Martha Lincoln's voice again held icicles. "I can take care of myself, thank you"

The land locator made his thin eyebrows rise slightly. "You jump to hasty ideas, young lady. Maybe this is my affair, you know. After all, my company put you farmers on this range and my company guarantees you complete protection."

"Thank you, but I don't need your protection, Mr. Martin."

Dab smiled at the girl's frigid tone. Will Martin saw this smile and evidently it angered him, for when he spoke his voice was somewhat harsh and the words were directed toward Dab Jones, not Martha Lincoln.

"Keep away from these farmers, Jones. They are here on this grass legally and they'll stay on their homesteads as long as they want to stay."

Dab didn't want any trouble. He had had enough trouble

the last twenty-four hours without looking for more with this land locator, even though there was no love lost between him and Will Martin.

"This is a purty girl," he joked, "and she'll be almighty hard to stay away from, Martin."

"You heard me, Jones."

The man's voice was openly insulting. Dab got the impression that Martin might want to cause him trouble and then blame him for starting a fight, for the land locator had the deputy sheriff with him, and Dab was out on bail.

"Did you hear me, Jones?"

Dab had held his anger long enough. Hot blood rushed to his head, driving away his splitting headache for a moment. Will Martin had his right hand lying on the fork of his polished saddle. Dab noticed that the man's braided quirt hung from the wrist on his hand, the rawhide band around the man's arm right above his hand. And the quirt was within reaching distance, too.

Dab grinned and grabbed the sixteen-plait rawhide quirt. At the same moment he whooped like a Blackfoot who had just stepped on a hot coal. With one boot, he kicked Martin's bronc in the belly; the horse jumped ahead. By this time, Dab Jones had both boots anchored, and he pulled with a sharp yank which loosened the land locator in saddle.

"Come in a hurry!" Dab yelled.

Boot heels digging, Dab held onto the quirt and Will Martin hollered something, making a grab for his saddlehorn, which he missed. Deputy Sheriff Turner was yelling something, trying to get his bronc around and drive

Trail to High Pine

him in between Dab and the land locator, but the deputy was too slow and too late.

For Dab, with another jerk, had pulled Will Martin from leather.

The land man did not have time to reach for the bone-handled gun that hung in the ornate holster with its hand-engraved surface. He came down on all fours, and Dab let go of the quirt. For some reason, Dab Jones sent a glance at Martha Lincoln, but to his surprise her face did not show horror or fear—rather, she wore a pleased expression.

Dab jerked his gaze back to Will Martin, but he had spent too much time looking at Martha Lincoln. Will Martin was as quick as a cougar, and he lunged forward and tackled Dab Jones around both knees.

Dab went sailing back and Martin landed on him. Dab could hear Deputy Sheriff Mike Turner bellowing like a bull being branded. Dab was not sure, but it seemed as though the deputy was encouraging Will Martin. Martin needed no encouragement, in Dab's estimation.

For Martin was hammering Dab around the head, and his knuckles were not soft. One of his fists hit Dab in the left eye. The blow was hard and it did his head no good. He realized he had to get Martin off him. He could not kick the man off, so he decided to roll. He went over and bunched on all fours and literally bucked the man off him. By the time Martin had got on his feet, Dab was also on his boots. Fists up, he was ready, and he spat blood.

"Come on, Martin!"

And Will Martin came.

Before it was over, Dab Jones knew he had really been in

a fight. Evidently Will Martin had done some boxing. Dab found this out to his sorrow when he led with a right. Martin crossed over it and knocked him down. Martin came in to kick and Dab rolled over, the boot missing him. When he got up, bells were ringing in his head.

The weight advantage was a few pounds in Dab's favour, so he moved in close to use this advantage. He got a hammerlock on Martin and, with his free hand, hit the man in the face twice, and felt the blood spurt out and hit his hand. Martin pounded his free hand into Dab's belly. Each time he landed squarely it was like a colt kicking Dab.

He heard Martha Lincoln hollering for Deputy Sheriff Turner to stop the fight. Dab pulled Martin around so he could watch Turner, who was still in his saddle. Six-shooter in one hand, reins in the other, Turner rode in, bulling his bronc forward, his short-gun raised. Dab saw the six-shooter come down, and he ducked; the blow caught him on a shoulder. It was a crushing, sickening blow and it broke his grip on Will Martin, who broke free and spun around and landed sitting down, blood on his thin face. The blow sent Dab to his knees and he knelt there, looking at Will Martin, who had his head down.

Martin said, "I've had enough . . . for now."

Martin didn't look up. He had both hands to his face. Dab got to his boots, looking at the deputy, who had reined in his horse and had his .45 on Dab Jones, the bore steady.

Turner's dark eyes were filled with anger and his thick lips spoke husky words. "You're under arrest, Jones!"

"What for?"

"You started that fight."

"Martin wanted to tangle horns, too. I just beat him to the draw." Dab Jones looked down at Martin. "Get on your pins, big boy, and we'll waltz around again a few times, huh?"

Will Martin looked up. Despite his split upper lip he tried to smile. "I'll sit this dance out, Jones," he said with difficulty. He got to his feet, almost fell down, his hands to his head. He regained his equilibrium and walked over to a boulder and leaned against it, head still in his hands.

"You're still under arrest," the deputy insisted.

"On what charge?"

"Disturbin' the peace. Pickin' a fight with Martin here, who is a law-abidin' citizen. You molested this girl."

"Dab Jones never molested me!" Martha Lincoln had hot irons in her eyes. "I was the one who molested him. I roped that cow of my own accord, and if I was so stupid I lost my outfit—well, that is my fault, not his. So just keep your big mouth shut, Deputy Sheriff!"

"You won't file a complaint against Jones?"

"Absolutely not!"

Dab grinned and said, "Good girl."

Will Martin spat, tested his jaw, and then brushed dust and sticks from his pants. He had a set of skinned knuckles. Deputy Sheriff Turner seemed undecided. Evidently he had hoped to be a hero in the eyes of two people— Martha Lincoln and Will Martin. He had failed with the girl.

"You got an open and shut case against Jones, Martin."

"What do you mean?"

"What do I mean? Why, he picked trouble with you—he made the first move. He jerked you from saddle. I'm takin' him back to Beaverton an' sinkin' him for good in the calaboose."

"You might be for that . . . but I'm not."

Turner studied the man. "Why not?"

"Use your brains, Deputy. We put Dab Jones here behind bars, it would be the same as the farmers putting him in jail, because I'm actually on the side of the farmers. You know what would happen?"

"Well, ol' Jim Jones wouldn't like it."

"You made an understatement there, Turner. Old Jim would do more than dislike it—he'd show some action. He'd take his riders and peel the jail off his nephew. Then he'd turn against us farmers. And we don't want bloodshed and death."

Turner rubbed his jaw; apparently this idea was new to him.

"This range will be ripped with gunfire from one end to the other," Martin continued, "Jim Jones is looking for an excuse to ride against us farmers with his hands. This would be the excuse."

Dab knew the land locator was correct. Turner chewed his Horseshoe, his jaws working thoughtfully.

"The Law can handle old Jim Jones," Turner said at length. "We can't favour cowmen over you farmers, you know."

"I swear out no warrant," the land locator said stubbornly. "I was wrong, too—you can handle your dukes, Jones."

"You ain't no slouch yourself," Dab conceded.

Grudgingly the deputy surrendered. "All right." He

shrugged and holstered his gun. "I can't arrest him unless somebody files a complaint." He sent a dark glance at Dab. "You got off lucky, Jones."

"I don't think so."

"Why not?"

"I'm the guy with the black eye, not you."

Martha Lincoln said, "Now that we have our arms all around each other, why doesn't somebody help me on my horse and I'll go out and look for my catch-rope and saddle"

"Where is your saddle?" Will Martin asked.

"On the end of my lasso. On the other end is a Double J cow. You help me on my horse and I'll tell you about it."

"With pleasure."

"I'll help her," Dab said.

But already Will Martin had beat him to it. He cradled the girl's bare foot in his hands and boosted her onto her horse; then he mounted his own bronc. Martha turned her horse and said, "Thanks for the help, Mr. Jones. Some day I hope I can learn to rope."

"So do I," Dab said.

Turner turned his horse and said, "Let's get out of here," and the three loped away with Martha in the lead. Dab rubbed his forehead and grimaced. His head still ached.

Gordo came riding out of the brush.

Dab Jones explained the situation to his obese partner.

"So this deputy he wants to put you in jail again, no?"

"Yes," Dab said.

Dab was washing his face in the water at the point where the springs came out of the rocks.

"I have seen this Lincoln girl."

"Where at?"

"Down in Beaverton."

"She looks all right," Dab said.

Gordo said, "She ees the beautiful girl."

Dab wiped his face gingerly with his neck scarf. Will Martin had packed a set of steel fists. "Never figured a city man would be that hard to handle," he said. "He's strong and tough."

"Me, I do not understand this deputy sheriff, this Mike Turner."

Dab looked at his partner. He had known Gordo Alvarez for as far back as he could remember. They had been reared together down in Texas. Around Pecos, to be exact. There Dab's father ran a small hen-chicken spread. Dab and Gordo had been kind of reckless and had got into trouble, so Dab's father had sent his son north to Montana to be with old Jim Jones. Gordo had trailed along, of course. Between the two was a fine bond of understanding, built through years of association.

"He sure wanted to get me into his clink again," Dab Jones had to admit. "He wanted me to tangle with that land man, too. I reckon I did some bad moves, Gordo."

"Nothing new . . . for you."

"What has that deputy got as a stake in this farmer outfit, I wonder? The way he wanted to press charges against me shows he wanted to get himself in good with these hoemen, I figure."

"Me, I do not like him."

"Neither do I."

Trail to High Pine

"He has got his friends on some homesteads."

Dab Jones nodded. He had not been too long on this range, but the months he had spent here around Beaverton had given him lots of information. A man named Walt Jorgenson had filed on a homestead over on Willow Creek. Walt Jorgenson and Deputy Sheriff Mike Turner seemed to be very good friends. Located in a strategic position on Willow Creek, Walt Jorgenson could dam that stream and control a nice head of water for irrigation, cutting off the supply of the farmers below him on Willow Creek, Dab realized.

Yes, and another good friend of the deputy's was homesteading on Porcupine Creek. His name was Matt Smith. Dab shrugged and said, "But that means nothing, Gordo. Look at old Jim now. He has about thirty of his ex-cowboys homesteading land in the valley. When they have their deeds in a couple of years, they turn the land over to my uncle, and he has it legally. Cowmen are doing it all over the West, they tell me. They've run cattle for years on gover'ment land—land they did not own—and now, with these farmers comin' in each day, the cowmen have finally decided they have to get control of land, holdin' it through deeds and not the ol' squatter's rights idea, which I understand the courts have thrown out as illegal."

"You think Jim he will fight the farmers? I mean will he go to his guns against them, Dab?"

"Lord, I hope not. I'd hate to have to shoot Martha Lincoln." Dab was only joking, of course.

"You like her?"

Dab shrugged. "What man couldn't?"

Gordo was very serious. "This war she is coming, Dab. We'll be caught in the middle. Maybe we should go back to *Tejas*, no?"

"And go to jail?"

"Maybe by now we can go into Pecos and not get in the jail. Maybe by now they have forgot what we do. Maybe they'll be glad to see us."

Dab had to smile. "Down in Pecos is warrants waitin' to be served on two gents, one Gordo Alvarez and one Dabney Jones. Thet town marshal will serve them if he has to get off'n his death-bed, too. They want you for bustin' up property and axin' down the marshal's son with your pistol barrel. They want me for ridin' my Baldy hoss, steel shoes and all, over that bartender in the Lone Star. He swore out a complaint against me, and the charge reads *attempted murder*. Oh, no, Gordo, I don't ride south again. No more bars for me . . . if I can help it."

The fat man scowled and rubbed his jaw. "But I do not like this Turner hombre. He wants the trouble between us and the farmers. We stay here and soon the bullets they fly, and then the cold weather come. I was born where it is warm—I do not like the blizzards."

"If you head south, you ride alone."

"Because of the girl you just met?"

"Heck, no. A woman is just a woman, man. Well, we better make tracks, and report this to old Jim."

"He might be mad."

"I don't think so. First off, he don't like this Turner gent; second, he hates Martin's guts, what with Martin getting in these farmers."

"The sheriff—this O'Mahoney—he might come out to the Double J and talk to Jim about us, and we are out on bail. You should not have got in this fight, Dab."

"Too late now," Dab said.

THREE

They came to the home ranch about one that afternoon. The big Double J Ranch buildings were located on Wild Creek at the foot of Wild Butte, an igneous outcropping of black rock that lifted itself out of the hills to a height of about three thousand feet, making a landmark visible for miles. They swung down off the hills and found the wagon road that led to Beaverton and they followed this through the cottonwoods and box-elders that grew along the creek, which was now almost dry except for some water standing in potholes.

"Old Jim he will be mad at us," Gordo said.

"Do his blood pressure good."

Now the big ranch-house came into view. It was long and low and rambling, and the trees shaded it and wild morning glories climbed the rough logs. Because of the time of the day the morning glory flowers had wilted, but the green veins were bright against the weather-coloured logs. The crew, Dab figured, would be out on range; even old Jim might be out in saddle. Dab Jones was wrong. Old Jim Jones was at home, and he was very mad.

Trail to High Pine

That was because a mule had just kicked him.

For old Jim and the flunky were shoeing a pack mule in front of the blacksmith's shop. They had nailed the shoes to the mule's forefeet and they were now shoeing him on the hind hoofs. His left hind hoof had lashed out and had caught old Jim in the loose part of his shirt. The hoof had scraped the hide on the man's chest and had torn the shirt and had knocked the old cowpuncher down. He had got to his feet, hammer raised, ready to commit mayhem on the mule, and now the flunky was holding him, telling him that if he hit the mule with the hammer he would kill him, and for old Jim to calm down.

Dab and Gordo could not have ridden in at a worse time. For when the old cowman saw them, he forgot the mule and glared at them, hammer still in hand.

"Don't use that hammer on us," Dab joked.

But his uncle was not in a joking mood. "What the heck you two buckos doin' on the home ranch? You two is in Siberia in exile. I told you two to stay out on Wine Crick an' ride them bog holes. Now you get out there just as fast as them two old horses will take you, savvy?"

Dab winked at Gordo. Old Jim saw the wink and got even madder. Dab said, "We got news, my lovin' uncle."

"Bad news," Gordo said, and shook his head.

Old Jim studied them, lips quivering. His anger faded slowly.

"Oh, bad news, huh? Jes' lookin' at you two is bad news for me. What trouble are you hellions in now, Dabney?"

"I jes' tangled horns with thet land locator, Will Martin, out on Wine Crick."

Faded eyes touched Dab's face, noticing his black eye. "Seems to me you might have come out second best, too, lookin' at your mug. You must have been drunk again, seein' you couldn't whup thet town dude with his soft hands."

"He ain't soft," Dab said.

The mule was forgotten. He stood with one hip up and his head down, ears back. He seemed also to be listening to Dab's story. Dab told about the fight, his run-in with Deputy Sheriff Mike Turner, and about meeting the nester girl, Martha Lincoln.

"Turner wanted to put me in the clink again," Dab said.

"Good idea," his uncle snorted.

"We got a mule to shoe, remember," the flunky said.

"That we have," old Jim said.

So the old cowman and the flunky returned their attention to the mule. The shoe went on, the hoof was filed down to ensure a perfect fit, and the nails were driven in.

"Trim them nails off shorter, flunky," Jones ordered.

The flunky got the nail-clippers and went to work, down on his knees. Old Jim Jones took off his leather blacksmith apron. He hung it on the hook and looked up at his nephew and Gordo Alvarez, and his face was glum and solemn.

"What do you think of the deal, men?"

"That deputy sure wanted to jug me," Dab said. "He doesn't like me one bit. Not that I love him, either."

"He's a dirty son," the old cowman said.

"He'll head hell-for-leather into Beaverton and report this to Sheriff O'Mahoney," Dab said slowly. "He'll want the sheriff and the j.p. to pull back our bail and jug us again, or I'm way off my beat. He even wanted Miss Lincoln to press a charge against me, but it was no soap. She said she'd rid in to rope thet cow on her own hook and would suffer the consequences, which was right nice of her, I thought."

"How about Martin?"

"He wouldn't file a complaint, either. 'Fraid it might break the war between our outfit and the nesters wide open, he said. Wants no gun play."

"He's lookin' for trouble," Jim Jones said. "And by hades, I'll give 'em a snoot full, when and if the time gets ripe."

"Lord, Unc, don't fight them farmers. You can't win."

"You keep your advice to yourself. When I ask you for your opinion, then give it—but not until then, savvy?"

"I wish," Dab said, "you were sixty years younger."

"I'd be eight years old," Jim Jones said. "You're in your twenties. I guess you could whip a kid of eight, at that."

"Your age changes. Last week you were seventy-two."

"I felt I was seventy-two that day."

"Turner is after me," Dab said, "and I don't know why. I ain't never done nothin' to him."

Old Jim was smiling now. "I sure wish I could have seen you land a fistful of knuckles in the face of that land man, nephew. I've seen thet Lincoln heifer down in town. She's worth fightin' over."

"We didn't fight over her, though."

"Well, anyway, whatever you fought over, I hope you won." The old man washed his hands in the horse trough. "I'm goin' to ride over to the Lincoln farm and talk to thet gal and her mother."

"Why?" Dab asked.

"Just to make sure she won't file a complaint."

"She won't press a charge against me. She ain't got no grounds. I told you she said she wouldn't."

Old Jim shook his grizzled head. "Cain't tell a thing about a female, be it a human or a hoss or a cow. You go to the house and change clothes, Dab. They ain't much left to them you got on—your shirt is tore to ribbons. Then what do you aim to do?"

"Head out in the hills for a few days," Dab said. "There might be a warrant swore out, and the sheriff'll have a hard time findin' me to serve it. He'd have to catch me."

"And that she might be a chore," Gordo said.

"Good idea," Dab's uncle said. "Pack some grub with you. Have plenty of ca'tridges for both your pistols and rifles. Always remember there is chuck at our line-camps. Keep your eyes open and your ears pinned back and your big mouths shut. And if either of you get hold of a bottle—"

"We've quit drinking," Dab said.

"Since when?"

"Since I met Martha Lincoln."

The faded eyes turned to Gordo.

"I no drink no longer, too, since I met Martha," the fat rider said, shrugging.

"Hogwash, both of you!"

Dab spoke to the flunky. "Get fresh horses for us, huh? Throw our kaks on them while we change clothes and get some chuck."

"Sure thing, Dab."

Dab went to the house, where he changed clothes while

Gordo went to the mess hall. The cook was taking his afternoon nap, so the Mexican prepared a meal and it was a good one—fried eggs, bacon, beans. Dab felt better after changing clothes; his old clothing had been a muddy wreck. He admired his black eye in the mirror over the wash basin as they left the mess-hall.

"Sure a lulu," he said.

"Almost as beeg and as black as that one Curly West gave you at the dance on the Pecos, remember?"

"Remember? How could I forget? He hit me so hard he knocked me into next week. Wonder if he addled my brain? I do some queer things sometimes and have queer thoughts, and sometimes I heard meadowlarks singing in the winter time."

"We get the bullets and some canned grub, and we ride."

"Sure thing, *amigo*."

Soon, their saddle-bags loaded, they rode out of the Double J, both of them astraddle fresh horses—tough Montana cayuses that could travel long circles and still come in fresh.

Dab and his partner drifted east, heading for the foothills. When they came to the crest of the first high hill they looked back and saw a horseman, little more than a dot in the distance, going toward the Lincoln homestead, over by Wishbone Springs.

Dab said, "Old Jim, huh?"

"Sure."

Dab pushed back his old Stetson and ran a callused hand over his rope-coloured hair.

"I don't understand all I know about this, Gordo."

"You tell me what worries you and I will explain."

"Now why would old Jim be in such a rush to ride to the Lincoln homestead? He's too old for a girl as young as Martha."

"Sure, but did you ever see Martha's mama?"

"No, I ain't."

"Me, I see her once, down in Beaverton. She is the older edition of Martha. *Hombre mio*, she is beautiful, no?"

Dab glanced at his companion and let him keep on talking. Gordo used plenty of adjectives—both Spanish and English—while describing Mrs. Lincoln. Dab got the impression that Martha's mother was indeed a wonderful and beautiful middle-aged woman.

"Down in Beaverton—ol' Jim he see Martha's mother—and he stand there and gawk, and his eyes they were out so far you could knock them off with a stick, you could. I almost laughed."

"How old is she, would you say?"

"About forty-five, maybe a little more."

"But old Jim must be sixty, if he is a day."

"Not too old for the *señora*."

"What the heck you blabbin' about, Gordo? Martha's father would shoot old Jim to latigo straps if he came shinin' up to her mother."

"Martha she has no father, Dab. He is dead."

"That old devil of a uncle of mine. His eyes was burnin' like two brandin' fires, he was so anxious to head for Wishbone Springs. Well, let's mosey over toward Beaverton, huh?"

"Why?"

"Check up on the sheriff."

"Good idea."

They did not have to ride all the way to Beaverton to check up on Sheriff O'Mahoney. They were about five miles out of the cowtown when Gordo said, "I hear the hoofs coming this way."

They drew rein and Dab cocked his head. "Sure enough," he said.

They were riding along Beaver Creek, which was almost dry. Mosquitoes were thick and so was the brush, and they rode into the high buckbrush, there in the cottonwood trees. They dismounted and went down and stood at their broncs' heads and waited, peering through the underbrush. Within a few minutes three riders loped by, heading for the Double J.

One was a stocky man who filled his saddle—Deputy Sheriff Mike Turner. The other was a slim man who had a face that was black and blue, his upper lip cut—the land agent, Will Martin. And the third man, the one heading the group, was none other than Sheriff O'Mahoney.

The trio thundered by, dust rising from under their broncs' hoofs, and then they slanted around a bend, the brush hiding them. Dabney Jones and Gordo Alvarez waited until the sounds of the hoofs had died against the distance and again found their saddles.

Gordo sighed lustily. "They head for the ranch, Dab."

"Our hunch," said Dab, "was right."

"For once only, though."

"I wonder," said Dab, "if Martin finally did file a complaint and if them two lawmen are heading out to serve it on us?"

"On *us*? You mean on *you*?"

"They're riding for the ranch, though, and we were exiled to the bog holes."

"They no know that. They think maybe each night we come back to the ranch. So to the Double J they ride."

Dab sucked his cigarette for a moment in deep thought. "There is more to this than meets the eye," he told his partner. "And I don't believe Will Martin is at the bottom, either."

"Who is it then?"

"The deputy, Mike Turner."

Gordo watched him, his dark eyes blank. "He has friends on the homesteads. Turner is no farmer. She does not make the sense, no?"

"Got me stumped."

"Where we go now?"

"Still into Beaverton."

Gordo rubbed his hands together, reins between his palms. "We can get the drink there. Just one, though. Nobody they will bother us. The law is out of town looking for us."

FOUR

They loped into Beaverton big as life and twice as bold. Old man Smith's dog came barking out, nipping at the hind legs of Dab's horse, and Dab leaned low, catch-rope doubled, and by luck, caught the cur around the middle. The dog went up in the air and yipped and turned and fled for the safety of his yard. The old man saw this and cursed them, but Dab only grinned.

They tied their broncs in the alley behind the Saddle Back Saloon and came in, spurs chiming. Dab was quick to notice that the saloon sported some new furniture—new chairs, six of them, and two new card tables. The barkeeper proved cordial enough, and Dab got the impression that he wanted them to ride their broncs through the joint again and break up the rest of the old furniture so Jim Jones could buy him some more new stuff. They ordered a whisky apiece, and Dab said, "This is all for me," and killed his drink.

"We no drink much more," Gordo said. "All she gets us is the trouble, this whisky does."

Dab had not come into town to discuss the weather. He wanted to find out if Will Martin had indeed got the sheriff to swear out a warrant. The bartender wiped the counter with a damp rag and told them all he knew. The sheriff had not sworn out the warrant because Will Martin had not been in favour of it, but the trio had ridden out to the Double J to talk it over with Jim Jones and Dab so the sheriff could hear both sides of the question.

"You are not a outlaw," the Mexican said.

"We fought fair," Dab said.

The towel made short revolutions, seemingly having a grudge against the varnished surface.

"So Martin claimed," the bartender said. "But Turner was hoppin' mad, they tell me—he wanted Martin to file the complaint. O'Mahoney don't like you two gents too good, nohow, and he seemed sort of in favour of servin' a warrant on you, Jones, but Martin still held back."

Dab decided he might look up Will Martin sometime and have a talk with him. It seemed odd that Deputy Sheriff Mike Turner wanted him jugged so bad. He had never had trouble with Turner.

"Martin su'prised me," he said. "He sure can handle his dukes."

"There'll be the devil to pay in this basin soon," the bartender said. "Farmers' ploughs and cattle don't mix."

"I think," Dab said solemnly, "that the days of the cowmen running on open range are numbered—done with for all time."

"Don't let your uncle catch you saying that," the bartender warned. "Turner says the cowmen got to learn this country is civilized."

"Turner," said Dab, "is too wide for his pants. He

oughta remember he ain't the sheriff, but just a deputy. Well, let's drift, Gordo."

"We no buy a bottle for the trail?"

"No."

"Well, all right."

They went out and climbed on their horses and rode out of Beaverton. This time old man Smith's dog did not try to nip their horses on the hamstrings. He sat inside his fence and watched, not even barking.

"Learned his lesson," Dab said.

"*Si*, until tomorrow, anyway. Dab, we see another range war, no, like the one we leave down on the Panhandle?"

"I hope not."

"Me, I hope not, too. Even if the farmers take up the basin land, there is always the hills to run cattles on. The farmers can raise the hay for winter feeding. Your uncle can buy hay from them and feed his cows. When the farmers get the water—the irrigation—they can raise lots of good hay. I sure hope your uncle he doesn't want us to kill Martha and her mother."

"My," said Dab, "what a consoling soul you turned out to be." But he was serious underneath. "We got to keep Jim Jones from going to war, Gordo. I sure don't want to be tangled up in another Wire Cutters' War."

"Where we go now?"

"Visit the Lincoln family."

Gordo smiled widely. "The good idea," he said.

When they loped into the yard at the Lincoln farm, the collie pup came out barking, warning the inhabitants of the house of their entry. Dab saw a henhouse, a brush barn, and house made of sod. Grass grew on the sod roof, and the roof beams, made of cottonwood trunks, were visible under the roof. The pup brought a woman to the door—Martha Lincoln.

She wore a housedress now. Dab and his partner dismounted, and Gordo swept off his hat in a grandiose gesture.

Dab looked at her ankles. She wore house slippers. "Get your boot sewed up yet?" he asked.

"I have not been to town to the cobblers."

Dab grinned, ground-tying his horse. "You don't sound too cordial," he said.

"I am not too cordial."

"You look even purtier when you are mad, Miss Martha," Dab said. "Aren't you going to invite us into your house?"

"I might . . . and I might not."

The collie came up and put his forelegs on Dab, who patted him on the head. "Your dog likes me," he pointed out.

"That is no sign that I—"

She never got to finish her sentence, for a woman's voice, coming from the open door behind her, said, "Invite the boys in, Martha."

"Oh, all right." She stepped to one side. "Come on in, you devils."

Now it was Dab's turn to bow deeply, hat sweeping the ground. "After you, fair princess," he said.

"Hogwash."

Nevertheless, she was smiling as she entered the house,

Trail to High Pine   47

Gordo following her and Dabney Jones following his partner.

They came into a house that had a dirt floor that was swept rock-clean. The furniture was hand-made from native lumber and the table had a gay tablecloth on it. But it was not the tablecloth or the food that interested Dab. What interested him was the sight of his uncle sitting at the table with a plate of grub in front of him.

"Thought you had gone home," Dab said.

"You're not my boss," old Jim said, bristling immediately. "Besides, these good women prevailed on me to stay for chuck."

"*Prevailed*," Dab said. "That's a good word."

"Meet my mother, men," Martha said.

Gordo had not been wrong. Mrs. Lincoln was as blonde as Martha. Her pretty housedress fitted her just right, and her waist was as small as her daughter's. She could have passed for Martha's older sister. Old Jim watched every movement Mrs. Lincoln made.

"I'm hungry," Gordo said.

Dab said, "Where are your manners?"

"I beat you to it," Gordo said. "You were on the edge of saying the same thing. When did we eat last, Dab?"

"Down in jail."

"No, at the Double J."

"Heck, I forgot. This has been some day."

Martha walked to her place at the table. She limped very little. Dab looked at her ankles sharply to see if the one was swollen more than the other.

The food was good—fried potatoes, boiled beef,

vegetables and coffee. Old Jim ate as if it were his last meal before mounting the gallows. Dab told about their ride to Beaverton and about meeting the sheriff, his deputy, and the land agent riding for the Double J Ranch. At this information, old Jim glared at him.

"Keep our family troubles to yourself, son."

"You don't mean *son*; you mean *nephew*."

"Do you two fight all the time?" Martha asked.

Gordo answered that. "Only when they are both awake at the same time."

Martha related how she had got her saddle back, and they all laughed about the cow upsetting her, saddle and all. Dab promised some day to teach her how to take dallies so she would not have to tie hard-and-fast. But there was an air of stiffness about the gathering. Dab was quick to define the reason: his uncle and Gordo and he were cattlemen and these women were farmers. Martha's mother loosened up a little but Martha remained pretty tense. Dab blamed some of this on her accident at the springs. She had hit the ground hard and had hurt herself, and he had a hunch the shock was still with her.

Dab sent her a glance and winked at her, but she looked away, stony of face. Her mother had seen the wink and smiled at Dab, who grinned and blushed a little. The meal was excellent, and they were just finishing when the collie started to bark again, this time way down the road.

Martha went to the door. "There is a rider coming," she said.

"Who is it?" her mother wanted to know.

"Looks to me like Deputy Sheriff Turner."

Trail to High Pine 49

Dab noticed that Mrs. Lincoln got a little red. "Sometimes Mr. Turner comes to visit," she said.

Old Jim bristled but said nothing. Dab pushed back his chair. "Time to go," he said.

Gordo Alvarez was also on his feet. "*Si*, we go—and *gracias* for the foods."

Martha's voice dripped ice. "Seems to me you boys are always in a hurry to get out of somewhere."

Dab grinned, but her tone had angered him slightly. "We don't want no trouble here in your home, Miss Martha. Turner, for some reason, don't like me. He might pick trouble."

"You'd best go," her mother said.

Old Jim said, "I'll stay here. See you boys later."

"Not if we see you first," Dab said.

Turner was out of sight, for the trees hid him at this point. Therefore he did not see Dab and Gordo mount and ride behind the house. A sharp *coulée* ran here, and they rode into this and circled around, hidden from the house and from the deputy sheriff. They came out in the trees at the point where Turner had been when they had come out of the house.

Dab said, "Take it easy, son."

Gordo reined in, face serious. Suddenly Dab began to laugh. He bent over his saddlehorn and laughed and then looked up.

"What she is so funny, Dabney?"

"Old Jim. He's courtin' the Widow Lincoln. Then in rides old Jim's bosom enemy, Turner. The old fellow got as red around the wattles as a turkey gobbler they was takin' to the chopping block."

"Wonder if they will fight?"

Dab held his horse in with tight reins. "You know, Gordo, all joking aside—I would like to have a powwow with this Turner deputy."

"Why?"

"Find out why he is after me."

"Well, he will ride away from the farm soon, I think."

"We wait," Dab said.

They dismounted and moved over to a point where they could see the Lincoln farm and still remain hidden. The afternoon slipped away and became dusk, and a lamp was finally lit in the sod cabin. So far nobody had ridden away from the farm. Dab grinned. He could see old Jim Jones and Mike Turner both sitting there eyeing each other.

An hour went by, then another. Gordo dozed with his back to a broad cottonwood, his jaw on his wide chest and his lips mumbling with each breath. Dab squatted and rolled cigarette after cigarette. He was puzzling over why Turner wanted to nail his hide to the fence. Well, if he could talk to the man, he might find out.

The moon came up and was very bright. About this time two riders left the Lincoln farm, and Dab's elbow prodded Gordo to wakefulness.

"Two riders," Dab muttered. "Old Jim should swing off there—then the deputy, if he is headin' for Beaverton, should ride past us."

"What we do?"

"While you was sleepin' I got the rawhide *riata* from your saddle. You get there along the trail and front-foot his horse as he goes by."

"Maybe I miss. The moonlight is not daylight."

"You never miss, remember?"

Gordo got to his feet and shook out a loop. Dab kept watching the riders. True to his prediction, one rider turned off—that was old Jim, heading for the Double J. Dab grinned. His uncle had stuck around until his opponent had left. Old Jim was not leaving Turner alone with the two Lincoln women. Old Jim rode at a lope, went over the hill, and then was out of sight.

"Here comes the deputy," Dab said.

"I fix him."

Deputy Sheriff Mike Turner rode at a long lope, whistling as he loafed in his saddle. Squat and dark, he rode through the moonlight, the cottonwood trees occasionally shadowing him, hiding him. He did not know there was any danger within miles and miles. His whistling was terrible—in an off key. Dab watched and held his breath. Gordo was an expert with that rawhide rope.

Turner loped even with the Mexican, who was hidden in the brush. Dab saw the loop snake out, hanging hungrily in front of the horse, just an inch or so above the dust. The horse saw it, too, and leaped, almost throwing Turner, who cursed and grabbed for the saddlehorn, his reverie broken. Gordo snapped up and back, and both forelegs went into the noose. Then Gordo planted both boots, rope across his hip; the horse went down heavily, throwing his rider belly down in the dust. Gordo let slack go into the rope and the horse struggled upward, forehoofs slashing to free themselves. Turner, cursing dazedly, sat up.

"What in the name of billy—?"

Then Turner was staring up at Dab, who had come out of the brush. The deputy's .45 had fallen from its holster and the deputy reached for it. Dab kicked the gun to one side.

"You front-footed my bronc," the deputy said.

Dab said, "Not us, Turner. Your bronc stumbled on that root there." By this time Gordo had thrown the *riata* back into the bush close to his saddle-horse, for the Turner bronc had cleared his forelegs and stood with his reins trailing. Evidently Turner had not seen the noose; his hands had been too full of horse to notice the loop close to the sod.

Gordo said, "Lucky we are here. The horse he fall over the root there. You are hurt, no?"

"No. But you front-footed that horse—"

Dab shook his head slowly. "Why don't you get on your feet, Turner?"

"Why?"

"I want to talk to you . . . and it embarrasses me to talk to a man sitting down in the dust."

Turner got to his feet, boiling inside. Moonlight showed his heavy, angry face with great clarity, for his hat had skidded off his head, revealing his dark thick hair. Now he beat his hat against his thighs to knock the dust off it.

"What do you want, Jones?" he demanded.

Dab said, "Neither the girl or Martin would file a complaint against me, yet you talked Sheriff O'Mahoney into riding to the Double J to talk to me or my uncle, and then you trailed my uncle over here to the Lincoln farm."

"Get to the point."

"You got it in for me. I've never done no wrong to you.

Trail to High Pine 53

Why do you want me behind bars?"

"I don't."

"Then why try to get me arrested today?"

"I'm a lawman, mister. I have the public to protect. I think you are a menace to the public. You proved it when you and this drunk here wrecked the Saddle Back Saloon and tried to ride your horses through the Mercantile."

Dab said, "You lie, Turner, and you know it."

Turner gritted, "Nobody is callin' me a liar, Jones!"

He flung out a right fist. Dab had not expected it and it hit him on the side of the jaw, turning him. The thought came then that this was one fight Dab Jones had not started. With this thought came another bothersome idea: Mike Turner wore a law badge, and he was going to slug it out with an officer of the law. But then Turner had hit first; hit, in fact, without provocation. And he, Dab Jones, had Gordo for a witness.

For the second time in hours, Dab Jones was in a rough-and-tumble fight. But this man, he found out, was even tougher than Will Martin. He outweighed Dab, for one thing; for another, he was all bone, gristle and muscle. Hours in the saddle had toughened him.

Dab had not wanted to fight the man, but now he was forced to protect himself. The suddenness of the blow had given the deputy the upper hand. Dab then realized what was in the man's mind. Mike Turner hoped to whip him and then take him and Gordo into town, saying he had run across them and they had caused him trouble.

Turner hit again, the blow coming off his boot tops. But Dab moved under this, letting it go around him. The first blow had knocked his hat sailing galley-west. Now, bareheaded, he went to work.

Turner fought from a crouch, his breath coming in short and terrible gasps. For a while, he had Dab Jones moving backwards; this, too, was something new to Dab. Usually he had the other fellow back-pedalling.

Dimly, as though from a great distance, came Gordo Alvarez's yells of encouragement; Dab hoped the women would not hear them, for he did not want any female onlookers. Turner hit him solidly on his good eye. For some reason, Dab's nose was not working properly—air was difficult to get. And when he opened his mouth to grab air, a fist always clicked it unceremoniously closed.

Then Dab connected twice—one, two, good clean blows. They stopped Turner and he went to one knee. He fell partly because he slipped and partly because of the blows. Dab hit again, missed, and lunged ahead. Turner, on his knees, tackled Dab around the ankles, and both men went tumbling to the Montana dust.

Turner came out on top. He was gouging his spurs into Dab's belly and was beating down with his fists. Dab tried to roll, but the spurs held him. He had to do something and do it quickly, so he bunched his back and threw Turner ahead. Turner's spurs ripped Dab's shirt as the man fell forward.

Both men by now were getting winded.

Dab knew that if he were to win, he would have to win fast. Youth was on his side, and he used this advantage now. He got to his feet and was standing when Turner got to his boots. He hit the deputy with a right, and Turner went

Trail to High Pine 55

backwards, crashing into a tree. This held him, and then he fell on his side in the dust.

Dab looked at Gordo. For some reason the fat Mexican seemed to waver in and out. "Did—the—women—hear?"

"They no hear."

Dab panted, "Good."

"Another black eye," Gordo said. His voice sounded closer and he did not move back and forth any longer.

"Not good," Dab said.

Deputy Sheriff Turner rolled over and sat up, holding his head in his hands. He moaned like a sick animal for a moment.

"More, Turner?"

Turner did not look up. His voice was thin. "No more . . . for now." He kept his head in his hands.

Dab had his breath by now, and energy came back into his muscles. He said, "Unload his pistol and get his gunbelt and hang them around his saddlehorn, Gordo. Take the ca'tridges out of his rifle, too."

"Sure."

The big Mexican hurried about his tasks. Dab squatted and knocked down the deputy's hands, and Turner had eyes thick with anger and hate. He had a bloody, ugly face, too.

"Why hound me?" Dab asked.

Turner did not answer that. He said thickly, "You'll go to jail for this, Jones."

"On what charge?"

"I'm a sworn officer of the law. You beat me up. Your man there took my gun and unloaded it. Both of you gents will go to jail for this."

"You started it," Dab said, "and Gordo is my witness."

"His word is no good in court."

Dab said, "We'll argue about that when the time comes." He felt defeated, and not by the man's fists—the fight had netted him nothing except more bruises and another black eye.

"Get on your cayuse and get out, Turner. If you got any brains you'll leave the country for good. O'Mahoney hired you because you talked big and could draw a gun fast. If word gets around we tangled and you came out second best, your balloon will be busted—your rep gone—"

"That's my look-out, not yours."

Gordo said, "His fangs they have been pulled, Dabney. The short-gun is without bullets and the rifle he has no bullets either."

"Get out," Dab ordered.

The man went to his bronc and swung up, moonlight showing his savage bestial face.

"This ain't finished," he said huskily.

Dab nodded. "Maybe not," he said.

Turner turned the horse and used his spurs, this time on the horse and not on the ribs of Dab Jones. He loped away, straight in the saddle, and then he went out of sight and the cottonwoods hid him. The echo of his hoofs rang out, and there was only the taste of dry dust in the moonlight.

FIVE

"We gain nothing," Gordo lamented. "Only now, for sure, we're the outlaws, no?"

"Yes, I reckon so."

"What we do now?"

Dab had a sudden hunch. "You trail the big son a mile or so, while I wash up in the crick—if I can find some water in a pot hole."

"Why I trail heem?"

"Get on your horse and get moving."

The Mexican shrugged. "All right, boss."

Dab went along the creek until he came to a pot hole that had some water which was not too clear. He wet his neck scarf and washed his face rather gingerly because of the sore spots. This done he decided his shirt was almost done for. Those spurs had really ripped the shirt to shreds, not to mention what they had done to his belly and ribs. He tore the shirt off and threw it away. His chest was black and blue in a number of places. He could hardly see out of one eye—the one blackened by Will Martin.

"Hope I don't get blinded in both eyes an' wander

around like a wool-blinded goat," he told himself.

Then he breathed deeply and decided he would live.

Would Turner report this fight to Sheriff O'Mahoney? He doubted if the deputy would go to the sheriff for aid. Up to now, Dab found, he had been underestimating two men on this Beaverton Range. One had been the land agent, Will Martin. And the other was Deputy Sheriff Mike Turner. Both were plenty tough.

He went back to his horse. Evidently the Lincoln women had not heard the fight, for the light was still on in the cabin and nobody had called out or had come down the road to investigate. He wished he had a shirt. He thought of Martha. What if she could see him now, with his other eye going closed?

He did not like that thought.

He got his horse and rode about half a mile down the road, and then Gordo came riding out of the brush.

"Turner he did not ride for Beaverton," the fat Mexican reported.

"Where did he head for?"

"He go for the homestead of the man called Matt Smeeth."

"Smith," Dab said.

"That is what I said. Smeeth, over on the Porcupine Creek."

Rimrock Line Camp, an outpost for the Double J, was to the south about four miles, a stone cabin set on the rimrock overlooking the valley. Here a narrow defile angled into the badlands, and stray cattle could be turned back at this point. Behind the cabin was a spring that came out of

Trail to High Pine

granite, its water clear and good. The cabin would be open, for a line camp was never locked, and Dab knew there would be grub on the shelves—canned grub—and also beans in the steel bin.

"Lead the way, Dab."

Within half an hour, they were at the cabin. They stripped their horses and put them out on picket-ropes, using their catch-ropes for pickets and sagebrush for picket-pins. Moonlight washed over the area below, sending rays of golden light dancing across the wilderness. Dab could see the farmstead of the Lincoln women; the sod house was dark.

Far in the distance, looking cold and unwelcome, were the lights of Beaverton, twinkling and yellow.

Dab said, "We'd best have a guard out, huh?"

"You think Sheriff O'Mahoney he look for us?"

"Not him so much as maybe Turner or Martin. They might get together and compare notes and decide to get us out of here . . . for good. A bullet in the back, out of the high brush."

"I'm sleepy."

"You go in and nap, little boy, and papa will stand guard."

"All right, Daddy."

The heavy-set Mexican waddled into the cabin. Dab climbed onto a boulder and sat there and wondered if he could keep watch with one eye. Time drifted on and he got drowsy. But the night turned chilly at this higher altitude and this kept him awake. Once he dozed and caught himself, and he gave the valley a sweeping glance.

Then it was that he saw the first fire. His eyes went from this fire to another, not too far from the first.

He called to Gordo.

They went out on the rimrock, and Gordo dug the sleep out of his eyes and then looked. Finally he said, "That one fire she is belong to Matt Smith, the friend of Mike Turner. The other . . . it might be the house of Jake Thomas. That other farmer, he live about a half-mile from Jake, you know."

Dab said, "Wonder if ol' Jim has jumped the gun."

"You mean, Jim burned down Smith's house?"

"Could be. Smith is a farmer. Jim Jones wants the farmers out. He might have took the bit in his mouth. He might have got mad at Turner—there at the Widow Lincoln's—and decided to hit Smith because he was a friend of Turner's."

"That would mean war."

"Range war," Dab said. "Just what we left in *Tejas*, Gordo."

"I do not like this one bits."

"Neither do I," Dab had to admit. "Doesn't seem logical ol' Jim would ride against a nester like Smith, though. Jim was shinin' up to the widow like all get-out. I figured the widow would convince him farming was a good deal. Jim should go down to Texas where we come from. Then he could see that farmers and cowmen can work good together and both make good money."

"Jim, he is a stubborn old woman."

"Old woman is right," Dab snorted. "You know one thing, Gordo?"

"What is that thing?"

"Those houses burn fast, don't they? I know the weather has been dry—no rain for weeks—but they sure burn almighty fast."

"We ride down there, huh?"

"Might just as well. Wonder if they can swing the blame of burnin' down Smith's joint around to us? We tangled with Turner, you know—and we know Turner and Smith are buddies."

"If it is possible, the people they will blame us," Gordo said philosophically.

They pulled in on their picket-ropes and got their horses saddled, cramming bits between their grass-discoloured teeth. Then they coiled their catch-ropes and tied them to the forks of their saddles and mounted.

"My horse she is tired," Gordo said.

Dab said nothing in reply. His bronc also had had the edge worn from him. They rode down the slope, with Dab in the lead and Gordo following.

Legs braced, Dab's horse crossed an area of loose shale, then came to the hard dry earth again. The trail broadened and they were on the basin floor, sagebrush standing out in the moonlight. Dab figured it was about two miles or so to the Smith farm, and he said, "Come on, pony; stretch," and the game horse started to lope. They moved across the sagebrush, and now dust was in the air, grey as the sage, but with a musty odour. They crossed the flat, and came to an area of greasewood, and here was white alkali that glimmered in the soft light, its crusty surface deceptive and dusty. Dab swung wide of this alkali bed, knowing that the crust could be broken through easily and a horse could stumble, and again he found harder ground, always driving toward the flame of Smith's shack up ahead.

They found Porcupine Creek, and then Gordo rode close, hand going out and getting hold of Dab's sleeve.

"I hear a man on horseback he come."

Dab said, "Follow me," and he drove his horse into the high underbrush and went down, moving to the head of his bronc. Gordo also hit the dust, and they stood there, hidden by the wild rosebushes and buckbrush, and Dab said, "You got good ears. I'd never have heard them hoofs," and they waited, the sounds of hoofs drifting closer.

"*Dos* riders," Gordo said quietly. "Two of them, Dab."

They came into view then. They slanted around a curve, running their broncs hard, the wind pushing back the brims of their hats, their quirts rising and falling against the labouring flanks of their running broncs. They ran past, and then they were out of sight, only the acrid dust hanging in the air, this being punctured by the rap-rap of their retreating hoofs.

"You see who I see, Dab?"

Dab nodded. "I couldn't be wrong."

"The deputy, Mike Turner, he was one. The other, he was the man named Matt Smith."

Dab stood for a moment, digesting this information. This did not make sense. Turner and Smith were riding away from the burning cabin, whereas by all rights, they should have been fighting the fire, pumping water from the well. Dab shoved back his hat and scratched his head and decided this range was full of crazy men, including one Dabney Jones.

"I don't *sabe* this," the Mexican said.

"Got me stumped, too."

They waited a while longer but no other riders came, so they mounted and rode toward the burning cabin. The flames had sunk down and the glow was much smaller against the sky. Dab kept thinking, did old Jim Jones and his riders burn this cabin? That did not seem logical. Surely Smith would have been inside the cabin—there would have been some lead thrown. He remembered that Mike Turner, after their fight, had ridden toward the Smith cabin. Evidently Turner too had been in the cabin when it had caught fire. There was much here Dab Jones did not understand.

Within a minute or two they were on the hill behind the burning cabin, the brush screening them. But nobody moved down there in that area lighted by the dying flames.

Dab said, "Do you smell something?"

Gordo sniffed. "She is smell like the kerosene to me," he said.

"Probably he had some kerosene in the house," Dab said. "It might have popped and sprayed the joint with kerosene from the can. That would make it burn faster, too."

"Nothing we can do here."

"Let's ride over and look at the other fire."

"By this time, that fire will be burned down, too."

"Come on," Dab said.

Again they took the trail; again moonlight showed two

scurrying ants, darting across the sagebrush, through the brush and greasewood. Again, when they neared the Thomas shack, they slowed down, just as they had done when nearing the burning Smith cabin. But this tine no riders loped away from the ruins. The Jake Thomas cabin was a mess of red ashes glowing in the moonlight.

"Nobody around here, either," Dab said.

"Maybe Thomas—he burn up?"

Dab said, "Can't see nothin' on the bed, an' you can see the ruins of that clear against that heat. And if he was in bed he would burn with the house, I'd figure; a man could see his carcass on the bed, huh?"

"I would think so."

"Maybe Jake Thomas wasn't home," Dab said.

Gordo shifted his body, stirrup leathers creaking. A cow bawled somewhere out on the range and the sound was lonesome.

"First, a farmer's house catches fire, then a house belonging to old Jim catches fire. That means that Jim hit at Smith, burning his spread; the farmers, to hit back, burned down this house. And then, by sheer accident, we meet the deputy sheriff and Matt Smith hightailing it away from Smith's outfit."

"No make the sense to me."

Dab turned his horse. "Only one thing to do, Gordo."

"And that?"

"Ride over to the Double J and see old Jim Jones, if the old bugger is at home. We got to talk to him."

"Our horses—our *caballos*—they are tired, Dab. They have been rid far and their legs are weak."

Trail to High Pine 65

"We'll change broncs at the Odum farm, then."

"All the time we ride."

"Either we settle this," Dab said, "or this range goes to war. You and me went through that once."

"Do not talk like that. The bullet hole in my ham—it is healed—but your words make it ache."

"They'll blame this Smith fire on you and me, I'll bet."

Gordo shrugged. "Makes no never-mind. All the time we get blamed for everything anyway."

They pushed their ponies to a lope. Mack Odum was a Double J cowpuncher who was proving up on a claim for old Jim Jones. He had settled on a good water hole—a spring that ran all the year around, its waters sinking into sand within a few rods from the source, there in the granite boulders.

Odum had a one-room shack—about twenty by fourteen feet—and fastened onto this, on the west side, was a lean-to barn. The shack was dark when Dab and his partner rode out of the brush into the moon-washed clearing.

"Odum," Dab called. "Mack Odum. Dab Jones and Gordo Alvarez."

"Back here, men," the cowpuncher said.

They turned on their stirrups and looked back at the brush, for the voice had come from behind them. Mack Odum, a short, bow-legged man, came out of the buckbrush, rifle in his hand.

"Saw the fires in the distance. Happened to get up to doctor my dog—he's sick and that is why he never come out barkin' at you—and I saw them two fires over yonder. You boys sure did a good job of burnin' down Smith's outfit, looked like."

"We never torched the shack," Dab said.

Gordo said, "We rode there but there was nobody around. We did not light it on fire."

Odum peered up at them, eyes hidden. "Figured sure ol' Jim had made his first move to run out the sodbusters," he said, "and you two hellions had been commissioned to burn Smith's shack."

"Not us," Dab said.

Odum shifted his chew, jaw bulging. "Then another thing struck me as a mystery—that looked like Jake Thomas' shack going up, so I figured the nesters had burned him down, hitting back at ol' Jim Jones. Was you over to Jake's place, too?"

"We were," Dab said.

"Was he there? Hope he never got caught in the fire."

"Nobody there, either," Dab assured him. "No corpse in either fire. We need fresh horses, Odum."

"Got three head in the night pasture."

"You run them into the corral," Dab told Gordo.

Gordo said, "I always do the work."

While the Mexican corralled the saddle-horses Dab unsaddled his horse and turned him into pasture. The pasture included the spring, so the horse had water handy. Odum planned to stay awake all night and stand guard around his property. Dab did not tell him about seeing Deputy Sheriff Mike Turner and Matt Smith riding away from the burning Smith cabin. Dab kept wondering about Jake Thomas. Had he pulled stakes or was he dead somewhere in the brush? Maybe old Jim Jones would have the answer.

Their fresh horses under saddle, Dab and Gordo swung up, and Dab reined his horse around, looking down at Odum.

"Tell ol' Jim I'll be watchin' his property here," Odum said, "but if he needs me to sling my gun, jes' come a-running after me."

"That talk is no good," Dab said.

"What do you mean by them words?"

Dab said, "That talk leads to gunfighting and gunfighting leads to graves, and that settles nothing—only makes things worse."

"Them words seem out of place comin' from you, Dab."

"What do you mean by that, Odum?"

"Well, you an' Gordo got drunk—wrecked the Saddle Back—rid broncs through the Merc—"

"Fun," Dab said. "Innocent fun, nothing more. This is range war, and a range war is not fun, believe you me. Gordo and I got smoked out in one once, down in Texas—the Wire Cutters' War."

"They filled my leg with lead," Gordo said.

Odum said, "The talkin' of guns might be the only words them nesters can understand, men."

Dab said, "So long."

SIX

Dab and Gordo loped out of the clearing. Once Dab glanced back. Odum, rifle in hand, was heading for the brush again. Dab suddenly came to life. His horse started to buck.

The horse almost threw him, for Dab had been riding a loose saddle, not expecting the horse to start to pitch—he had figured he was on a well-broken old saddle-horse. The first jump loosened him in saddle and he grabbed and missed the horn, but the second jump was an error on part of the horse—he bucked back in under Dab, thereby slamming the cowboy back in leather.

Dab had his seat now; he used the fork of his saddle, knees pressed down firmly. He hit the horse in the neck every jump with his spurs. The horse could pitch, but Dab could ride; Dab won. Soon the bronc was running wide open, stretched out like a quarter-horse, tail behind him. And a jump behind the horse came the lunging horse of Gordo Alvarez.

Dab slapped the horse across the flanks with his quirt. "You asked for it, horse!"

Trail to High Pine

They rode then. They went about a mile and then Gordo held up his right hand, pulling his horse to a halt.

Dab asked, "What's wrong?"

"Me, I think I hear hoofs."

Dab knew how good his partner's ears were, so he listened. There were but a few small sounds: the hard breathing of their broncs, the creak of leather as the ribs of their horses rose and fell, the sounds of the night. Gordo Alvarez sighed with Latin gusto.

"For once my ears they no tell me true."

Dab said, "I hear no riders. You might have heard range horses running. Our coming might have run some out of the brush—horses behind some hill so we could not see them."

"I do not know."

"Come on," Dab said.

Again they took the trail.

They left the valley and entered the *coulée* through which twisted the road that led to the Double J Ranch. The road was a dusty ribbon of grey, coiled and leading through the moonlight. They were about a quarter-mile from the big outfit when a guard came out of the brush, rifle raised slightly.

"Hold in, men."

They reined in, lifting dust. Dab said, "Dab Jones and Gordo Alvarez." He leaned over his fork and studied the man. Then he said, "Hello, Jack."

Jack said, "What the blazes is eatin' you two hellions? The old man said you were exiled to Siberia for two months or until snow came."

"Where is ol' Jim?"

"Poundin' his ear in his bunk, I reckon. Why ask?"

"Any Double J riders out tonight?"

"Only Smoky. He went to town for the mail an' never come back. Ol' man is mad as a hen with saddle-boils about it. Smoky prob'ly went off on his annual drunk."

"The curse of hard liquor," Dab said, and grinned.

"Why all the questions?" Jack wanted to know.

Dab realized something then. Set in the hills as it was, the ranch had not seen the two fires down there on the basin floor. Anyway, Jack had not seen them, for the brush was between him and the fires.

"Got to see Jim," Dab said, and rode forward.

The big ranch seemed sound asleep. The bunkhouse was dark and the barns were heavy silver shadows suspended against the luminous air. Down at the corral the stallion smelled their sweaty horses and ran around his enclosure, his hoofs making dull sounds against the dust of his prison. Dab and Gordo rode to the long tie-rack in front of the house and dismounted and went inside. The door, of course, was unlocked. Dab knew where the lamp was, and he lit it, and the yellow rays showed the stone fireplace, the hand-made furniture, the stone floor. Dab said, "Come on," and he went down the hall, carrying the glass lamp by its stem.

Dab knew that if his uncle were home he would be alone in the house. He said to Gordo, "Make lots of noise," and they clomped down the hall, boots rapping the rock floor, spur rowels clanking. Jim Jones had had about twenty housekeepers during his ownership of the Double J, which dated back more years than twenty. But he had managed to make their lives so miserable they had fled the spread. Now twice a week a squaw came over from the reservation and swept and ironed and cleaned the house for him.

Lamplight made shadows against the wall as they walked. They came to the door of old Jim's bedroom and Dab unceremoniously kicked it open for it had been left ajar. The door flew back and hit a night stand and knocked it down; it made quite a racket.

Jim Jones came out of bed like a bullet. He had a .45 under his pillow and one bony claw went for it. He sat on the edge of the bed looking at his nephew and Gordo.

"What in the name of all that's holy is wrong with you two fools?"

"Were you asleep?" Dab made his tone innocent.

"You know darned well I was asleep." The hand brought out the .45, and it dangled as Jim Jones fought to come wholly awake. "You two drunk again, huh?"

"No," Dab said.

Gordo said, "Not even a sip of tequila."

"Then what the—" Jim Jones was wide awake now. He made revolutions with the .45 and the hammer was eared back, too. He cursed in English, some Spanish, and Sioux, with a smattering of Blackfoot. "What the devil do you want?"

"Two cabins burned down," Dab said.

The .45 stopped making circles. The eyes widened, the jaw quivered.

"Whose cabins?"

Dab told him. The old man pulled on red underwear and rubbed his whiskery jaw. "Now who set them buildings on fire?"

"They sure burn fast," Gordo said, his eyes round in the lamplight. Then his eyes rested on a pint of Old Saddle on the dresser, the cork and seal undisturbed. Dab saw it, too, and he knew why Gordo slowly worked his way in that direction. He decided to keep his uncle interested so Gordo could snag the bottle and put it in his pocket unnoticed.

"Thought maybe you or some Double J men had set Smith's cabin on fire," Dab said. "Can you see Smith's cabin from the window?"

He walked to the far window that looked out on the yard. He knew full well the cabin could not be seen from this point. Old Jim hobbled after him, and this gave Gordo his chance.

"You cain't see nowhere from here," the cowman muttered. He hobbled back to bed, sat down. Gordo was back in his original position but the bottle of Old Saddle was not.

"You order Smith's cabin burned?" Dab asked.

"Heck, no, Dab. I never ordered nobody to fight no nesters. And that cabin of Jake Thomas—I owned that. Would I burn down my own property?"

Dab said, "We figured that way, too. This is a mystery to me, Jim."

The old man put his head in his scrawny hands, legs dangling over the edge of the bed with its dirty bedding. Dab listened to old Jim's words, seeping out between his fingers.

"Me, I've decided not to fight the nesters because, like the Widow Lincoln says, I can't whip them—they're bound

Trail to High Pine 73

to come. I drive one bunch off; here comes another. But I had made my mind up on thet point even before conversin' with the Widow today. That's why I put men on homesteads."

"Sure Mrs. Lincoln never persuaded you to that conclusion?" Dab asked.

He knew right away he had asked the wrong question.

"I don't like the tone of voice you said that in, young man. I'm so ol' no handsome young woman, widow or single, or any way they come, would look at me, and it don't bother me one bit. I like the Widow Lincoln and I hope she likes me—I think she does."

"Turner likes her too," Gordo said, "and Turner is a young man, no?"

"You ain't asked to put in your oar, Gordo. The Widow Lincoln don't cotton to Turner one bit—she done tol' me so!" Jim Jones looked at his nephew's face again. "You got lots of new bruises, it looks to me. Another hoss kick you with both hind laigs?"

"My bronc fell with me."

"Tear your shirt off you, did he?"

"Ripped it from aft to stern," Dab said, "so we boiled it and made soup out of it, Reckon I'll get some new duds in my room."

Dab was very, very sleepy. But evidently there would be little if any sleep this night; last night, too, had been without sleep.

Old Jim started to pull on his socks.

Dab shook his head. "You and your men stay close to home, Jim. Then you won't get into trouble."

"You're runnin' this spread, or am I?"

Dab grinned. "Don't get huffy with me or I'll toss you on your back and gag you with one of your own crusty socks. Listen to reason, Jim. You move out and look at them shacks that got burned down—nesters will be on you, man. Stay home and mind your own knittin', Unc."

Jim Jones stopped, looked at his sock, let it drop. "Reckon you are right, nephew," he admitted. "We'd best stick close to the home ranch. They might try to hit us, all armed and in a body. But there's something behind this— somebody else—"

"We think so too," Gordo said.

The old man continued dressing. "I'd best warn the men and get more guards out. You two stayin' here to help me, ain't you?"

"You sentenced us to Siberia, remember?" Dab prodded.

"That sentence is withdrawn, as of now. Stick on the home ranch and help your old uncle."

"Poor old uncle," Gordo moaned.

"You keep your sarcastic tongue still, Mexican, or I'll tie the can on you and send you down the road talkin' to yourself."

"You fire Gordo," Dab said, "and you have to write my time, too."

"Oh, Lord, I'm not cannin' him." The faded eyes bored into Dab's. "You got somethin' on your mind, son?"

Dab said, "I sure have, and I just happened to think of it. Last night it seems to me thet me an' Matt Smith had some **hot words, down there in the Saddle Back Saloon."**

Trail to High Pine   75

"I remembers that," Gordo said, and added, "Very dim, though."

"What do you struggle over?" Jim Jones asked.

Dab shrugged. "I don't know. Smith an' I almost fought, if I remember rightly."

"You do," Gordo said. "I had to hold you back so you not fight him. He cussed you and you cussed him back. You fight because you were drunk, nothing more. But lots of peoples they hear you two."

"And now Smith's cabin is burned," Dab said.

"I holds you back," Gordo said. "Like this."

He pinned Dab's arms behind him by running his own arms through Dab's elbows.

"They might lay this onto you, then," Jim Jones said.

"I better go to town and talk with Sheriff O'Mahoney, huh?" Dab asked.

"Might be a good idea." Jim Jones snorted like a whale surfacing. "You two danged idiots. One night on a drunk, and you tip this whole basin toward war. And because you're my bone-headed nephew, the whole thing will come back to my henhouse to roost. Far better you'd stayed on the Texas Panhandle."

"Maybe I should go back?" Dab said.

"Nah, stay here, you fool."

Old Jim started to stand up and Dab pushed him with the flat of his hand, sending him rocking back on the bed. Before the old-timer could straighten Dab and Gordo were in the hall, leaving the lamp in Jim's room. Dab closed the door to Jim's room and locked it, tossing the key down the hall.

"How will he get out?" Gordo asked.

Dab shrugged. "Climb out a window, I guess."

When they turned from the hall to the living-room, old Jim started to whoop at them from behind the locked door, rocking it as though pulling on the knob with both hands. They paid him no attention. They swung up again, hit their saddles, turned their cayuses, and loped out of the yard, whooping like drunk Sioux bucks on the warpath. A lamp came to quick life in the bunkhouse. The hounds, penned down by the barn, howled and barked. The bunkhouse door was ripped open and somebody screamed something at them, but their hoofs drowned the words. They slanted around the bend, the house and buildings fell out of sight behind them, and Dab pulled his horse to a long trot, the Mexican making his horse also seek a similar mile-covering gait.

SEVEN

Beaverton slept in moonlit slumber. Dab figured that in an hour or so the first light of the new day would break across the sky. Sheriff O'Mahoney, they knew, stayed at the town hotel, a two-storey frame building badly in need of paint and new shingles. They left their broncs in the alley and went up the rickety back stairs, Dab in the lead and Gordo puffing behind.

"These stairs they are not strong."

"They held Fatty Wellman and he weighs more than both of us," Dab pointed out.

"But that was a year ago, or so. Hope they don't fold up."

"You got lots of worries."

The stairs swayed, moved an inch or so, but held them. Gordo breathed deeply. They went down the hall—it was lighted by dirty-chimneyed bracket lamps on the walls—and the light showed Number Nineteen, which was Sheriff O'Mahoney's room.

Dab put his ear to the thin door. "Keep your breathing down," he ordered. "Better yet, stop breathing."

He listened. Gordo held his breath. They could hear the snores of a man from inside the room.

"He is there," Gordo said.

Dab pounded on the door with the butt of his six-shooter. The sound was loud in the corridor.

"Who is there?"

"A couple of convicts," Dab answered.

"Go away and pull that joke on somebody else." Sheriff O'Mahoney's voice was loud and angry.

"Dab Jones and Gordo Alvarez," Dab said. "We want to get back in jail. Safer than on the outside."

"Dab Jones, eh?"

They heard a rustling, a squeaking of springs, and then feet padded across the floor, and the door opened to reveal the sheriff in b.v.d.s.

"What do you devils want?"

Dab said, "We want to talk to you, Sheriff. Enter, fair Gordo. After you, *amigo mio*."

Sheriff O'Mahoney asked, "You two drunk again?"

"Not a drop," Dab said.

The lawman sniffed. "Must be the blackenin' liquid I used on my boots afore going to bed. Sit down and tell me the tale of woe. Everybody brings their miseries to me."

Dab realized that the sheriff had not been notified about the two cabins burning down or the lawman would not have been in his bed. Therefore he told the man about the two fires.

"Smith's cabin burnt, an' so did the shack of Thomas, huh? Now how come none of them two rid into town to tell me?"

Dab shrugged. "I don't know."

"How come you boys saw the fires?"

Dab said, "We were up on the Rimrock Line Camp. I never wanted no trouble with that land locator, but he egged me on. Did he swear out a warrant for me?"

"No."

"Then how come you an' him an' Turner rode for the Double J after that ruckus?"

"I wanted to talk to your uncle. We didn't ride out there so much to talk about you and Will Martin fightin' as we did to talk about the nester-cowman situation."

"Ol' Jim had no hand in these fires," Dab maintained stoutly. "We just came from the Double J. Jim was in bed, sound asleep; all his hands were accounted for, too. No Double J man lit them fires."

"Then who did?"

Dab shook his head slowly. "I don't know. Wish I did know. Smith an' me had a argument in the Saddle Back when I was drunk night afore last. The argument was over nothing. Seemed to me this Smith button wanted trouble with me."

O'Mahoney watched him with cat-yellow eyes. Dawn was sifting through the window, turning the morning to sunlight.

"Heard about that, Dab. Talked to the bartender about it, too. Asked some questions. Bartender said Smith egged you on. Bartender finally warned him to lay off you, they tell me."

Dab said, "It's kinda hazy to me. That's why I come into town, Sheriff, to report I had nothing to do with burnin'

Smith's cabin. I ain't mad at him. Why he should want trouble with me is somethin' I can't comprehend. Smith and Turner are good friends, eh?"

"Turner?"

"Your deputy."

"Oh, Mike Turner. Yes, I guess they are friends. Turner seems to have a lot of his friends located on homesteads, now that you mention it."

"Smith might hate me because ol' Jim is my uncle. Smith hates Jim. Ol' Jim says I've caused him a heap of trouble, but him bein' my uncle has made it hard for me, too."

The sheriff pulled on his pants. He threw questions at them. Was old Jim ready to hit the warpath against the farmers?

"No, he met the Widow Lincoln."

The sheriff stared at him. "Lincoln's widow is dead, ain't she?"

"Not the President's widow," Dab explained, grinning. "This is Martha Lincoln's mother, over on Wishbone Springs."

"She's a beauty," the lawman said.

Gordo yawned and showed his dark tobacco-stained teeth.

Dab said, "Well, he went over to visit her. He decided, then and there, that nesters were here to stay, and I believe he would like to roost on the same roost with the Widow Lincoln."

"That would be nice," the sheriff said.

Gordo said, "Your deputy—Turner—he come along. He picked a fight with Dab. Dab, he have a hard time

Trail to High Pine 81

defending himself. Turner, he report that to you, Sheriff?"

O'Mahoney scowled, tightening his gunbelt. "Turner never told me that. I haven't seen him since yesterday when the three of us rode to the Double J. When did this happen?"

"Yesterday evenin'," Dab said. "Right out beyond the Lincoln farm. I wanted no trouble, but Turner seemed intent on fightin' me, why I don't know, Sheriff."

"Did you win?"

Gordo said, "It was the draw."

Dab decided to skip the fight. His ribs were sore from the deputy's rowels; first time a man had ever used him for a horse.

Sheriff O'Mahoney had gone over to the thick white washbasin and had poured some water from the enamelled pitcher.

"Who would stand to win by burnin' down them two houses?" he asked.

Gordo shrugged.

Dab said, slowly, "How about Will Martin?"

The sheriff studied him over the towel, eyes narrowed. "On what premises do you base that statement, Dab?"

"All of them nesters, they tell me, owes Will Martin money. If he gets them into a fight with the Double J, they'll lose and the Double J'll lose, too. The nesters couldn't pay Martin and he could foreclose. Then, too, some would get scared and leave—they would forfeit most of their claims to him, improvements and all."

The sheriff looked at the towel as though suddenly interested in it, dirt and all.

"Jim's Double J hands have some good homesteads," Dab continued. "Homesteads some of those nesters really want, too. Jim settled them first; that's how he got them. Some of those farmers are right dissatisfied with the locations that Will Martin picked out for them."

"So I have heard."

Dab stopped, hand on the doorknob. "You ain't got no further charges against him and me then, huh?"

"Nobody has sworn out any more complaints. You are still out on bail. I should have made that bail out so that you couldn't tote your weapons, but it is too late now. I'll go to your funerals, though."

"Bury us in one casket," Gordo said. "Me on the top."

"Put us both on our sides in the casket," Dab said, and he and his partner went into the hall.

"We are almost the free mans again," Gordo said huskily.

Dab said, "Don't worry, we'll get back into more trouble again. I feel it in my shinbone."

"Which one?"

"My right one, of course."

Gordo said, "One thing he bother me. Why you not tell the lawmans we see the two men—Turner and Smith—riding away from the burning cabin?"

"That's our ace in the hole, I guess."

Gordo shook his head. "Me, I do not see that point."

"Only one thing you see good," joked Dab Jones, "an' that is a full bottle of tequila."

Gordo grinned. "More than the bottles I can see. I can find good the *Señora* Carmeleeta in the darkest night."

Trail to High Pine 83

Dab said, "Let's have a gabfest with Will Martin. I feel sure he'll hug me when he sees me after yesterday, especially this early in the morning. His room is Twelve. Here it is."

"I knock this time."

Gordo beat on the panel, almost shaking the old hotel. No answer came, so he beat with both hands and kicked with one foot at the same time. Heads popped out of doors, glared at them, and Old Maid Williams, who worked in the Merc selling corsets and women's wear, stared at them, her hair in paper curlers.

She pulled her head back in a hurry.

One head said, "He must be dead in that room. Otherwise he would be awake by now. You'd wake up the dead."

Gordo listened, ear to the panel. "Somebody she move in there," he said. He showed a triumphant smile. "At last I wakes him up, no?"

"You did good," Dab complimented him.

"Who is there?" Will Martin demanded.

"Dab Jones and Gordo Alvarez," Dab answered.

"Drunk or sober?"

"Both."

"What do you mean by *both*?"

"One drunk; the other sober."

"The door, if you happened to turn the knob, is unlocked, you idiot. Come in and leave your bottle outside."

Gordo said, "Never did I think to try the doorknob."

"He don't sound too mad," Dab said.

Gordo opened the door and they entered. Land Locator Will Martin sat on the edge of the bed rubbing his eyes. He wore smooth silk pyjamas. They were a violent red.

"My friends," he said sarcastically.

Dab said, "We came to find out if you burned down Smith's shack and set fire to Jake Thomas' dump?"

Evidently the land agent figured they were drunk. "Sure, I burned them down." His voice was sarcastic. "Burned them both, I did. I set them on fire with some hot coals I carry on a little shovel. Always have the shovel full of hot cinders in my hind pocket—you've seen the handle sticking out. Now, after receiving all this sterling wisdom, will you please move your carcasses to some other room—anybody else's room."

Martin crawled back between the covers. "And close the door behind you," he said, and showed them his back.

Dab said, "But it's the truth, Martin. Both cabins burned a few hours ago."

"Ah, go on out of here."

"Man, I'm serious."

Something in Dab Jones' voice made the land locator roll over and sit up and stare at him. Martin's lips were swollen and one eye, although not yet black, was almost shut. Out of the other eye he regarded them with an owlish and heavy stare.

"When did this happen?"

"A few hours ago, like I said."

Will Martin rubbed his jaw and his fingers brushed against whisker stubble to make a dull sound.

"Who burned them down?"

"We don't know."

"Jim Jones?"

Dab told his story, watching the man carefully. Again he made no mention of seeing Deputy Sheriff Mike Turner and Matt Smith riding away from the burning Smith cabin. When he had finished, Will Martin was wide awake.

"I been in my bed all night," he said in self-defence. "This looks like a range war—and a ripsnorter—to me. Jim Jones has burned down the Smith cabin."

"Him and his men and you had one thing in common last night," Dab informed him. "They were all home in bed."

"Well, did the farmers burn down Jake Thomas' place?"

Dab shrugged. "We don't know."

The man swung his legs over the bed and rubbed the silk knee of his gaudy pyjamas and did some deep thinking. Gordo Alvarez went to the window, looked out, glanced at Martin, saw he was not watching him. The bottle left the shelf and found a home in Gordo's pants pocket, under his chaps.

"I better get out to see my farmers," the land agent said, stripping off the top of his pyjamas, showing a torso battered black and blue by Dab's fists. "And you two get out of my room."

"You don't like us, huh?" Dab asked.

"It isn't a matter of dislike or like. You two ride too much, raise too much ned, and I don't want to associate with you."

Dab glanced at Gordo. "Bad boys we are," he said.

Gordo said, "He can go to and stay put."

They went down the hall.

EIGHT

Dab and Gordo ate at the Bullhide Café. Both were dog-tired and Dab's ribs hurt from Turner's spurs. The bacon and eggs tasted good, though—so did the coffee.

Within a few minutes, they were riding out of Beaverton. Dawn had changed to day and the threat of sullen heat was in the air. Freeze to death nights; boil to death days.

"Good old Montana fall weather," Dab said.

"Somewhere we catch some winks, Dab?"

Dab nodded. They were not riding the wagon road; they were cutting across the sun-browned, dusty hill. No use meeting any of the farmers. They would be suspicious of them because they were Double J men, and doubly so because Dab was Jim Jones' kin. Also, Dab had fought Will Martin, and he had quarrelled with Matt Smith. Things had sure piled up against him.

Gordo's head came down, and he dozed and almost fell out of the saddle. Dab reached out and steadied him.

The Mexican lifted his head. "I was almost asleep," he said. "We get to the Sunken Spring, and the grass is thick there, and we take the forty winks, no?"

Trail to High Pine   87

"About a hundred winks," Dab said.

"A drink of tequila she would keep me awake."

"Hit the bottle you stole from Martin."

"Stole? Gordo he never steal—he just borrow."

Within an hour, they were at Sunken Springs, back against the rimrock. Here grass was rather high, for few cattle got back this far and the spring water irrigated the area. They picketed their horses and immediately fell asleep, lying on the thick and matted grass. Dab was the first to awaken. The hot sun had awakened him; he consulted his dollar Ingersoll.

They had slept about four hours.

He left Gordo there, sound asleep, and he climbed the ridge, the sun bringing sweat out on him; the sleep had done him worlds of good. From the ridge he could see the numerous roads leading to Beaverton from the farms. Rigs and riders moved along these roads, heading for town. Evidently the farmers were heading in to demand protection from Sheriff O'Mahoney. Dab grinned and thought, the sheriff'll be in hot water from now on until this is settled.

He went back down to the Springs, and he saddled their horses and bridled them, and then he held his hand over Gordo's mouth, pushing down hard.

Gordo awakened, started to struggle, then looked up, his eyes big and round.

Dab released his hand.

"What she is the matter, Dab?" the Mexican whispered.

Dab grinned. "Nothin'. Just tricking you."

"What a terrible trick"

Dab said, "We're saddled and ready to move. Come on, man; day is wastin'."

Gordo sat up and yawned. "I wash first my face." He bent over a pool of clear water and washed and said, "My whiskers are far out."

"Don't expect them to grow in, do you?"

Gordo wiped his face on the tail of his blue chambray shirt. "Now I feel better. That whisky that Will Martin he drink is bad whisky. She has upset my stomach. Where we ride for, Dab?"

"I thought we'd ride over and talk to Walt Jorgenson."

Gordo reined his horse around, found his stirrup. "Why we ride over and talk with that dumb Swede?" he asked, finding his saddle.

"Walt ain't dumb and he ain't a Swede, either—he's Norsky."

"Why we talk to Jorgensons?"

Dab touched his horse with his rowels. "Walt is pretty level-headed and steady. These farmers will blame us—me, that is, not you—for burning down Matt Smith's spread. Jim will say, of course, he never burned it down, nor did any of his punchers—then the farmers will say I did it for revenge on Smith."

Gordo nodded. "Wonder where the deputy sheriff, this Turner, he is? And where is Matt Smith?"

"Hard to tell," Dab said.

They were careful not to meet any farmers' rigs. Once they even reined in and hid in a *coulée* to let the Elkins buggy go by. Mrs. Elkins was alone. That meant that Fred Elkins and the boys were home, on guard with rifles and shotguns, Dab figured. She was going into town to see what the sheriff would do to protect the hoemen, Dab reasoned.

Jorgenson was on lower Buggy Creek. He had built a log homestead house, set in thick cottonwoods. Dab and Gordo dismounted, hidden by the brush, and watched the house. Within a few minutes the Norwegian left the house and went to the log barn. Dab and Gordo swung around and entered the barn by the back door. Nobody in the house could see them, for brush screened them.

The barn smelled of harnesses, sweaty horses, and manure. Jorgenson had a span of sorrel mares tied in a manger. He was in the act of pouring a bin full of oats into each oat-box. Dab noticed that the sorrels had sweat-marks from a harness, and that told him they had been hooked up to a rig and driven that morning, for the sweat was still damp on their glossy coats.

Jorgenson heard them and turned, oat bin poised. His sturdy, weather-grooved face showed surprise.

"What you two do here, Dab?"

He spoke in a thick Scandinavian accent. Dab figured he was a good solid man, just in his actions, level in his thinking.

"We didn't come for trouble, Walt," Dab said reassuringly. "We got enough of that without getting more from you. Judging from the looks of them sorrel mares you've driven them some distance this morning, probably into Beaverton."

"I drive them there."

Dab squatted, picking up a spear of hay. He bent it and talked. He told the Norwegian everything that had happened the night before except for his seeing Turner and Smith ride away from the burning Smith cabin. Gordo sipped his flask, and a wry taste was on his tongue. Jorgenson glanced at the fat man, and showed his antipathy toward whisky by a grimace.

"What are the farmers thinking?" Dab asked.

The man spoke slowly, apparently weighing each word. Besides being slow of speech, he was uncertain—he had been in the United States but two years, and one of those had been spent in Minnesota, where they spoke mostly Norwegian.

But the gist of his narrative was clear. The farmers had demanded that Sheriff O'Mahoney arrest old Jim Jones and his riders, put them under a peace bond. They claimed the Double J had burned down the Smith cabin. They also had demanded that the lawman throw two men back into jail and throw away the key. They could have burned down the cabin, also.

Dab knew, without asking, who those two men were.

"That line of reasoning," said Dab Jones, "don't make good common sense, Jorgenson."

"And why not?"

"Well, if the Double J did burn down Matt Smith's shack—which the outfit did not do—then who burned down the Double J where Thomas was hibernatin'?"

"The farmers—some of them—say that the Double J burned down its own cabin," the farmer said.

Gordo said, "That does not make sense to this mans."

Jorgenson laboriously explained. According to the thinking of the farmers, the Double J wanted them off their

Trail to High Pine

homesteads so the big cow outfit could run cattle on land they claimed. To gain back this land the Jones outfit would have to have a wire-cow war. Dab nodded; so did Gordo. Well, to lay blame on the farmers—to incite the war—was it not logical they burn down their own cabin? This way, they could lay the blame on the farmers, just as the farmers blamed the Double J for burning down Smith's shack.

Dab said slowly, "Sounds far-fetched, but it could be possible, only the Double J burned neither shack, Jorgenson."

"The farmers think different," Walt Jorgenson said.

Dab asked, "Why don't they talk to Smith? Where is he, anyway?"

"Matt Smith can't talk, Jones." Jorgenson looked down at his oat pail, his face long and glum. "You see, Matt Smith is dead!"

Gordo let his mouth open slightly. Dab stared at the man in amazement. Just a few hours ago he had seen Smith and Turner riding away from the burning cabin, and now the farmer was dead?

"Dead? What do you mean by that, Walt?"

"Just what I said. Turner came into town this morning and got the sheriff and they went to Smith's cabin. About an hour after you two left, I guess."

"After we leave from where?" Gordo asked.

"After you left Sheriff O'Mahoney down in Beaverton," the farmer replied. "The sheriff rode out with Turner. The body was in the burned-down house. A wagon has already taken the body to town."

Dab was somewhat bewildered; he hoped his face did not

show his utter surprise. This did not make sense. Two men *riding away* from the fire, and then the deputy sheriff finding his companion *dead* in the fire! He was glad now he had told nobody about seeing Turner and Smith leave the scene of the burning shack.

"Could they tell for sure it was Smith's carcass?" Dab asked slowly.

Jorgenson gave him a quick look. "Who else but Smith would be in the cabin?" He did not wait for an answer. "The body was burned a lot but the sheriff—he's coroner, too, you know—said for sure it was Matt Smith."

"Wonder if there was any bullet holes in him?" Dab asked.

Jorgenson did not know. The body had been badly burned. Gordo sniffed suddenly, as though smelling kerosene; Jorgenson looked at him.

Gordo asked, "Who they think kill Smith—or burn down the house? They have to kill him or knock him out to burn him in house. Or maybe the smoke she suffocate him, and he cannot get out of bed."

"I don't know about that," the farmer said, "but they blame it on the Jones outfit, of course. But there is another angle, too, and it has you in it, Dab."

Dab nodded grimly. He knew what the farmer meant. "They think I might have killed Smith and burned down his cabin because him and me had an argument in the Saddle Back, huh?"

"There's talk along that line."

With an effort, Dab Jones held back his flaring anger. "These people sure have a low opinion of me," he said, his

Trail to High Pine

voice thick. "What do you think, Jorgenson?"

Jorgenson did not want to give his opinion. He was not relying on the Law to fight his battles, he said. He had two rifles, a shotgun—he had his two sons, his wife, and he would fight until he died for his property. The grimness of the man registered on Dab and Gordo.

Jorgenson was in a solemn and dangerous mood.

Dab and Gordo left. They were in the foothills before either broke the silence, and then it was Gordo Alvarez who spoke, and his voice held no happiness.

"The sheriff he say in town he no want you, Dab. But now, with the farmers wanting you for murdering Smith, he wants you again, no?"

Dab was not happy, either. "Bet there is a warrant out for me right now. Or if there ain't no warrant, the sheriff wants to question me. And if I get in jail again . . ."

"They throw the keys away."

They rode for a distance without speaking, only the steel-shod hoofs of their horses making a noise occasionally on a rock.

"Ghosts they do not ride the saddles, no?"

"Guess they do," Dab said. "We seen one when we seen Smith riding away from that fire with Turner."

"Maybe Smith he not a ghost at that time."

"Maybe the dead man—the burned man—he is not Smith."

Gordo shrugged. "I no know nothing."

"You got company," Dab said.

They were on a windswept ridge. They had decided to ride the ridges; that way, they had the advantage of altitude, and they could see the range below them—see every movement of man, horse, or coyote. And Dab figured there were a number of coyotes on this range. Two-legged ones, though—not the four-legged variety.

Gordo pointed, said, "There is a rider down there. About half a mile away, and it is ridin' like a woman—bouncing in the saddle."

Dab focused his field glasses. Gordo watched his partner's face. He saw a smile touch Dab's lips.

Gordo said, "The girl, Martha Lincoln."

Dab put his glasses back in their case and buttoned down the flap. "You're a mind reader, Gordo. What say we go down and jaw with her?"

"She might not like us, after last night."

"She can't do nothin', even if she dislikes us."

They rode down the slope. Their horses zig-zagged, fighting the incline, being careful in the loose gravel. The girl saw them and reined in and was waiting in the sagebrush when they rode in.

She was lovely as a picture, Dab thought.

"I was riding to the Double J to see you, Dab," she said, smiling prettily.

Dab looked at Gordo. "The women are chasing me now," he said. "My life is complete."

Martha smiled. "I am not chasing you, Mr. Jones," she said sweetly. "I was riding over to the Double J hoping to find you there so I could thank you for the new boots." She held out her left foot. A new boot was hiding the pretty ankle. A justin boot, made of cream-coloured leather, with bright green and blue stitching. Dab was surprised. He glanced at Gordo. Gordo looked at him and said nothing. Dab put his attention back on Martha's face.

"Glad you like them," he mumbled.

"Your uncle brought them over this morning, Dab. Said you were too bashful to give them to me. You shouldn't have done it, Dab. But I sure thank you, and I mean just that."

Dab made an extravagant gesture. "Let's not talk about it any longer. We're heading for the Double J. Why not ride with us?"

"*Si*," Gordo said. "Ride between us."

"You boys are sure good to me," she said.

Gordo said, "We're good to all the lovely womans."

"Go easy," Dab warned his partner seriously. "She'll think we give a line like this to every woman."

"We do, don't we?"

"Shut up," Dab ordered.

They did not follow the wagon road. They cut across the hills to gain the advantage of the rimrock again.

Martha frowned. "Why don't we follow the road?"

Dab answered that. "They found the body of Smith in his cabin. Me and Smith had some words down in town. There is a rumour out that I might have done away with him."

"Oh, how terrible."

"I didn't kill him."

"I know you didn't, Dab."

Dab grinned tightly. "One person believes in me," he told Gordo.

"I believes in you."

"Two," Dab said, and smiled.

NINE

The guard was out at the Double J. He came out of the brush and said, "Pass by, men," and went back into the brush, carrying his rifle.

"He must be blind," Martha said. "He referred to me as a man."

Dab said, "He's so dumb he can't tell a goat from a sheep."

They rode into the yard—hoof-packed, boot-tromped, with the windmill squeaking, lifting water from the barren earth. Saddle-horses were tied to every hitchpost or rail on the *rancho*. The cowpunchers, all carrying sidearms, sat in the shade of the bunkhouse, and there was an air of grimness about them. Dab was quick to notice one thing: all the cowpunchers Jim Jones had established on homesteads were at the home ranch.

Nobody spoke. A few cowboys nodded; two lifted their hands; the rest sat in watchful silence. Dab had a feeling of great concern. This reminded him of Texas, of the bitter and deadly Wire Cutters' War.

They rode up to the ranch-house with its long porch. Dab

Trail to High Pine

had expected to see old Jim sitting there, rifle across his lap, but the porch chairs were empty. They dismounted and Martha shivered.

"Cold?" Dab asked.

"Oh, this terrible, terrible war," she said.

They crossed the porch, bootheels tapping. The big living-room held some cowpunchers, and Dab asked, "Where is my uncle, Charlie?"

"In his room, I reckon."

"What's going on?"

"Gonna give us a talk, I reckon."

They heard boots coming down the hall from old Jim's room, and soon the wiry rancher entered, gunbelt sagging. Usually his uncle did not pack a gun, Dab knew. The first person Jim saw was his nephew.

"So you came home to eat, huh?"

"No, Uncle, no." Dab was bone serious. "I came home to die. I am mortally wounded."

"You'd joke on your way to the gallows," his uncle said. Now his eyes rested on Martha Lincoln and he smiled, evidently remembering Martha's pretty young mother. "Sorry, girl, but you have to leave."

"Why?" Dab asked.

"She's a farmer, and what I got to say is for cowmen, not for farmers," his uncle pointed out, still smiling at the girl.

Martha said, "I'll go."

"You don't have to," Dab said.

"Your uncle is right," she said. "I'll go back and help the squaw make some coffee."

Every male eye in the room followed her to the door.

Old Jim called the meeting to order. First he outlined the problem. Then he asked for suggestions. He was a wise old boy, Dab saw. He aimed to listen, keep his mouth shut and then, after all the suggestions were in, he would make his decision.

Two or three of the cowpunchers—young men, all of them—wanted to fight it out with the farmers, smoke them out of the basin with rifles and short-guns. The other cowpunchers—the older and more level heads—advocated letting the law have full jurisdiction, and letting Sheriff O'Mahoney get to the bottom of this trouble. And to this plan both Jim and Dabney Jones nodded agreement.

"That is the best," Gordo said.

Jim then extracted a solemn promise from the cowpunchers he had settled on homesteads that they would not fire on a nester unless the farmer forced the trouble. They could only protect Double J property in case of attack. Old Jim added, "Don't take no back-talk when on your property or if your life or property are in danger. Shoot and shoot first, and the Double J will fight every inch of the way for you."

Dab said, "But who burned down Smith's shack and who fired Thomas' house, and where is Jake Thomas?"

Nobody knew the answers.

"Somebody—a third party—is working in this deal," Dab said slowly. "I don't know who it is, but I aim to find out."

"You'd best stay away from O'Mahoney," his uncle warned. "There's a rumour around that you kilt Smith and burned his shack."

Trail to High Pine

"So I have heard," Dab said.

"What do you know about this, Dab?" asked a cowpuncher.

Dab took the floor. He told them everything he knew except the fact that he and Gordo had seen the two men riding hurriedly away from the scene of the fire.

"You men ride to war," he said, "and you'll be playing right into the hands of this third party, whoever he is."

"He's right," a man said.

Old Jim said, "Never knew you had that much brains, Dab. You su'prise me, son."

"Nephew," Dab corrected him.

Old Jim grinned. "What do you aim to do from here on out, Dab?"

All eyes were on Dab Jones. "From what I hear, the sheriff might swear out a warrant for me, charging murder. I got some plans of my own, men."

"Like what?" Jim Jones asked.

Dab smiled at his uncle's impatience. He hesitated a moment, almost disclosing his plans; then the thought came that there might be a traitor in this group—therefore it was best he kept his ideas to himself. So he said, "I'm playing my cards close to my chest, Jim. You're an old hot-head, and if you knew what was on my mind you might tip my hand off to somebody and spoil the whole pot."

"What a nephew," Jim said, but he was angry underneath, for his eyes were blue glacier ice and his bottom lip trembled slightly.

Dab winked at Gordo.

Jim Jones said, "Meetin' is adjourned."

The cowpunchers trooped outside into the bright sunlight; Dab and Gordo went into the kitchen. Martha and the squaw had a meal cooked, and they sat down and ate fried antelope steaks, potatoes, string beans and good biscuits.

"I made the biscuits," Martha said.

Dab bit into one. It was soft as silk. "Hard as a stone," he said. "You didn't have time to make these, did you?"

"You were in there an hour," she said.

Old Jim came in, snagged a chair, settled across the table from his nephew. "Now you can tell me what your plan is, Dab."

"I might . . . and I might not."

Old Jim got mad, then hesitated. "Look, some day you'll inherit this spread—cattle, buildings and all."

"Even the debts, huh?"

"No debts against this property, whippersnapper. Sometimes I think you're so loco you cain't be kin of mine."

"Maybe I don't want your spread," Dab said, buttering a biscuit. "Sure nice cooking, Martha."

"Glad you like them, Dab."

For all that Dab cared, apparently his uncle was dismissed. Old Jim shoved back his chair, snorted like a bull walrus, and stalked from the room, his back poker-stiff.

A few minutes later, the trio rode away from the ranch and took to the hills again, Martha riding between the two men. Gordo was chewing industriously on a biscuit.

"You must have a wooden leg," Dab told the Mexican. "Your belly sure can't hold all that grub."

Trail to High Pine

"Both legs are hollow."

Martha said, "Your uncle got mad, Dab."

"He's mad all the time. He'll ride over and court your mother, Martha. He's fallen for her, I'd say."

She glanced at him. "You mean that, Dab?"

"I sure do."

Her eyes were serious. "I believe you are right. I am sure she has fallen for him."

"He's got lots of property," Dab pointed out.

She said, "Dab Jones, don't talk that way."

Her face was flushed, not so much with anger as with annoyance, Dab figured. Dab smiled and said, "You sure look purty when you get mad, Miss Martha. Your mother sure is a lovely woman. Almost as purty as you are, by golly."

Gordo said, "Pass the biscuits, please?"

They all laughed then. The day was slipping into late afternoon, and the sun had lost some of its heat as it sought refuge behind the western mountains. Dab pulled his horse in and wiped his forehead with his bandanna.

"Time you went home, Martha."

She studied him. "Why?"

"We got some riding to do, little woman. And besides, don't forget one thing—us and you are enemies. You're a farmer; we're cowmen."

"I have to get home anyway and find the cows and milk. The mosquitoes chase them into the buckbrush and they are hard to find."

"Some day," said Dab, "we'll hunt cows together."

"Maybe," she said, and turned her horse. "So long, and

good luck. And thanks again, Dab, for these splendid boots."

"You are sure welcome," Dab said.

She loped away, sitting her saddle nicely. They watched her until a hill hid her from their view.

"Where we go now, Dabney?"

Dab said, "There's a dead man on a slab down in Beaverton, Gordo. Came out of a burned-down shack, and when we saw the fire burning the shack the dead man was not in the flames."

"We ride to Beaverton?"

"That is right."

The Latin sighed. "Even now my rump has the saddle-boils."

Dab grinned. "Come on, old man."

"Our horses they are leg-tired, and there is no rush. We dare not get there before dark. The sheriff, if he sees us, he puts us in jail, maybe no?"

"Maybe yes," Dab corrected him.

They single-footed along the hills, keeping hidden by the brush as much as possible. When they came to Beaver Creek, the stream that flowed on the south side of Beaverton, they did not follow the wagon road—they rode along the creek, following trails made by cattle going to water in the pot holes. The sun gave way to dusk, and night started to move in on its silent and cool feet.

Dab said, "The way I figure, Matt Smith is still alive."

"Then who is the dead man?"

"I don't know . . . But Jake Thomas is among the missing."

Trail to High Pine

They squatted in the brush, watching the wagon road, and waited for night to come. About an hour later, a rider came along the road, and Dab said, "Are my eyes deceivin' me, or is that the honourable deputy sheriff, big as life and twice as stupid?"

"He is Turner," Gordo affirmed.

"You hold a rifle on him, Gordo, and I'll go out and talk to him."

"Talk? About what?"

"The weather," Dab said dryly.

Turner saw Dabney Jones standing there in the road, and he drew in, the dusk failing to hide the look of surprise on his face.

"What you doin' on foot, Jones?"

"My horse is in the brush. There's a rifle on you from the brush, too."

The deputy showed a lop-sided smile and sent a glance at the tall underbrush; he could not see Gordo Alvarez, though, for the Mexican was hidden securely, rifle barrel poked out in front of him.

"How come you didn't tell Sheriff O'Mahoney about our little tussle out in the brush, Turner?"

Turner studied him. "You lookin' for more trouble, Jones?"

"Yes, if you want to furnish it."

Turner caught his anger in time, and his smile was smooth, despite his swollen lip.

"There would have been no use my reportin' the fight to my boss. First thing, it was a personal affair—not part of my office as a deputy. Second, I had no witnesses to the effect you two picked on me. It would have been your word against my single word, and even if I tote a star it would not have been convincing—not when your uncle is a rich man, Jones."

Dab said nothing. Mike Turner's word did not ring true.

"Keep riding," Dab said.

Turner said, "You go to blazes, Jones."

Turner touched his horse with the spurs—this almost made Dab Jones wince—and he loped away, squat and dark and full in the saddle. Dab went into the brush.

Gordo said, "I heard every word said."

"And it all adds up to nothing."

"The dead man," Gordo said. "The guy on the slab."

Dab said, "Not night yet. We got to play this safe. You don't suppose Turner will tell the sheriff about meeting us and O'Mahoney will come out and look for us?"

"We move camp right now."

They led their horses down the path, then rode them across the creek; the ford was shallow, the creek-bottom of water-washed gravel. They rode along the timber some more, then halted in the brush. From here they could see the wagon road. Two wagons came into town, each carrying a farm woman and her family, and Dab said, "Some of them are sendin' their wives and little ones into town for safety."

"The Merc sells lots of ammunition," Gordo said.

"Ol' Jim said the town ain't got a rifle or shotgun in it for sale. Every arm in the burg has been sold to the farmers. No ammunition, either. Jim has a arsenal out to the ranch."

"I know. In the cellar."

Trail to High Pine

"Don't look like Turner is goin' squeal to O'Mahoney on us. Either that, or the sheriff ain't in town."

Gordo only grunted. He put his head down, and soon he was snoring softly, chin on his heavy chest.

TEN

It was after midnight when they led their horses down the road and came to the outskirts of Beaverton. They put their horses in a barn belonging to an old pensioner who, by this time, would probably be sound asleep in his tarpaper shack at the front of the lot. The interior of the four-stall little barn was dark, and Dab lit a match.

"What you look for?" Gordo asked.

"A shovel or something we can use for a pry under a window. That fork is not strong enough, I'd say."

"Crowbar hangs from the hook there. Over your head."

Dab's fingers explored the dark post, went through some cobwebs, and met steel. "Not a crowbar," he said. "A wrecking bar."

"No argue over small matters."

Armed with the crowbar, Dab went down the alley, Gordo following him. The Mexican carried his quirt. The town was quiet—sleep was on the land. A dog slunk across the alley, a dark shadow moving through other shadows, and when they came to where they could see the main drag, Dab saw there was not a horse or rig at any of the hitching-racks. When they went past Mrs. Jackson's yard, her dog started to bark. He came rushing out, a fox-terrier, and he meant business. So did Gordo's quirt when it came down over his rump. The barking changed in one second to a terrified yapping as the dog scurried home, kicking himself in the ears with his hind feet. Mrs. Jackson opened a window.

Dab pulled Gordo back into a shadow. They waited there, watching the window; evidently she wore a white nightgown, for something white glistened against the darkness of the window.

"Laddie, what in the world happened to you?"

The dog jumped in through the open window. He had had enough adventures for one night. The white patch of nightgown moved away from the window. Dab said, "Now we can continue."

"I do not like this. Dead mans are not good."

Dab joked, "You are to go in and look at him."

"Not me, *amigo*. You."

"You'll be dead yourself some day," Dab told him.

"Sure, I know that. I go to Heaven. And I don't have to look at myself, either. I'll be dead."

"Heaven wouldn't have you," Dab grunted.

They came to the back of the hardware store. Gordo stationed himself at the far corner of the window. There was a night watchman in town—an old broken-down cowpuncher—and both hoped he would not hobble along. They had enough troubles as it was. Dab moved close to a window and went to work.

He jammed the straight end of the wrecking-bar under

the window and pried upward. The first time the bar slipped upward, tearing the wood; he had not jammed it under sufficiently far. He pushed it under the window again, using more force. The sharp end cut through the dried pine. He put his weight on the end of the bar, hearing the wood softly tear. Again the bar slipped, ripping free of the wood.

"What is the matter?" Gordo said in a low voice.

Dab did not answer. He jabbed the pointed flat end again, and this time he laid harder on the end of the bar, and heard the wood give. To his satisfaction, the prong-catches on each side of the window slipped out of their bases, and the window suddenly went up, screeching like a banshee wolf.

"Holy smokes," Gordo muttered. "What a racket."

Dab said, "Close your mouth."

For a moment he and his partner felt tension, and then this vanished as no alien sounds or voices were raised.

"Nobody they hear you," Gordo whispered.

Dab said, "You watch. I'm going inside."

Dab again gave the alley a glance and saw nothing out of the ordinary, and then he climbed into the gloomy, dark interior of the room. Right away he was aware of a strange smell, and he catalogued it mentally as the smell of something burned. He stood there in the dark and sniffed: Was it kerosene he smelled? Maybe the undertaker used kerosene in embalming a corpse. Dab didn't know a thing about embalming and had no desire to learn anything, either.

Silently he stood there, letting his eyes grow accustomed to the gloom. He saw the door leading to the hardware

Trail to High Pine

store's main section. He went across the room, and his hands found the key and he slowly locked this door. The thought had come that perhaps somebody slept in the store proper and might hear him and come to investigate.

To his right was a window. This looked out on the building next door, and he opened this, for the closeness of the room nauseated him. The other building was very close—about two feet away—and therefore nobody could see the window from the street.

He saw two chairs. On these lay some planks, and the dead man lay on these, not even a sheet over him. Dab gritted his teeth and moved over to look at the corpse, but the darkness was very thick.

Taking a chance, he lit a match, and what he saw almost made him bolt; with an effort, he controlled his stomach. The head was burned the worst, and the identification was impossible, he realized. His attention was attracted to the man's left knee. Below the knee cap was a scar. Fire had marred it and seared it, but it was clear, none the less.

The match burned down and he almost yelped when it hit his thumb and forefinger. He lit another match and again looked at this scar. He studied it and then broke the match. There had been no bullet-holes in the corpse; at least he had not seen any. Suddenly he stiffened.

"Hey, where is the watchman? There's a light in the back of the hardware—in the morgue!"

Dab froze in his tracks. Now who was up at this hour of the night? The voice had belonged to a man—it had been sort of squeaky and high-pitched.

Gordo was at the window. "Make the tracks, Dab."

Then he was gone, boots pounding down the alley.

"There runs a fellow," the old voice hollered. "Hey, town watchman—robbery—looting—"

Dab hit the window on the run, hooked one leg over the sill and hit the dust, stumbling as he landed. He ran down the alley, running as he had never run before in his life. Behind him he heard the town watchman yelping. The town was coming to life in a hurry.

Gordo had their horses out of the barn. "Hit the stirrups," he grunted.

Dab landed in saddle with one leap. "Hope nobody recognized us," he panted, turning his bronc on its hind legs.

"Get out of town," he hollered.

But already Gordo was doing just that. Bent over his bronc's neck, riding like a jockey, rump sticking up, the Mexican was whipping his bronc for speed, quirt rising and falling. Behind them somebody let go with a shotgun. The roar sounded like that of a small cannon. Dab instinctively ducked and wondered if any beebees had even come close to him or Gordo.

They skidded around a corner, moonlight silvering the dust; then they were in a grove of cottonwoods, out of sight of the townspeople. They rode through this dark avenue, moonlight dappling the soil, and they were in the sagebrush, about a mile out of town.

All this time, Gordo had been in the lead, working his horse the way a jockey works a mount, but now the crisis was past, and the Mexican slowed down his labouring, sweaty horse.

Trail to High Pine

"Did you know the dead man?" he asked.

"Yes, I did."

"Was he Matt Smith."

"No, he was not Matt Smith."

Gordo breathed deeply. His ox-like eyes were on Dab. "Did you know who he was, then?"

"That dead man was Jake Thomas."

Dab heard the swift, harsh intake of the man's breath. "Jake Thomas? The cowpuncher who work for your uncle, who settle on the homestead, who lose his shack to the fire last night?"

"Only one Jake Thomas on this range, Gordo."

"And that was him, dead? You sure?"

"I know it was Jake."

"How, for sure?"

"Mind last spring on calf roundup? I roped with Jake Thomas, remember? We were brandin' a heifer calf—over on Flat Mesa, it was—and Jake was flanking. The calf's mother come in behind him, horns out, and caught him in the knee."

"I remember. Ripped a hole in his hide."

Dab nodded. "We had him go into town and Doc took some stitches in the cut. About eight, I think. Well, that scar was on this corpse. Burnt some, but not enough to hide the scar."

"Then the corpse he is Jake?"

"That's what I told you. His skull had been fractured, too. Somebody had slugged him with something big and broad, looked like."

"What you think happened?"

"Well, Smith is in on it, and so is Turner. Turner wants to control the basin. He's working the Double J against the farmers to get them in one whale of a big fight, and when it is over Turner will be boss. Most of the farmers will be dead, the Double J will lose men, and everybody not dead will be in jail. So, with some capital, Turner could step in, buy for a song."

"He has some of his friends on homesteads, too, remember."

Dab said, "Seems this way to me. They slug Jake Thomas and kill him. Slug him from behind. Then they tote him to Smith's cabin, throw him in the flames, or else they put him in Smith's bed, then set fire to the joint. We smelled kerosene, remember? We saw Turner and Smith riding off, too."

"But they burn Thomas' cabin, too."

"Good thinking. Blame it on the farmers. Some might think even now that Thomas burned with the spread—some have looked for his bones in the ashes, they told me at the Double J."

Gordo rubbed his jaw thoughtfully. "That makes sense," he had to admit. "We were up on the rimrock. You saw the two fires. First they kill Jake, then tote his body to Smith's cabin."

"You're on the right track."

"They put Jake's carcass in the burning cabin. They got a man about the same size and build as Smith."

"They sure did."

Gordo let his mouth drop. "But where," he asked, "is Matt Smith?"

Trail to High Pine

Dab said, "That is one thing we have to find out."

"Maybe they have him hid out."

"Maybe," said Dab, "Turner killed him and buried him to silence him forever. It has been done before, you know."

Gordo gave this dark and gloomy thought. "But the farmers—they no want to fight; neither does the Double J. What would Turner do in a case like that?"

"Raise more ructions to blame on Jim Jones. Burn more of Jones' homestead shacks to blame it on the farmers. But one thing still puzzles me, Gordo."

"What she is that?"

"Why would he want to kill Jake Thomas?"

Gordo shrugged. "That is simple. He wants farmers to be real mad. Farmers liked Smith. they are real mad 'cause Smith is dead. Good move . . . for him."

"But rough on Jake Thomas," Dab had to admit.

"Maybe Smith he jump out of the country?"

Dab stared at his thick-set partner. "My God," he said, "that's the only thought you have had since I met you. How far is it from here to Willows?"

"The town where there is no buildings, just the depot?"

"That's the burg."

"About ten miles, maybe eight. Across the country, that is. Why do you ask?"

"We're going to Willows."

"For why?"

"You'll find out when we get there."

ELEVEN

Willows was in another county. It was a railroad point where the locomotives stopped for water and coal. The town consisted of a signboard with the name WILLOWS, MONTANA, and a single little telegraph office which Gordo had called a depot. The office had a telegrapher all hours of the day. Dab and Gordo did not know him, for the trading post at their end of the range was Beaverton. Telegraphers came and went; they did not stay long in this dull dreary outpost. They dismounted in front of the weather-beaten little shack with the semaphore over it and went inside. The operator was eating a sandwich, and that made both Dab and Gordo realize how hungry they were.

"Cowboys, hug?" the man asked, smiling.

"Lawmen," Dab corrected. "Dropping in to send out a message, Clerk. Been out hunting a murderer and he got away. Got a pencil and a pad?"

"Here you are, Sheriff."

Dab scrawled laboriously and slowly, for he was no hand with a pencil or pen. But finally he got the message written. Gordo, who could read quite a bit of English, followed the slowly-moving pencil, his mouth moving to form the words. When Dab had finished, Gordo looked up with a smile, comprehension showing in his dark eyes.

"Good work," he said.

"Here it is, Operator."

The man read the message aloud:

To all Law Officers, on Great Northern or Northern Pacific Railroads,
Heed this message:
Wanted for murder: one Matt Smith. Dark hair, six feet tall, heavy, coarse face, scar on right cheek, seldom shaves, talks rough. If caught, wire collect:
    Mike Hastings, Sheriff,
    Beaverhead County, Montana.

"Long ways from home," the operator said.

"Chased him quite a piece for quite a spell," Dab agreed.

The man went to his key, nimble fingers working. When he had sent the message over the wire he came back and said, "Odd thing, Sheriff."

"What is odd?" Dab had a cold feeling. But the man's next words chased it away. The man still believed him sheriff of Beaverhead County.

"I just sent out another message, almost like this, trying to find this same Matt Smith. About an hour ago, a man rode up here and had me send it to all points on these two lines."

"Who sent it?"

Gordo listened, mouth opened slightly.

The man described the man who had sent the telegram. Dab and Gordo exchanged glances. The man was describing just one: Land Locator Will Martin. Dab had to be sure, though.

"Was this gent a lawman, too?"

"Not that I know of. Never mentioned it. I got the telegram here." The man reached down and got a spindle that had a telegram impaled on it. He turned it and squinted. "Signed it by the name of Will Martin."

"Don't know him," Dab said.

He and his partner went outside, after paying the man.

"This I do not understand, Dabney," said Gordo.

"Martin is wise, too, I guess. Playing on his own hook. No use in notifying Sheriff O'Mahoney."

"I do not think Smith he had gone, nor do I think he is dead."

They got their saddles under them. "Why do you say that?" Dab wanted to know.

Gordo put his horse even with that of his partner. "Smith is in on this. There is a basin—an empire—at stake. Lots of money. Smith would not run out on it."

"He might be dead. Killed by Turner. Buried somewhere in a badlands grave that nobody will ever find."

"He was the tough man."

"Any man can be killed."

"I still think he is alive. He will lay low and let this blow over and then come back, maybe."

"Lot of guesswork."

"What else have we been running on? Nothing but the guesses. I still think Smith and Turner they are partners.

We watch Turner and he lead us to Smith. I feel sure of that."

"He might lead us into a gun-trap, too."

"We chance that."

Dab said, "I'm starving. My belt buckle is rubbing on the inside of my backbone. My stomach thinks my throat is cut. I could eat a skunk, hide and all."

"We can eat at the Flying W *rancho*. She is over the hills about three miles that way."

"We head that way."

They had breakfast at the Flying W, a spread not as big as the Double J. The foreman knew them, for each roundup the Flying W sent a rep over to work with the Double J, and he asked what they were doing in that neck of the timber, and Dab said Jim Jones had run them off. The man laughed and said Jim was probably trailing them, hurrying to catch them to bring them back.

After breakfast they set forth again.

"We had better not ride into Beaverton," Dab said.

Gordo suggested, "There might be the warrants there for us. Maybe somebody he recognize us last night when we rob the grave."

"I doubt it. We ran like kids with their parents chasing them. And we made a fast getaway."

"Still, we no go into town."

"You're right. No use tempting fate too far."

They changed horses at the same camp. With fresh broncs under their saddles, they felt better. When noon came they ate at the Rimrock Line Camp. Dab did the cooking. It all came from mason jars. Beans, some soup.

"From here we can see all the roads, huh?" Gordo commented.

"Every wagon road in and out of Beaverton," Dab said. "You watch with the field glasses, and I catch the shut-eye."

"Sleep and eat. Just like a hog."

"I didn't hear you," Gordo said.

Dab went outside and sat on a boulder.

He swung his field glasses down and to the west, and Beaverton came into their circle. The town was situated on a small bluff overlooking the basin and roads ran into it, looking like dusty snakes loafing in the sunlight. Beaverton was the hub of the wheel; and roads were the spokes running out.

Men and women and children moved along those roads. They moved on horseback, in buggies, in wagons, in democrats. Some of the farmers were going into town for supplies, perhaps expecting a long siege from the Double J. Others wanted more cartridges, perhaps a rifle or shotgun. Dab viewed the traffic in glum silence, and thought of the grim and deadly Wire Cutters' War.

So the afternoon marched into the mystery of other afternoons, and the shadows moved in and the night came. And in shifts the partners watched, and saw nothing of interest.

TWELVE

Night moved in again, possessing the earth, filling the contours and *coulées* with thick blankness. Again Dab saw the dim far lights of Beaverton, yellow and tawny against the night; again, the shacks of the farmers were dark. Dab again felt the chill of approaching autumn. He let Gordo sleep and sat there alone in the dark. About midnight, despite the chill, he dozed and he slept about an hour—he was exhausted and weary to the bone. The marks left by Turner's ugly spur rowels had crusted over and were itchy. His face was losing the swelling put there by the fists of both Will Martin and Mike Turner. He came awake slowly and looked out over the basin; now Beaverton, too, was dark. The moon on this night was thin and dull, for high clouds had moved in. A harsh wind sent these clouds scurrying across the upper reaches of the sky. There was no wind here on the earth, and Dab was glad of that. He got to his boots and walked along the rimrock to loosen his muscles. About an hour later, a fire came into sight below him.

First it was a red light—an evil eye. Then, within a minute, the flames moved upward, red and sullen and strong in the moonlight. Dab went to the cabin and hollered inside, "Gordo, *vengá*."

"*Si*, I come."

Soon his partner was standing beside him.

"Fire, Dab."

"What cabin would you say?"

"That is the cabin of Joe Yokum, that tall farmer. It has to be his cabin. He has no neighbours and he is in that section of Wild Rose Creek, Dabney."

Dab said, "He had some trouble with Jim Jones once, down in town. Accused Jim of cutting his pasture fence, wasn't it?"

"He did that, and they argued."

"Now we know why his cabin got burned," Dab said. "Next thing is to catch the man who burned it."

"Hit the saddles, no?"

"Yes."

Soon they were riding down off the rimrock, following the trail more by practice and instinct than by sight. Old Jim Jones would get the blame for this, Dab knew. Turner and Yokum were good friends. Dab built the rest of it in his mind. Turner and Yokum had burned down the farmer's shack. Everybody in the valley knew that Jim Jones and Joe Yokum had had an argument. The finger of suspicion, flat and ugly, would point at his uncle.

But the main thing was to find Turner, following him into the hills. Smith might be with the deputy sheriff, Dab realized. Then another thought came and he shouted back to Gordo, "Yesterday I saw a rider leave Yokum's shack. My glasses picked him up. He didn't go into Beaverton."

"Where did he go?" The Mexican's voice could hardly be heard above the rattle of their broncs' hoofs.

"Rode straight across the basin. Headed for Canada."

"You see who he was, Dabney?"

"Distance too far even for my field glasses. But I get it now. They've paid Yokum off and he's drifted. Now Turner has burned his cabin. They'll look for Yokum and they won't find him, of course. So Jim'll get the blame of doing away with Yokum."

"So she could turn out, Dab."

"I never saw the rider come back to Yokum's shack and—"

Dab never got to finish his sentence. His horse stumbled over a rock and started to fall. To Dab's left was darkness; here the cliff tumbled off into a drop of about a hundred feet, he knew. Behind him, the horse carrying the Mexican stepped over the boulder, warned by the fall of Dab's horse. Dab was fighting to control the plunging, stumbling horse.

He hauled upward on his reins, boots braced in ox-bow stirrups. One moment it appeared that he had control of the horse; the next, the bronc was stumbling and falling again. Time seemed aeons long. Finally Dab had the horse on all four hoofs and the horse trembled in the night. Dab patted him on a sweaty shoulder.

"Good boy," he said.

Gordo said, "He fell over the boulder."

"You don't need to tell me." Dab pushed back his hat and wiped his forehead. "And just a minute or so back I was cold. I'll get killed yet."

"Unless you die before you get killed."

Dab said, "Very funny."

They were on level ground at long last. The fire was not so bright now, because they were even with the land; they were not looking down at the fire now—they were level with it. They loped off the foothills, following a mesa's curving base; then they were on the prairie proper—level and sweeping and wide. They could see only glimpses of the fire now. That was because the cottonwood and box-elder trees of Wild Rose Creek had moved between them and the flames.

Dab rode a pace or two in the lead, his partner running his pony behind his. Dab hoped they could find some trace of the men who had burned the cabin. They were staying away from the travelled wagon road because it would lead them past the houses of two nesters. And these farmers would be ready to fling lead at any night riders.

Despite their precautions they still drew the fire of a farmer's rifle. That was because a farmer had recently taken up a claim on this creek. He had not yet built a house; he lived in a dull-coloured old army tent. Suddenly this reared out of the night, and Dab said, "Swing right," and reined his horse in that direction. The flame of a rifle came out of the tent.

"Farmer . . . in a tent."

Dab said, "Ride, but don't fire back."

He did not know where the three rifle balls went. He only knew they missed them—and that was what counted. Then they were in the timber, and the farmer was behind them.

Gordo rode close. "You are all right, Dabney?"

"He missed me. You?"

"I no get hit."

Mosquitoes came buzzing out of the swampland along the creek They came out in thousands, anxious for some supper—human and equine. Dab batted at them and said, "We swing away from the crick."

"They make the meal of me."

They left the brush and the wind on the hills brushed the mosquitoes away. They were close to the Yokum house. The flames were down now—the house had been small, made of dried pine, and had burned with great rapidity. They came in behind it and moved through the buckbrush, glasses in hand. Nobody was around the burning house. Soon Dab and his partner watched from the brush. The bedding was a glow of fire against the bent iron bedstead. But no bodies were inside.

Dab said, "We swing south, into the hills."

"Why?"

"Turner rides out of the south hills. Smith might be with him. They'll go back there and lay around a day or so, I figure."

"All she is the guesswork."

Dab shrugged. "What more have we to work on?"

"Nothing, Dabney."

So they turned toward the badlands, and behind them the house of Joe Yokum was ashes.

The moon came up even higher, and the yellow light became more strong. And it was Gordo, the man who could hear anything, who heard a horse moving somewhere to the right, off in the hills.

"Listen, Dabney."

He had reached down and taken the reins of Dab's bridle, compressing them between the horse's jaw and neck. Dab listened and heard nothing—only the talk of the gentle wind in the branches of some bullberry trees.

Dab said, "They"re gone now, Gordo."

Gordo straightened. "They might have been made by the wild horses, Dabney. And they might have been the hoofs of a saddled horse, too."

"Only a fool would ride this mesa," Dab said, and looked at the badlands around them.

"Or a person who is hiding from the law," Gordo said.

"Maybe we ride a cold trail."

"We have no other way to go."

Dab said, "Come along."

Dab took the lead, for the trail petered out here, running along the edge of a sandstone ledge, a dark canyon below them. Dab knew they had to find Smith, either Smith in the flesh, or in his grave.

Gorgo said, "I hope we no get killed. I am a young man yet." And he laughed, but the laugh was not a merry one.

"You're a cheerful son."

By the time dawn had come, they were quite a few miles into the badlands. They squatted and waited for the sun to rise, and the air was cold. Dab figured by this time they were on a wild-goose chase. They had seen no trace of any rider, they had heard no hoofs in the distant night. They were hungry and cold and disgruntled. Gordo hunkered on the sunny side of a boulder, his blue overall-cloth jacke pulled around him, and the chill made his face take on a bluish hue.

Dab said, "Seems to me that that thick layer of fat around you would turn the cold, Gordo. Gordo means *fat man* in Mexican, don't it?"

"Fat does not turn the *frio*—the cold."

Dab said, "Oh, for hot coffee and ham and eggs. And you say I should not marry Martha Lincoln!"

"You do as you want."

"I do that anyway."

Gordo said, "This is the only trail leading back into this country. And yet it turns out to be a cold trail."

Dab shivered. "Darned cold, too."

"We go back to the rimrock camp, huh?"

"First we do some scouting."

Gordo shifted his weight to his other leg and stretched his leg slowly. "I have the cramp in the leg."

"Good."

Gordo fought the pain, lips twisted. Then it left, and he pulled his leg back under him.

"Turner and Smith, now."

"Yes?"

"We say that Smith he is alive. Turner he has him hid out somewhere. That does not mean that Turner he is with Smith now."

"You're talking sense, for once."

"We say that last night Turner and Smith they burn down Joe Yokum's house. Yokum he has already left the country and the house she is vacant and nobody he is to guard it. Smith and Turner they come and burn down the house. Then Turner he ride back to Beaverton—he is the innocent man, the deputy sheriff, you know—and Smith ride back into the badlands where we are."

"You still sound good, Gordo. Go on."

"Maybe Turner he not burn down the house. Maybe Yokum's house is burned down by Smith. Turner he is in town, and somebody they come in and tell the sheriff that Yokum's house is burning. That looks good for Turner, no?"

Dab pulled his forefinger across the dust. "It sure does. There he is—big as life— and this rider tells about Yokum losing his house, and Yokum is nowhere around. Maybe this gent says Yokum might have burned in the fire, or the Double J have killed Joe Yokum."

"What would Turner he do then?"

"Ride out to investigate, I'd say. After all, he's deputy sheriff."

"Then what he do?"

Dab gave this a moment of deep thought. "Prob'ly meet Smith somewhere back in the hills."

"Then maybe we on the wrong racetrack, Dabney."

"You mean we're looking for Smith and we should be looking for Turner. Is that what you mean, Gordo?"

"*Si*. Yes."

Dab asked slowly, "What brought on all these deep observations?"

"One rider . . . last night. He pass somewhere in the dark. But only one rider she was—I know for sure my ears they tell me."

Dab said, "You think that was Smith?"

"He could be. He could have gone down on the basin

bottom and set the shack on fire and then come back to his hiding place."

Dab nodded. "Turner will contact him later, huh?"

"I think so . . . if Smith he is alive."

Dab said, "Then we are wasting our time here. The thing to do is go back to the place where this canyon comes out and watch there. If Turner rides out, he is the man we heard in the dark. If Smith was the man, Smith is hid somewhere back in this wilderness and we prob'ly couldn't find him."

"So I think, *tambien*."

"Then if Turner rides in, he is going to contact Smith, and Smith was the man riding in the dark. So we follow Turner, and he leads us to Smith?"

"Smith he holds the key to the whole thing."

"And he might be dead, and we might be barkin' up the wrong tree."

Gordo got to his feet and brushed dust from his chaps. "We have to take that chance, Dabney."

"We'll ride back," Dab said.

THIRTEEN

They mounted and headed back down the trail. The wind was chilly and snow was not far off, and this reminded Dab that when this trouble had started he and Gordo had been ordered to ride bog holes and pull out cows until snow came and two months passed, whichever was sooner. The old ringy cow had sure started things when she had rushed his horse.

Suddenly he remembered how Martha Lincoln had roped the cow with a loop big enough to snag a young dinosaur and how she had sailed into space, saddle and all. He'd never let her forget that incident.

When they reached the point where the trail left the bottom land and started into the hills, the sun had risen enough to gain some warmth and the chill was slowly leaving both of them. They came to the level ground, the badlands behind them, and Dab said, "That rider sounded like he rode to the west of us, didn't he?"

"*Si*, the west."

Dab turned his horse in that direction. "We do some scouting," he said.

Trail to High Pine   129

They rode over the hill, and here was another trail running up a different *coulée*. They followed it about a mile, and it joined the trail on which they had ridden, but the juncture had been hidden by trees—therefore they had ridden directly past it without noticing it.

"The man he ride ahead of us, and then swing in on the trail," Gordo said. "But he did not ride a shod horse. His horse he was barefooted. He has big hoofs—they are round."

"He rides a horse from the valley," Dab said. "Down there where there're so few rocks a horse grows a round hoof—no boulders to chip off his hoofs. Up here in the hills, with all this rough country and gravel, a horse has a small hoof—nature trims it for him."

"Smith would ride a horse that had been on the bottom land," the Mexican said. "But we cannot trail him. The wind she has blown the trail clear of hoof marks, even those we left."

Dab looked at the twisted badlands ahead. "A man could hole up in them crevices," he said, "and hold back an army. We'd ride right into Smith's rifle, if that was him—and it must have been him. Or it might have been Turner."

"No hoofs they come out but ours. Here where the brush broke the wind, there is this set of hoofs, and those left by our shod horses."

"He's still in there," Dab agreed.

Gordo Alvarez frowned.

Dab said, "Smith is on the spot. He can't stay in this country. He's supposed to be dead, you know."

Gordo nodded. "Only one thing Smith can do, if he has

not already done it—and that is leave the country. You are almost accused of his murder—maybe there is a warrant out now. We have been in the badlands for some days. If he shows his face again around Beaverton, the whole plan he has with Turner is exploded like the rifle bullet."

"Maybe those tracks are leaving the country for good."

Gordo gave this deep thought. "We have telegrams out—you and me and Will Martin, and some lawman he pick up Smith."

Dabney Jones agreed with this. They went back to their original programme of watching Turner, hoping he would lead them to Matt Smith. They decided to split up temporarily. Gordo Alvarez would return to the Rimrock Camp and watch from that high vantage point with his glasses. Dab said he would stick around Beaverton, and if Turner left that cowtown, he would swing in behind the deputy sheriff. To this plan the Mexican expressed some opposition. He pointed out that Dab might be seen and caught and sent to jail. Dab grinned and said he could take care of himself. He wanted to be closer to Beaverton to make absolute identification of every rider who entered or left the cowtown.

"We can see them good from Rimrock Camp, Gordo, but the distance is too far to be absolutely sure who the riders are."

"You are right there, Dabney. We should arrange some signal, no?"

Dab said, "What would it be? He might ride in the night. I couldn't fire my pistol—that would warn him—and if I stopped to build a signal fire, I might lose his track. Besides,

Trail to High Pine

he might see the fire."

Gordo said, "I have the answer."

The answer was simple. Gordo would stay on the camp on the rimrock in the daytime, but when dusk came he would descend into the basin and watch the trails leading into the badlands.

"And if you do trail Turner, I can meet you along where the hills come down, where the big cottonwood tree is in the wash, Dabney."

"Good idea."

So they parted company, with Dab riding toward Beaverton and Gordo turning his horse toward the higher country overlooking the basin to the south. Dab knew now what it felt like to be a drifting coyote—always on the alert, watching the skyline, listening, tense.

He spent most of the day in the brush along Beaver Creek where the road came across the creek, running south. From the high buckbrush's cover he watched the rigs move—springwagons, buggies, buckboards, lumber-wagons. These were the farmers, and they were armed—they sat on the seats with rifles close at hand and short-guns strapped to their waists. He saw not a single Double J cowpuncher. That told him that Jim Jones was keeping his hands close to the home camp.

And there were not many farmers abroad, either. About six rigs all day was the count; this told him that they, too, were staying close at home to guard their property. Turner had a fine scheme; his net was secure. He had his hired hands on homesteads, and these would revert back to him when the time came, and the farmers would sell to him—

that is, some would. But some would be stubborn and stick it out. Turner's scheme was unsuccessful in one thing, though—Jim Jones and the farmers were not having open warfare. And Turner's scheme called for them to fight and annihilate each other.

To win, Turner would have to get the Double J fighting the homesteaders. Then Dab saw a rider come from the direction of Beaverton.

This rider was a slender man dressed in a neat blue suit, the legs tucked into justin half-boots, and a Tom Watson stetson was on his head. He rode a midnight black gelding that tossed his head against the bit and the flies. He was the land locator, Will Martin.

Martin rode within a few rods of where Dab Jones was hidden. Dab thought back to the day he and the land locator had fought and Martha Lincoln had watched them fight. Despite his easy-going manner and soft appearance, this land locator was tough. Dab grinned.

The thought came that Martin was riding out to cheer his farmers and talk to them. The militia might be called in, Dab realized—that would be a good move. He decided to trail the land locator for a distance. He rode up-creek, came to the hills, and there left the brush, going into the huge sandstone rocks on top of a hill. From here with his glasses he watched the man. Martin rode south toward the badlands, and the rising hills cut him from view. Dab wondered why he rode toward the rough country. Possibly had some farmers located in that area, although Dab did not know of any.

How deep was the land locator in this? Was he working

with Turner? But Will Martin had ridden to Willows and sent out a telegram, signing the sheriff's name to it, to apprehend and stop the man called Matt Smith.

This put Will Martin against Mike Turner.

Dab figured that Gordo, up there on the dim and hazy rimrock to the south, would follow the land locator through his glasses, so accordingly he gave his thoughts over to different subjects. He was raw inside, for impatience was a grindstone, and he wanted to move, to settle this. The day moved away, as all days must do, and then there was dusk—as only Montana can have dusk—silent, clinging to the sun-parched earth, blessing the soil and the trees and the earth, blessing the soil and the trees and the land.

And out of this dusk there came a rider.

FOURTEEN

Dab was not hiding along the creek in the buckbrush when he saw this rider. Down there the mosquitoes were fierce, for the wind had died down and given them the opportunity to rise from the pot holes with their green and slimy water. Accordingly Dab Jones had moved back into the rocks. He was sitting there in the darkness, watching the dimming ribbon of the trail, when the rider came jogging along, heading south.

And that rider was Deputy Sheriff Mike Turner.

Dab stared at the man. Turner rode at a slow trot, sitting solid in his saddle, big body anchored between fork and cantle, boots deep in the visalia stirrups. He rode a black horse, too—just as had Will Martin.

The light was still strong enough to show the rifle in the saddle boot, the Winchester with its stock up, ready for the rifleman's hand to lift it, sweep it out of the leather holster. He could see, too, that Turner now packed two guns instead of one.

The man was ready for danger.

Turner rode straight east about three miles and then,

Trail to High Pine 135

once behind the black protective cover of rocky Black Butte, he rode south toward the badlands. By this time, the night was very dark, and Dab lost the man's trail. He knew only that Mike Turner had ridden toward the rough country. He hoped that Gordo would be watching the badlands trails and that the obese man would again come through by picking up the trail of Mike Turner, if Turner actually entered the badlands.

Dab turned his horse south. This was a hard task, for the night carried sounds, and the man ahead might draw rein and listen, and there was a chance of an ambush. He therefore rode with caution. He worked his way across the rangelands, heading towards the badlands, and soon the moon came up—but on this night when they really needed the moonlight, the clouds were high and lazy, and the moon seemed reluctant to get from behind them.

Dab rode toward the east, intending to come in along the edges of the badlands. He did not want to ride directly along the trail, for Turner might have holed up and he might be watching his back-trail.

When he came to the edge of the hills he judged it to be close to midnight. He was tired of the saddle, tired of his thoughts—he longed for hot coffee and his bunk at the Double J. He knew now how an outlaw felt—furtive, watching, hoping, tired. The hills came out, he reined to the west, and he rode along the rim of the steep cliffs, their shadows throwing him into darkness.

He came at last to the point where the two trails entered the badlands. He pulled his horse down, and the horse was tired. He dismounted and left the horse in the brush of a *coulée* and went ahead on foot. He hoped that Gordo would not shoot at him. Maybe it had been wrong to go in on foot. Had he ridden in openly the Mexican would have hung back and watched and come out when recognition became certain.

"Who goes there?"

The words were soft and yet they penetrated the night. They came from the direction of some big boulders to Dab's right.

"Gordo?"

"*Si*. Over here, Dabney."

Soon they were close together, each glad to see the other.

"What have you seen, Dab?"

Dab told about seeing Land Locator Will Martin heading toward the badlands. Then he told about seeing Deputy Sheriff Mike Turner also riding south, presumably heading for the rough country.

"First Turner went east; then he circled around Black Butte. That was to throw off anybody following him. If anybody saw him leave town they would think he aimed to ride east, instead of swinging south again."

"He ride into badlands, I think."

"What do you mean by *think*?"

The Latin was not sure. A rider had moved along the trail. The night had been dark; the rider had resembled Mike Turner. But certain identification was impossible because of the night.

"Did you see Will Martin?" Dab asked.

Gordo had seen the land locator. He had watched him from the rimrock area with his field glasses.

"He rides into the badlands, Dabney."

Dab frowned. "Did he ride out again?"

"Not that I could see. Did you see Martin ride back towards town?"

"No."

"I think he is still in the badlands."

Dab pushed back his hat. "This has got me up a stump." He rubbed his forehead slowly. "Martin rides into the badlands; later, Turner follows him. Why would they be heading into that rough country? No reason for them to ride into that God-forsaken stretch of nothing."

"They must have the reason."

Dab said, "If we rode in there on horseback we'd be like ducks sitting on a pond. They'd skyline us and pick us off with rifles before we even knew one of them was in the vicinity."

"Me, I hates to walk."

"Either walk or run," Dab said.

So they left their broncs in the brush and went along the trail on foot, carrying their rifles. Dab was in the lead. They had taken down their spurs and had hung them on their saddles, and this eliminated that noise. Still the sounds of their boots on the dust sounded loud to Dabney Jones' ears. Dabney did not like walking; he had been born to the saddle. The badlands were about five miles across. What if they had to leg it all this distance? What if Turner and Martin had used the badlands only for a short-cut and were not in the area's boundaries but had merely ridden through to get on the other side. Five miles to the other side; five miles back. That added up to ten long wearisome miles . . .

on foot.

Behind him came his fat partner, who puffed and wheezed with each step; plainly walking did not agree with Gordo either. The trail was narrow as it moved along the base of the hill, and then it reached an area where it fanned out somewhat, making a small flat about two hundred feet wide, the trail running along the west side. This flat was rough with bumps and held some tall clumps of sagebrush that looked silvery-grey under the moon. And they were on this flat when they heard the rap-rap of rifle bullets up ahead, the sound sharp and ugly on the chilly night air.

Dab grabbed back at Gordo, caught his sleeve, held him. "Rifle shots," he whispered, his voice hoarse.

"You count them, Dab?"

"Four, I think."

"Four there was, I think."

Dab said, "Let's hide in the brush."

He darted off the trail, heading for a clump of high sagebrush, and Gordo was on his heels, moving like a dark, thick shadow. Once behind the sagebrush, they hunkered there, watching the trail, and their voices were husky with excitement. Gordo asked, "What do you think she has happened?"

Dab said, "Somebody shot at somebody else."

"That much is certain. The shots they sound to me like they were all fired from the same rifle—they were rifle reports because they were not as loud as those made by a six-shooter. If they were shot by one rifle, then only one man he do the shooting, no?"

"Yes, so I would say."

"Who shoot at who? Turner and Martin, they shoot it out, maybe?"

Dab said, "Here comes a rider."

They lay on their bellies, rifles out, and waited as the hoofs became louder. The rider was coming out of the badlands and would pass in front of them on the trail. Dab's mouth was dry. It seemed a long time until the rider came around the curve and rode in front of them. He came without great haste, hitting a lope that was not too taxing on his horse, and he carried a rifle in his free hand. They got to see him but a fleeting moment, nothing more. Then he was gone and out of sight in the neck of the badlands.

Gordo said, "He rode a black horse."

"So did Martin . . . and Turner."

"He carried a rifle."

"The land man, Will Martin?"

Dab said, "Did you know who he was?"

"Turner, I think."

Dab said, getting to his feet, "I think it was Turner, too. He's done some shooting. Maybe he has killed somebody. Who?"

Dab said, "Martin rode into this area. Could be." He was moving down the trail, heading in the direction whence the rider had come. These badlands, with their scarlet walls, their blue ledges, their orange streaks, held a mystery. Dabney Jones was sure of that. A man did not ride all the distance from Beaverton to this spot just to stage midnight target practice with his rifle.

"Sure hope he doesn't find our horses cached out," Dab murmured.

Gordo whispered, "They are hid back in the brush and far off the trail, Dabney. This has me stumped. I hope I do not get killed."

"We'd render you for lard," Dab said, "Make hotcakes for a whole winter at the Double J out of your suet."

"My *amigo*—my friend."

Dab hoped the rider would not see their horses. If he did then they would be bottled here in the rough country. But there was no time for such conjecture. They moved forward, bent over, with Gordo behind. They passed through a narrow part of the trail and came to another wide area, this one even wider than the spot where they had crouched and watched the rider leave.

Dab said, "You trail in behind me . . . cover my back."

"*Si.*"

Dab went ahead, working through the brush. He was sure that the shots had been fired on this flat area. His ears had judged them to be about this far distant. He swung around through the sagebrush, working toward the east wall of the canyon, and he felt stiff and worried. But Gordo was watching his back, he knew; this helped him some. This seemed like a crazy wild dream. Would he wake up soon in the Double J bunkhouse? He stubbed his toe on a rock and almost hollered. He knew then for sure it was no dream.

He paused, dark against some underbrush. Had anybody heard his boot hit the rock? The sound had been very loud in his own ears. He listened but he heard nothing. The wind did not move the brush here because they were at the bottom of the canyon.

He went ahead and then stopped in the brush that

Trail to High Pine

rimmed a clearing. Here a man had evidently made camp—he saw the dark outlines of a rock-rimmed campfire, the ashes cold, and beyond it a bunk-roll on the ground. But he was interested in none of these things.

What interested him was the form of the man lying there on the ground. From this distance it looked as though the man lay on his face, belly down. Dab took a long look around, saw no danger, and went to the man, going to his knee and turning him over.

The body was limp, which meant the man had not long been dead, and bullets had punched wicked holes in his chest. He had blood on both the front and back of his blue shirt. His mouth sagged open, and moonlight showed his grey flesh.

Dab stood up then, wiping his hands on his chaps. He studied the face and was opening his mouth to call to Gordo when he heard the sound of brush crackling behind him, the ring of a boot heel on gravel.

Dab turned, gun rising.

Then he stopped his upward lift, for two men came into the clearing, one walking ahead of the other. The man in the lead had his hands raised shoulder high, and his thin face was grim. Gordo had his .45 in the man's back.

"I find him back in the brush, Dab. He watch us."

Dab said, "Will Martin."

Gordo looked at the dead man. "I cannot see from here who he is, Dabney."

"Matt Smith."

FIFTEEN

They got the story from the lips of Land Locator Will Martin. He also had grown suspicious of Mike Turner. He was, after all, working for his farmers—hadn't he located them and nursed them along as a mother would rear her children? He too had wondered if the corpse taken from the fire had really been the body of Matt Smith.

Dab thought of the telegram the man had sent, and nodded. This all added up and gave a true and accurate total. He listened to the land agent talk. The moonlight was brighter now, for the moon was straight overhead. It showed the stern thin face of the dead man.

"Turner hired Smith to help him kill Jake Thomas and then heave Thomas' carcass into the fire," Dab said slowly. "We saw them ride out—Gordo and me saw them. And now you say he rode in here a while back to pay off Smith?"

"He did that. I watched from the brush. He paid Smith and told him to get out of the country, and Smith started to count the money—it was paper money. And when he got interested counting, Turner shot him with his own rifle—shot him four times through the chest."

Trail to High Pine

"How did he get hold of Smith's rifle?" Gordo asked.

"Smith had it leaning against a tree. He never saw Mike Turner pick it up, for he had his head down counting the money. Turner got his money back and he got rid of Smith and then he rode out. But first he turned Smith's horse loose from picket—the bronc is back in the brush grazing—"

"I saw him," Gordo said, "right before I come in behind you, Land Man."

"You walk on silent boots, heavy man."

"My mother she was a little woman and she was quick like the cat. My father he was a big man—"

Dab said, "Forget your family tree, Gordo."

"I am the nut from that tree," Gordo said.

"An old stale joke." Dab looked at the dead man. "We saw Turner head out, but we weren't sure it was him. Both you and him rode black horses."

"Night horses," the land man said.

Dab got to his feet, whistling tunelessly. "Well, we got the thing solved, and we got Turner where we want him—but we need the help of one man, and that man is you, Will Martin."

Martin said, "I'm afraid. I've gone too far already. I got an old mother in St. Louis. I have to send her money—support her. I want to back out, men. I'll drift, if needs be. Turner is a killer. I saw him pump lead into this poor devil. He never hesitated, never wavered. Just lifted that rifle, sighted it, and killed him—got his money back and rode away."

Dab shook his head.

Gordo was lump-faced, silent, watching Will Martin.

Martin said, "What is the plan, men?"

Gordo looked at Dabney Jones and let his shoulders fall, and remained silent. He was letting Dab make the decisions.

"You can't pull out on us, Martin."

"This is a free country, Jones. I can do what I want."

Dab shook his head slowly. "Not this time. If we let you go we throw this basin into a range war. Gordo and I were just kids, but we went through one, and it was no fun. I've seen them in the Pecos, bodies with bullet holes like Smith's body here—swishing back and forth, back and forth."

Gordo canted his great dark head, listening.

Will Martin was thin, razor sharp, hard as steel.

Dab said, "They think I might have killed Smith. There is that rumour, you know. O'Mahoney is riding a cold trail and his horse's shoes are ice. They lay the blame for these burned down shacks on me and my uncle and the Double J. Only you know the truth—saw the truth—and you'll testify to that, even if I have to beat you silly to get you into town to talk to the sheriff."

"Turner will kill me."

"No, he won't. We'll see to that. Turner put the killer label on me, and he tried to run my partner in under the same brand. I don't like it. I'll kill Turner if I have to. He's got some yellow in him. He hides behind a badge—he's a disgrace to men like O'Mahoney who might be not too bright in the head but is honest up the backbone, like a law officer should be."

"Where do I come in?" Will Martin asked.

Dab got to his boots. "You ride with us . . . to Beaverton."

Dabney Jones gave the problem deep thought on the ride into Beaverton. Mike Turner had not buried Matt Smith because he had had no shovel on his saddle, according to Will Martin. Turner had ridden out to pay Smith for his part in the murder of Jake Thomas and the mutilation of Thomas' body in the fire. But he had changed his mind about Smith . . . and four bullets had recovered his money for him. He had left Smith's body and Smith's saddle behind.

"He probably figured on coming back to bury Smith sometime," Will Martin said. "He probably figured on bringing out a shovel, burying him and the saddle together."

"We could wait out by the body," Gordo said. "Then when he came back we could call his hand."

Dab shook his head. "He might never come back. He might never bury Smith. Nobody ever rides that country—cattle don't go back there. No cowboys ride back there in those badlands. Smith and the saddle could turn to dust and nobody would ever find them."

"Reckon that is right, Dabney."

"He had me fooled," the land agent said. "I thought he was an honest guy. Then when things broke and I got to thinking—The main clue was when you boys broke into the morgue to look at the body. That got me thinking. They buried the corpse yesterday, still thinking they were burying Matt Smith."

Dab said, "That is logical. No one would know unless he knew about the scar on his leg, and if nobody saw the scar . . . well, the secret would go into the grave with Jake Thomas' body."

"He never knew I watched him from the brush," the land agent informed Dab. "I got suspicious of him riding out of those badlands, so I did some investigating, and the odd thing is that you boys had the same suspicions I had. I checked the results of my telegram from Willows, and the telegrapher told about you two sending out a telegram like mine. That clinched the idea we were both working on the same track, Dab."

Dab said, "You were lucky that Mike Turner never caught you in that canyon, Martin. He'd have gunned it out with you."

"And I'm no hand with a gun, either pistol or rifle."

"This points to only one thing, men," Dab said.

Gordo glanced at him. "And that thing, Dabney?"

"Only one person knows that Turner shot down Matt Smith. That man, of course, is Will Martin here. Martin's evidence could send Turner to the gallows."

"It might not," Martin said.

"You saw it," Dab said.

"But it would just be my word against his, Jones. One man against another, and my reputation is new here—not too strong. It might not hold up. I doubt if it would hold up."

Gordo said, "He talks the sense."

"You're no lawyer, Gordo."

Gordo shrugged, smiled. "What plan have you,

Dabney?"

Dabney looked at Will Martin. "Did Mike Turner look at Matt Smith to make sure he was dead, Martin?"

"That he did, Dab. He felt of the man's wrist to see if he had any pulse. I could see it clearly. A cold-blooded affair, with Smith being given no chance. I'll remember it until I die."

"He might have seemed steady enough," Dab said, "but I'll bet he was cold inside, and his thinking wasn't any too clear. A man might put on a poker face in a deal like that, but his nerves were hollering inside, I'll bet."

Gordo asked, "What is behind all this?"

"Martin is built a lot like Smith," Dab said. "In the night, it would be hard to tell one from the other, if they had their heads covered when anybody happened to look at them."

"What's the deal?" Martin asked.

"I've got a plan."

"Spill it," Gordo said.

They drew rein and Dab explained. They had to get Turner to come to them, for, as Will Martin had said, they could not prove he was a killer just by putting Martin's word against his. The fact that Smith lay dead in the badlands meant nothing—it did not point to Turner as his killer.

"We have to get Turner to make a play that will be the same as a verbal confession," Dabney Jones said.

"But how?" Martin asked.

Dab explained his plan. Gordo listened, nodding occasionally, agreeing with his partner. It was the land locator, Will Martin, who objected. His objection was based on the danger that he might get killed. And as he said jokingly, he was too young—far too young—to die.

"Gordo will guard you all the time," Dab said.

Martin glanced at the obese dark-skinned man. "That is no comfort," he said, and grinned.

"You'll be armed," Dab reminded him.

Martin considered the plan and said, "All right, I'll go through with it. It might not work, though. We might run into O'Mahoney."

"He's prob'ly asleep in his hotel room," Dab said.

Martin said, "Let's go, men."

They rode faster then, sweeping across the prairie. Dab Jones took the lead, the land locator riding on his nigh-side, his partner on his off-side. Dab tried to put himself in Mike Turner's shoes. He guessed that the man would be raw inside, his nerves jumpy under a tough exterior, and that there would be little sleep for Turner on this night. A dead man who had been Turner's friend lay there in that canyon with sightless, bulging eyes. Turner would remember that dead man, that friend, the man he had blasted into death. The memory of those straining, opened eyes with terror scrawled across them, the memory of the sagging bloody mouth—would they not return through a man's dreams and bring him sitting upright in bed, his mouth twitching and his brain hot and feverish? Dab hoped so.

Gordo was thinking that this would soon be ended, or so he hoped. Soon he could live a normal life again—punch cows for old Jim Jones and sleep in the feather-tick bed he had in the bunkhouse. He could squat and sip coffee and not keep an eye on the horizon for a lawman. Martin and

Trail to High Pine   149

Jim Jones would get together, and the cowman and the farmers would patch things up. Martin has suggested this and Dab had agreed, and if Dab agreed old Jim Jones would agree, too. Gordo was sure of this. Accordingly his thoughts had taken on a brighter hue.

Will Martin was mentally checking Dab's plan for loopholes. Back East a young woman was awaiting him. His success here on Beaver Creek would determine the date of his marriage to that girl. Martin had been misled by Turner. He had at first admired the man, but now he remembered the ease—the killer-ease—with which Turner had murdered his friend, Matt Smith.

And the memory put ice in Martin's veins.

Martin believed in the future of this Montana basin. He believed in it from the bottom of his heart. He had a homestead himself on which he was proving up. His plans went beyond dry-land farming. He had no faith in dry-land farming—one summer would bring twenty inches of rain and the next would bring four or five. Check-dams could be built in *coulées* to hold spring run-off water. A big dam could be constructed in Beaver Creek. Water could be run through ditches onto hungry fields of alfalfa. Yes, and corn, wheat, oats, barley—other head crops—Yes, and root crops, too.

Martin would develop this farm, and the girl would work with him. Then would come the day when from the doorway of her kitchen she would see her first-born ride his pony for the first day of school. Martin looked forward to this day, and other good days. He had come from poor parents. His only hope of freedom was to make contact with the soil, to work with his hands, to build his fences and plant his crops. So he gave Dab's plan deep consideration. And he found it as good as any he could have proposed.

Besides, he would have a pistol with him at all times.

This conclusion reached, Will Martin awaited the results of time and fate. He looked at Dab Jones, who rode high on stirrups, angled forward. He remembered fighting with Dab. They had been fools to fight. They had really had nothing to fight over. Turner had had a lot to do with that, too. Now that he looked back, everything centred around the big crooked deputy sheriff, Will Martin thought with grim wryness.

Dab said, "My ribs still ache."

"He use you for the rodeo horse," Gordo Alvarez said. "He rake you fore and aft with his hooks, like the cowboys does the buckin' horse."

'Don't rub it in," Dab growled.

Gordo glanced at his partner and realized Dab was only kidding.

SIXTEEN

They came to the limits of Beaverton, there on the mesa overlooking Beaver Creek, and Dab pulled his horse around, untying his blanket from back of his saddle, and handed the blanket to Will Martin.

"Cover your head with this, just leaving enough to see out of," he said. "Drape it around your shoulders and ride bent over in saddle, like you was sick or shot or both."

"Or half-shot?" the land locator joked.

Dab grinned. "Don't even think of hard drink, fellow. Hard drink got me and my partner behind this eight ball."

"I wish I had a drink of Red Crown," Gordo said.

Dab said, "Old Saddle for me."

"Thought you two had sworn off hard drink," Martin reminded him.

"I forgot," Dab said.

The land locator rode bent over in his saddle, the blanket covering him the way a shawl covers a woman on a cold and windy day. They stopped their horses at a log shack on the edge of town. The shack was owned by the Jones Double J outfit. Jim Jones had built it so his men could have a place to stay when in town.

"Your disguise is a good one," Dab quietly told Martin. "Nobody can see your face—if somebody is watching us—even at this hour of the morning. Here, totter into the cabin, like you were out on your feet. Gordo, get on that side—put your arm around him—"

"Make the knees slack," Gordo said softly.

Together they got the land locator into the shack with Martin sagging between them and looking like a man spent. Then, once inside, they got him in the bunk with its dirty covers and put his six-shooter beside him. The cabin was rather good-sized—about thirty by twenty feet. It had a pine ceiling and an attic hole.

Now Gordo looked at this attic hole.

"You think I can squeeze through that, Dabney?"

"You'll have to . . . or I'll jam you through, fat man."

"Get the chair over here, and you give me the boost."

"I could help you," Martin said from the bed.

Dab said, "I can get this ton of suet up there—you stay where you are. You're Matt Smith, remember, and we found you on the range—wounded—"

"Sure, I remember."

Gordo said, "I am ready."

He had pushed aside the cover over the attic hole. Had the aperture been bigger he could have pulled himself into the attic by his own power, reaching up and pulling himself upward like a man chinning himself on a bar. But the hole was too small. Therefore Dab had to push him up into the opening. Once inside, though, a fat man could use his hands, pushing down; he lifted himself into the attic and looked down, his face round and owlish in the dim light.

"I can see the door and the bed both," he said.

"Don't ruin things," Dab warned, "by poking your mug out of that hole. Keep it back and not below the level of the ceiling."

"I got a little brains."

"I doubt that." Dab looked at Martin. "You all set?"

"Sure am."

"Goodbye for now, then."

Dabney Jones led Gordo's horse as he walked toward the main section of Beaverton, and left the horse in a barn behind a house. This was merely a precaution, nothing more. He hoped he could find Mike Turner somewhere around town. For once, luck was with him. This amazed him. His luck had been running muddy for so long a single stroke of good fortune was like a cold breeze across the desert. For a light burned in the Idle Hour Saloon. Four men were there playing poker. They were the only men in the long, silent saloon.

The owner looked up from his cards, said, "Dab Jones, sure as heck. You might get into trouble comin' into town, friend."

"My lookout, not yours." Dab was brusque. He spoke now to Deputy Sheriff Mike Turner. "I'd like to talk to you, Turner."

"Go ahead," Turner said, glancing up from his cards.

"Alone, not with listeners."

Turner said, "We're all friends."

"Alone," Dab said. "Law business."

"Go tell Sheriff O'Mahoney."

"He's out of town," the saloonman said. "Rode out yesterday and never come back. Some say he's out scouting."

Dab said, "If you won't talk to me I'll take the law in my own hands, Turner. That's a warning."

Turner said, "You do, Jones, and I'll ride you next time with real rowels, not just my short rowelled spurs." He pushed back his chair and glowered. "I should take you to jail."

Dab walked to the back of the long room, his face hidden from Turner who followed him. Turner was angry because he had been taken from his cards. When they were at the extreme far end, Dab turned and talked in a low voice.

"Gordo and I—we were headin' across the range—and we found a man—crawlin' and shot—"

"Who was he?"

"Matt Smith!"

Turner studied him, and Dab admired the man's calmness. "You never found Matt Smith out on the range, Jones. We buried Matt Smith, remember?"

Dab shook his head. He spoke softly; so did Turner. The men at the card table did not hear. Dab did not want them to hear.

"No, this is Smith. We toted him into town—he's down at the Double J shack now. My pard is out looking for the doc. I thought I'd report this to you. I don't understand this, Turner—I thought Smith was burned in that fire."

"So did I," Turner said.

Dab built up a cock-and-bull story. Smith had been shot four times, he said—in the chest. Turner was dark, short, savage—he received this information stoically, unmoved. Dab told about taking Smith into town.

"Did he say who had shot him?"

Turner's voice might have wavered a little on this question, but Dab was not sure.

"He's out cold. Loss of blood, I guess. He was out when we found him. He never regained consciousness, but he's still alive. His heart beats good. We bound him to stop the blood."

"He never got to talk to you, huh?"

Did the man's voice hold satisfaction? No, it was the same—low and heavy, and devoid of emotion.

"Never said a word. Bet when Doc brings him to he'll have an interestin' story. He'll tell what is behind all this trouble. Wonder who was buried in place of Smith?"

"This sounds crazy to me."

"Go down to the shack and see for yourself. I'll go out and help Gordo—he's over to Doc's house, I guess."

"I'll go down to the shack and check."

Turner went out the back door, after snagging his hat off the rack. Dab knew a moment of wild satisfaction—so far, the plan was working.

Dab went over the plan again, and found no flaw. No horses were in front of the shack; he had led Gordo's bronc into the barn, and the black horse of Will Martin had wandered off, going down the alley of his own accord, head held to one side so he would not step on his trailing reins. Dab swung across a vacant lot and then ran hard, coming to a barn. He darted into this—this was the barn where he had stabled Gordo's horse—and he looked out a hay-window at the cabin. Within a minute or two Turner came striding along. He gave the cabin a hard raking glance, then went inside, and Dab noticed he was in a hurry.

Dab left the barn, slid along the side of the cabin, and pushed open the door. He came inside, and Turner turned and looked at him, and now his face showed expression.

"I thought you had Smith here," the deputy said hoarsely, "and you have Will Martin."

Dab said, "Martin, talk to him."

Martin swung out of bed fully dressed and sat there with his gun in his lap, his young face hard.

"You killed Smith, back in the badlands, Turner. I saw it. You shot him four times with your rifle through the chest. You paid him for helping kill Jake Thomas, and then you got your money back. You stripped the saddle off his horse and turned the bronc loose, and the horse wandered off, and you left the saddle there and rode off."

Overhead, Gordo watched. Turner did not see him. Turner had eyes for Martin, then for Dab. Dab wet his lips. There was a steel band around this cabin, and it was contracting, squeezing shut. Dab watched the man, and his hand was on his gun.

"You talk crazy, Martin."

"In the badlands," Martin said, "it happened. Dab saw it, too. We trailed you—we were suspicious of you—"

Turner spoke to Dab Jones. "And you saw it, too—you *claim* you saw this?"

"You kind of tipped your hand." Dab controlled his voice with difficulty. "We pulled you out here to trap you, Turner. We know your plan. You worked the farmers against Jim Jones. You got me and Gordo tied into it. We've got two charges against you, Turner."

"And what are they?"

"Murder, both of them."

"Who do you claim I murdered—besides Smith?"

"You and Smith killed Jake Thomas. They never buried Matt Smith—they buried Jake Thomas. Gordo and me saw you ride away from Smith's burning cabin that night. And Matt Smith rode with you as you headed for Jake Thomas' spread."

"You saw that?"

"Yes, from the brush—by accident, a man might say. But it started us thinking, and then when we identified that corpse as belonging to Thomas and not Smith, we knew for sure something was wrong. You didn't know about that scar on Thomas' leg, huh?"

"What scar?"

"Under his knee, where a cow hooked him on roundup. The fire didn't burn the skin much there. We can dig that body up and prove it is Jake Thomas' carcass, for we have Smith's body in the badlands—"

Turner said huskily, "You got me outnumbered—but it only takes one bullet to kill a man—"

Then, gun rising, he pivoted, low and crouched. His face was ugly with hate, and he drew with terrible speed. But this speed, wild and uncontrolled, threw his shot wide. By this time, Dab Jones had his own .45 out.

But Dab never got to shoot.

For Will Martin had moved in, fast as a wild cat. His gun lifted and fell with savage hardness.

Dab could not shoot because he might hit the land agent. And Martin missed Turner's head. His gun barrel smashed down on a burly, muscle-thick shoulder, and Turner turned, shooting at Martin.

The bullet hit Martin in the forearm and his gun fell from his hand. Turner had him out of the play and he whirled to face Dab, still hindered by the fact that Martin was behind the killer. For a moment, the world stood still. Dab Jones knew that he would have to shoot, Martin or no Martin in the line of fire.

But he reckoned without Gordo Alvarez.

Turner had moved directly under the ceiling opening. He did not see the heavy gun swing down behind him. His eyes, harsh with hate, were on Dab. Dab watched with terrified intensity. Gordo's face was wide and wore a huge grin. He swung the gun, the blow sharp—and it smashed across the base of Turner's head. It made a sickening crushing sound.

Turner never knew what had hit him. One moment he had been on his feet, boots spread wide, face tough and deadly. The next moment he was on his face on the floor, blood on the back of his head.

He went down like a bull that had run his head into a .30-30 bullet.

Gordo said, "Did I knock him cold, Dabney?"

"Cold as a iceberg, Gordo."

The smile widened. "I am the good partner, no?"

"Yes!"

Within an hour two riders were loping toward the Double J Ranch. The dawn was bright, and it rolled across the sun-blistered hills and lighted the *coulées* with their underbrush and cottonwood trees.

"Well, Dab, things they turn out okay, no?"

"They sure did, *amigo*."

"Those farmers they are mad at Turner. Maybe they try to hang him from the tree today."

"Sheriff O'Mahoney can control them."

Gordo chuckled. "The sheriff, he mad at Turner. He mad at us, too, in a way. We make him look like the fool. We are free men now—not the longriders. I wonder if old Jim will make us ride the bog holes again?"

"If he does that, we quit!"

"We go to Canada, work there. We quit if we have to ride bog holes. But if we go to Canada you can't marry Miss Lincoln."

"Maybe I don't want to marry her."

Gordo said, "She wants to marry you. I can see it in her eyes."

Dab spoke with youthful earnestness. "I'm too young to get married—babies, diapers, bills to pay. We both are young yet. We got more wild oats to sow, and a married man—he ain't supposed to sow wild oats."

"We got acres of them to plant, Dabney."

Dab grinned at his partner. "Next Saturday night there's a big shindig over to the Wild Rose schoolhouse. We'd best start this farming scheme of ours, this idea of planting them wild oats. Be some good-lookin' farmers' daughters over there."

"Good place to start sowing," Gordo said, and grinned.

WEST OF THE BARBWIRE

One

The stage driver rode like a maniac, his long whip popping, four sweaty horses lunging against their collars, the June dust of Montana hanging in the hot afternoon behind the lumbering Concord. Attorney Ric Nelson, his blond head close to the dirty window, glimpsed a deep rut crossing the prairie road ahead.

"Brace yourself, lady!" he yelled to the stage's only other passenger.

Hurriedly, he anchored both boots solidly against the floor rail, but the lovely young girl next to him acted too slowly.

The lunging Concord hit the rut, smashed its heavy weight against thick leather thorough braces, and heaved the girl against Ric, who caught and steadied her.

"How'd you like that one, Nelson?" the driver yelled.

Ric, his lips compressed, said nothing.

"What's wrong with this crazy driver?" the girl demanded. "He's suddenly gone insane!"

"He's doing this for my benefit!" Ric clipped. "He's trying to show off entering Sagebrush. He doesn't like me."

"Why?"

Blue eyes questioned Ric. Again, he wished he knew the girl's name. On the twenty-mile ride out from the rail junction back at Sun Prairie, he had hinted after her name, but she had parried each time.

He had loaded her two bags in the stage's boot, too. Neither valise had a name tag or identification embossed on its expensive cowhide surface.

Had he ever seen a lovelier young woman? A blue hoopskirt draped her curvaceous young figure, and a tiny black hat, perched on glistening black hair, accentuated her olive-coloured skin and sea-blue eyes.

"I asked a question! But you only stare at me!"

"You're beautiful."

"You've told me that before, Mr Nelson. Now why doesn't this stage driver like you?"

"How do I look to you?" Ric asked boldly.

She blushed slightly. "Oh, stop that. Okay, here goes. You're six feet, you've got blue eyes, too – and you're perspiring under the coat of that nice brown suit, but you're too much of a gentleman to take it off in a lady's presence."

"And I'm not married," Ric added. "And you have no wedding ring, either."

Her small jaw tightened. "We're off the subject. Why does this crazy man hate you?"

"From about two weeks back," Ric said. "Poker game. Sullivan's Saloon, Sagebrush's only watering spa."

"Yes?"

"This driver – Mack Wilson's his name – was a little drunk. He was in the game. I caught him palming a card."

"Oh."

"I called his hand. He swung on me, and I knocked

him down."

"That simple?"

"That simple," Ric said. "Do you have any kinfolks in Sagebrush?"

"I might have," she answered with that same impish smile. "And I might not have."

A sudden terrible thought hit Ric, and he put his head in his hands. Had this beautiful girl come to work over Casey Sullivan's saloon?

"Are you ill, Mr Nelson?"

Ric raised his head, for the stage had entered Sagebrush, the driver still whooping like a turpentined Sioux buck. While unpainted frame buildings flashed by, town curs yipped at the stage's spinning wheels.

"Hold 'er, boys!" the driver screamed to his horses.

Sixteen steel-shod hoofs came to a skidding stop before Sullivan's Saloon.

The driver yelled down, "Well, here you are, *shyster*."

Shyster! Anger tightened Ric's muscles. A shyster was a crooked lawyer – the biggest insult to an honest attorney.

"He deliberately wants trouble with you," the girl said.

Ric nodded and helped her down. She glared up at Wilson and then went to the rear of the stage to gather her luggage from the boot; a townsman helped her.

Sagebrush loafers had congregated before the saloon and shouted noisy encouragement up at Wilson, who sat nonchalantly on his box, grinning down at Ric.

Eyes narrowed, Ric studied the tobacco-chewing Wilson. Wilson, just small fry, merely tooled stage for Pete Brookhaven's immense Circle Y cow outfit. Circle Y owned this stage line and every building in Sagebrush.

Sagebrush had been built some twenty years ago by Pete Brookhaven's father, Big Ike. Big Ike had been dead two years, a bronc going over backwards on him. Now his only son, big Pete Brookhaven, ramrodded the Circle Y. Wilson wasn't hard to see through; Pete Brookhaven had given him orders to pick a fight.

"You owe the lady an apology," Ric told Wilson. "You scared her half to death with your wild ride."

"You don't say?" Wilson taunted. He spat a huge gob of tobacco juice down at Ric, who had to leap back. "I'm right sorry about that, Nelson; you was the one I wanted to jostle aroun'!"

The girl said pleadingly, "Please, men, let's have no trouble. Forget me, please."

Ric, deciding then and there to ignore Wilson's insult, turned to leave. At that moment, Pete Brookhaven came out of the saloon, followed by his top gunhand, Bat Malone.

Brookhaven was twenty-eight, six years Ric's senior. A gaudy, red silk shirt covered wide shoulders. He stopped on the plank sidewalk, looked at Ric, grey eyes level.

Ric glanced at Bat Malone, who stood at his boss's right – a tall, angular man, his muscular body seemingly relaxed. Two black-handled .45's were tied low on his thighs. His expressionless black eyes touched Wilson, then moved back to Ric.

Brookhaven looked at the girl. "Hello, Sis," he said. "We didn't expect you on this stage, Susie."

"Hello, Brother," the girl said.

Susie Brookhaven! Ric's mind swung back to his conversation with Pete's sister. He had told her he was an attorney, yes – Sagebrush's only lawyer – and he had arrived on this range from St Louis only a month ago.

Relief flooded through him. He hadn't told her he had gone to Sun Prairie to make arrangements to receive the first homesteaders. They would file on land now claimed by Pete Brookhaven's Circle Y.

Nobody in Sagebrush knew these farmers were arriving; he had told Susie nothing important.

He had heard about Susie Brookhaven, now in her last year of college in California.

"Is this girl your sister, Pete?" Mack Wilson's voice held awe.

"She certainly is," Brookhaven assured him.

"And I treated her to that rough ride!" Wilson's mouth hung open. "Dang, I never knowed, Pete."

Everything was now clear to Ric. Susie had been gone all winter, he understood, and Mack Wilson had bummed into Sagebrush two months back. He turned to leave. Brookhaven was the enemy, not loose-mouthed Wilson. If he tangled with Wilson, he would be doing Pete Brookhaven a favour and gain nothing.

"Leavin', shyster?" Wilson taunted.

Ric froze in his tracks, then slowly turned, fists knotted. He was surrounded by a sea of snickering, cynical faces, for Sagebrush stood solidly behind Brookhaven. Sagebrush citizens *had* to stand behind Circle Y; if they didn't, Brookhaven ran them out of town.

"He's callin' your hand, Nelson," an onlooker jeered.

Ric realized he couldn't walk away and be branded a coward. If he left, living in Sagebrush would be impossible from this moment on.

"Come on down, Wilson," he invited.

Wilson leaped from the high box, landing on bended knees, his face dark and twisted, his fists up and ready. "With pleasure, shyster," he rasped.

"Please, men —"

Ric scarcely heard Susie's words. Wilson, already on him, led with a wild, overhand right. Quickly, Ric moved inside the blow, Wilson's hard fist thudding harmlessly across his back.

Ric realized Wilson had made two errors: first, leading with a right; secondly, not knowing that he, Ric, had been heavyweight champ of his college's conference.

His left boot automatically crossing his right, Ric Went to work on Wilson's solar plexus, with blows that had won him his championship. A smashing left whammed into Wilson just below the ribs; a crashing right followed.

Agonized breath tore from Wilson's tobacco-stained mouth and his faded eyes turned glassy. Ric's left came in again.

Only, this time, the left did not bury itself to the wrist in Wilson's belly. It whammed sharply upward, colliding with Wilsons' gaping jaw; dirty teeth clicked savagely.

Bent in the middle, Wilson was out on his feet. His knees sagged, broke, and he landed face down, unconscious, in the dust.

Ric heard the onlookers gasp in surprise; Wilson had a rep as a tough, rough-and-tumble fighter. He had laid Wilson in the dust with three blows.

Suddenly, he heard Susie scream. "Ric, watch out —."

Ric spun to face Brookhaven and Malone, but never completed the turn. Something round and hard bounced off his skull, and he knew no more.

Two

The world spun, then cleared. Ric looked into a wide, bearded face. "Doc Smith," he said. His words sounded miles away.

"He's coming out of it," Doc Smith said.

Ric sat on the edge of a cot momentarily, head in hands, his memory sweeping painfully back.

He raised his head. Susie, who sat across the small room, and Doc Smith were the only others in the office.

"How'd I get here?" Ric asked.

Doc Smith boomed, "We carried you. Susie and I."

"Who slugged me?"

Heavy-set, middle-aged Doc Smith glanced at Susie, who twisted her handkerchief in her small hands. "Sooner or later somebody'll tell him," he told Susie.

Susie nodded. "Bat Malone."

Ric nodded dully. His back had been turned to Pete Brookhaven and Bat Malone. "Your brother ordered his gunman to knock me cold," he told Susie.

Susie frowned. "Why would Pete do that?"

Ric's head pounded. Malone had really bent his gun barrel over his head. He felt his scalp gingerly, where Doc had shaved quite a surface.

"Eight stitches," Doc Smith told him.

"What has Pete got against you?" Susie asked again. "You're a newcomer, a lawyer. Sagebrush needs a lawyer. There's never been one in town before. What have you done against my brother?"

"Your brother sent Wilson against me. I knocked Wilson cold."

"Wilson means nothing to Circle Y," Susie said. "You've had no trouble with my brother before, they tell me. Why should he suddenly move against you?"

Ric's memory swept back two days. The morning he left for Sun Prairie he had received a letter from the U.S. Department of Interior addressed to U.S. Land Commissioner Richard Appleton Nelson.

Only he in Sagebrush had known he was a U.S. Land Commissioner. He had asked Washington to keep this secret until he had moved in enough farmers to present a solid front against Circle Y.

Also nobody else knew he was on Montana Pacific's payroll, hired to bring settlers to this virgin prairie. When he had fifty farmers located, the railroad had promised to run a spur line out from the main line at Sun Prairie.

Somebody in Washington had erred, and put his official title on a letter. But didn't a U.S. post office keep matters secret?

He thought of Sagebrush's postmaster – crippled, talkative Gabby Jackson. Big Ike Brookhaven had gotten Gabby his easy job.

One year after the end of the Civil War, Big Ike and his hard-riding Texans had choused ten thousand head of longhorns onto Montana grass. For eighteen years, Big Ike had ruled Sagebrush with the iron fist of a feudal lord.

Gabby Jackson had helped Big Ike trail in

longhorns. Then a bronc had hit a badger hole, crippling Jackson.

Ike had established Jackson in the post office.

Jackson had told Brookhaven about that letter. Knees shaky, Ric got to his feet and looked out on Sagebrush's main street. The stage had left Sullivan's, the horses now in the livery barn. It would return to Sun Prairie the next morning.

Six saddled horses switched flies in front of Sullivan's. Ric recognized Pete Brookhaven's big buckskin; the blocky-shouldered roan was Bat Malone's.

Suddenly he remembered that two days back, when he was on the stage going to Sun Prairie, a hard-riding Circle Y cowboy had overhauled the Concord a few miles out of Sagebrush. He and Mack Wilson had held a brief conference out in the greasewood beyond earshot.

He had wondered what the talk had concerned – now he knew. The cowboy had been sent out by Brookhaven to tell Wilson that Ric was a U.S. Land Commissioner. Wilson had spied on him in Sun Prairie.

Ric bolted into the alley, running up the Mercantile's back stairs. He plunged down the hall and stopped in front of his office, staring.

The door hung on one hinge, its lock broken. His desk lay on its side, drawers open. Drawers had been jerked from his file cabinet, his papers scattered. Circle Y had read his correspondence. Brookhaven knew farmers were coming.

"What happened?" Susie Brookhaven had followed him.

"Your loving brother's work," Ric said sourly. He

righted a chair and sat down, studying the destruction.

"Why would Circle Y do this?"

He told her about the letter from Washington.

"Gabby Jackson broke a federal law," she said.

"I'll break his jaw!"

"He's an old, blundering man, Ric."

"Makes no difference." He studied her carefully. After all, she was Pete Brookhaven's sister. "Which side you on?" he asked roughly.

Her jaw stiffened. "I've got Brookhaven blood in my veins. I was reared on Circle Y."

"Then that makes you my enemy. Why not leave?"

"I really believe, Ric Nelson, that you've gone loco. These eastern plains of the Rockies are not farming country. Winters are hard and long, and summers have little rain. I learned that in college, too. And from experience here on Sagebrush."

"College texts can be wrong," he said. "Water can change this land into a Garden of Eden."

"Where will the water come from?"

"That's for me to know and for you to find out."

He had already filed on his homestead, where Sagebrush Creek came out of Sagebrush Canyon – the ideal location for a dam. Brookhaven wouldn't know this because his application was on a desk in Washington; he had written no letter with his homestead application.

Anger flashed in her dark eyes. She bit her lip. plainly boiling inside.

"Circle Y cannot win," he said.

"Why do you say that?"

"I was born and reared on the lower Panhandle of Texas. My father ran the STO iron on the Pecos River. Farmers started moving in – about ten years back – and foolishly my dad started fighting them."

"Did he run a big spread?"

"He ran over a hundred thousand head."

"Circle Y runs about thirty thousand," she said. "Did your father win?"

Ric laughed shortly. "You can't whip barbwire and windmills. Barbwire is the end of open range. Windmills bring free water up for irrigation. You can't stop westward migration."

"Where's your father now?"

"Under six feet of Texas sod. He pitched open battle with the sodbusters. It only takes one bullet to kill a man. The man who made the first gun made all men the same size."

"He got killed?"

"Two years after the trouble started. They call it the Wire Cutter's War. My only brother went down, too."

"How awful!"

Ric walked to the window and stared out on main street. "They died the way they wanted, Susie. Shock killed my mother in a year. Had I been an idiot, I could have carried on."

"What did you do?"

"I was the only Nelson left. We owned no patented land. We'd run over open range. I sold the herds, the ranch house – and went to St Louis, where I lived with an aunt and uncle."

"And that range today?"

Ric turned, face glowing. "Susie, you'd never recognize it. Irrigation ditches, farmhouses, alfalfa to a horse's knees, head crops. Families in peace, children, schools, towns where there were none before."

"Now you're on the other side of the fence," she reminded him.

"The right side. Circle Y is doomed," he repeated.

"You can't convince my brother. Nor could you convince my father were he alive."

"Then we're in opposite camps?"

"Ric, let me think, please." Her beautiful face showed anxiety. "I'll talk seriously to Pete," she finally said.

"Please, not on my account," Ric said. "I don't want your brother to think I'm using you in any way."

"You're not, Ric."

"How long do you expect to be around?"

"I have a teaching certificate, Ric. Teachers are very scarce in California. I thought I'd spend just a few weeks. I have a teaching position open in San Jacinto, California."

Ric's heart fell, and he told himself he was a fool, for this girl could never mean anything to him. Fate had lunged in, sending everybody sprawling.

He deliberately made his voice hard. "I want you to say nothing on my behalf to your brother. You understand that?"

Anger flared her blue eyes. "You're a stubborn, bullheaded man, Ric Nelson. I believe I'll just let another stubborn, bullheaded man – my brother – and you revel in your stubbornness!"

"Thanks," Ric said dryly.

She whirled, hoopskirt flaring, and disappeared, leaving Ric listening to her heels beat a retreat on the uncarpeted floor of the hall. Ric grinned twistedly, his fists knotted.

Within minutes, he was downstairs in the Merc. Proprietor Ira Beeson was alone.

The emporium smelled of yard goods, bologna, and leather. "When my farmers come in, you'll have a lot of trade," Ric told the beefy storekeeper.

"Farmers?"

"You know all about their coming, Beeson. Maybe you won't trade with them, huh? Maybe you still want to starve to death on Circle Y's small trade? Or should I start a store for the farmers?"

"What're you drivin' at, Nelson?"

"Circle Y raided my office, huh?"

Fat fingers trembled as they played with a spool of thread. "I know nothin' about it," Ira Beeson said.

Ric laughed shortly. "You must be deaf besides being ignorant. You'll have to jump one of two ways soon, Beeson. There won't be a middle path. Brookhaven won't allow it."

"Your farmers aren't here yet," Beeson reminded him.

"They'll soon be here, though." Ric saw he could gain nothing here and went out the Merc's front door.

Sagebrush also needed a lumber yard. His farmers would need lumber to build houses and barns. He would start a lumber yard himself, and a general store, too, if Beeson never came around, for this town had a big future.

Heat hung over Sagebrush. Out on the prairie whirlwinds played, sucking up sagebrush twigs and bits of paper. The air was bone dry. Old-timers claimed Sagebrush range had never before seen a drought of this intensity.

There had been very little snow last winter, little water runoff this spring. Waterholes were going dry, and Sagebrush Creek now merely consisted of muddy potholes.

Ric went down the street to the post office, a small log building set at the street's end. Big Ike had built it.

Gabby Jackson slept, swivel chair slanting backwards, his scuffed boots on the battered desk. Gray head back, he snorted, his open mouth showing scraggly yellow teeth. He didn't hear Ric enter.

When Ric batted Jackson's boots to the floor, he came instantly awake, teeth clicking shut.

"What the hell—?"

Jackson stared at Ric, fear colouring his sun-faded eyes. When he reached hurriedly to open a drawer, Ric slapped it shut.

"I know you got a gun in there," Ric said coldly, "but just forget it. You're due for a stretch in a Federal penitentiary."

"For what?"

"For releasing private information you learned through the mails. You told Pete Brookhaven I'm a U.S. Land Commissioner."

"I never ..."

Ric felt wry disgust, as he eyed an open ink pad lying on Jackson's desk. Ric grabbed the oldster's head, rammed his thin face down on the pad, rasped Jackson's face back and forth a few times, then released him.

Jackson's face was blue with ink. Ric shoved the swivel chair backwards hard. As Jackson spilled on the floor, Ric took the old .44 from the drawer and threw it out the open door.

"Washington'll know about this," he said.

"Notify 'em if you want!" Jackson stormed. "You cain't git me outa this job. Pete Brookhaven still runs Sagebrush."

"He won't for long."

Ric left, a wry satisfaction rising. Even his head had lost its throbs, for Doc Smith's headache powders had done their work.

Suddenly he stared at Sullivan's Saloon. Pete Brookhaven, red shirt flapping in the endless wind, had come out. Behind him came Bat Malone. Behind Malone trooped seven Circle Y punchers.

They turned and started toward the Merc. Then Brookhaven saw Ric. He called, "We've got business for you in your land office, Land Commissioner."

Bat Malone threw back his head and laughed.

Three

Nine gun-slinging riders charged into Ric's office. They righted his desk and shoved his chair into position.

"Now get to work, Commissioner," Pete Brookhaven said.

"On what?" Ric asked.

Brookhaven grinned wolfishly at dead-faced Bat Malone. "We're filin' on homesteads," he told Ric. "An' seein' you're U.S. land agent, we naturally come to you."

Ric's eyes narrowed. Circle Y riders would file homestead entries on valuable waterholes. Whoever controlled water controlled Sagebrush range. His incoming farmers would have little, if any, water.

"Maybe I won't take your applications?" Ric said.

Bat Malone tapped a holstered gun. Brookhaven sent Malone a hard glance. Malone's homely face again became dead.

Brookhaven said, "You have to take 'em, Nelson. We're all U.S. citizens an' over twenty-one. We got our votin' records to prove our qualifications."

Ric wet his lips.

"You can't escape your duty to Uncle Sam," Brookhaven continued sneeringly. "If you turn us down, we'll make a howl to Washington an' you'll get booted out of office."

Ric knew this could be done. Bigwigs in Washington, sitting safely behind shiny desks, had no conception of the danger riding this desolate range. And if he lost his government job, he was through in Sagebrush. Again, he silently cursed old Gabby Jackson.

Spurs clanging, Pete Brookhaven strode to the big wall map. For the first time, Ric noticed red circles marked on the map.

"This homestead is in my name," Brookhaven said. His thumb covered the area holding Circle Y buildings.

Ric leaned back, stalling. "I have no homestead entry forms," he said.

Brookhaven whirled, studied him. "What do you mean?" he demanded.

Ric designated his correspondence and printed forms, scattered over the floor. He hadn't sorted out the mess. He had glanced at it roughly, noticing the letter bearing his official title missing.

Brookhaven grinned. "That can be solved. Pick up his papers, men."

All went to work but Brookhaven and Malone. Brookhaven gazed absent-mindedly out the window. Bat Malone leaned against the wall, cold cigarette hanging on his underlip, eyes and face without thoughts. Circle Y punchers laid papers on Ric's desk, clearing the floor.

"They're all mixed up," Ric said.

Brookhaven turned quickly. "You can pick out the homestead entry forms," he said shortly. "You're pullin' a windy on us, Nelson!"

"Your men wrecked my office," Ric reminded him. "You've got to straighten it up."

Brookhaven's face hardened. A gun jumped into Bat Malone's right hand, the big bore centring on Ric. Brookhaven looked at the gun, then at Ric, then back at Malone. Brookhaven smiled tightly. "That the only way you know of to settle an argument, Malone?"

"This and my fists."

Ric studied Malone's weapon. "You're behind time, Malone," he said. "The day of the gun is past. Law has come into Montana."

"That why you don't pack a gun?" Malone countered.

Ric looked at his .45 and gunbelt hanging on the wall. The old Colt, which had a well-worn black handle, was the only possession of his father that he had.

"I might be wrong," he said.

Brookhaven spoke sharply. "Put that gun away, Malone!"

Ric watched Malone's gun. One moment it was pointed at him; the next, it was in its holster. Grudging admiration arose in him, for Malone had a fast gun. He had seen only one that had been faster – his dead father's.

Circle Y men made an effort to sort out his correspondence, but he noticed two stood aside. "I take it you two can't read?" Ric asked.

Neither of the two spoke, but one flushed slightly under his tan. Brookhaven said, "Shorty an' Slim never went to school."

"The Federal law says only literates can file on homesteads," Ric informed.

A Circle Y cowboy said, "A literate is a person what can read an' write, ain't it?"

"It is," Ric clipped.

Brookhaven's jaw tightened. "What kinda sandy you tryin' to run on Circle Y, lawyer? You'll have to show me that in your book."

"That book over in the corner," Ric said. "That big one, with the red binding, Brookhaven."

Brookhaven eyed the book, chewed on a cold cigarette, but made no effort to pick up the book.

"Shorty and Slim can't file," Ric said.

"Not even if they sign an X an' somebody signs witness?" Brookhaven asked.

"Read the book," Ric said.

He was lying. He hoped, through fabrication to save two choice spots for his incoming farmers.

Brookhaven hesitated, then said, "All right, we'll let that ride. You win that point, landman."

"I'm goin' down an' get a drink," Slim said, and he and Shorty left.

"That leaves seven of you," Ric said. "You'll have to pay a seven-hundred-dollar filing fee, Brookhaven."

Brookhaven's face tightened. Unconsciously, his hand moved to his holstered gun. "That's too much," he said stoutly.

Ric shrugged. The usual fee, government regulations said, was ten dollars per entry filed, but he couldn't remember the book setting a limit on the size of a fee. Circle Y had him penned in a badger hole. He would get all he could out of Brookhaven.

"Read the book," he repeated.

"I don't pack that kind of money on me," Brookhaven said. "No man walks around with that much cash."

Ric leaned back. "One hundred dollars has to be paid with each entry when original homestead papers are drawn."

"A cheque good?"

"No cheques accepted," Ric said. "Government regulations."

"You'll take a cheque an' like it!"

"I might be forced to like it," Ric assured, "but Uncle Sam won't – and he has the final say on homestead entries."

"You mean Washington might cancel the homestead entries?"

"Washington *will* cancel," Ric assured him.

Brookhaven spoke to Malone. "Go downstairs and get seven hundred bucks from Ira Beeson." The Merc's owner also acted as town banker.

"Okay," Malone said.

Circle Y punchers had finally straightened Ric's papers. They had them stacked in categories on his desk. He pulled entry forms in front of him. "You're first, Brookhaven?"

"I want to homestead the land I put my thumb on."

"Have you got a legal description of that land?" Ric asked.

Brookhaven looked at him. "What'd you mean by that?"

"I'll start from the beginning," Ric said. "Land is measured first in townships of thirty-six sections. Sections numbered eighteen and thirty-six are school sections."

"What's them?" Brookhaven asked.

"These two sections in each township cannot be homesteaded or sold. They can be leased, though. Money coming from them must go to support public schools."

"This map don't show sections, then?"

Ric shook his head. "That is a rough map,

Brookhaven. You rushed the gun, fellow. The true map – showing township and sections lines – hasn't come from Washington yet."

Brookhaven wet his lips, watching. "Go on," he said.

"Each section consists of six hundred and forty acres. Homestead law says a man can file on one fourth a section – one hundred and sixty acres. But first he has to have the actual boundaries of his homestead surveyed by a licensed surveyor."

Ric had found his way out. His heart thudded as his eyes travelled from cowpuncher to cowpuncher. They were a taciturn lot. Were their loyalties to Circle Y wholehearted? Did they stand solidly behind Brookhaven?

His mind flicked back to his father's big Texas spread. He remembered then the loyalty cowpunchers held to the immense STO, his father's iron. Every man on the STO payroll would have died for his father. These were Texans merely transplanted to Montana Territory. They had carried north with them, through dust and storm and stampede, a Texan's loyalty to the iron paying his wages. They stood – fists and guns – behind Circle Y.

Malone's boot heels clomped down the hall. Malone handed Brookhaven a leather sack.

"Gold," he said.

Malone leaned back against the wall again, watching Ric. Malone said nothing.

"Then you won't file our entries?" Brookhaven rasped. "Even if we pay the fees?"

"I have to have a competent land survey," Ric said stubbornly.

Malone snarled, "This can be handled right now, Pete! We don't need this man! The land is there – an' ours for the takin'!"

Brookhaven disregarded Malone. "When will a surveyor make this survey?"

"Two government men are due any day now. I expected them in on the train today in Sun Prairie. You must know that; you read my correspondence."

Brookhaven's lips were solid.

"Or did you read only the letter that bore my official address?" Ric asked softly.

He played with dynamite. He knew this. Tension held this group, coiling and uncoiling. All eyes bore down on big Pete Brookhaven, who would have to make the vital decision. Brookhaven pulled air into his lungs, his massive chest arching.

Finally, he spoke, voice level. "All right, Nelson, we leave it right there. But just one thing, lawyer –"

Ric nodded, eyes on Malone.

"When them gover'ment surveyors come, they'll find Circle Y squattin' on them rings we made on your map. An' the minute them men finish that survey, Circle Y files. An' if a would-be farmer steps in, he's right now dead. Squatter Rights still count."

Ric shook his head. "You're behind times, Brookhaven. Two big Montana cow outfits have taken the issue of Squatters' Rights into territorial court. The Pothook S, down on the Yellowstone. The Running M, up on Milk River. And both lost in court."

Brookhaven tapped his holster. "This won't get into court," he said huskily. He waved an arm. "Come on, men. Let's get outa here. We got work to do."

Ric got to his feet. "Sorry," he said mockingly.

Circle Y clanged out angrily, Brookhaven clutching the gold bag, Malone taking up the rear. Ric followed Malone. For once, Malone forgot to watch his back. Also Circle Y boot heels made so much racket

Brookhaven riders never knew Ric accompanied them.

Circle Y went down the stairs, Brookhaven leading. Malone was in the act of taking the first downward step when Ric touched his shoulder.

Malone whirled like a cat, instantly crouched, hand flashing to each gun grip. He was chain lightning, but so was Ric's left fist. Ric's left thudded upward on Malone's jaw. His right zoomed in, also connecting. Malone went backwards, arms flailing. He crashed through the stunned Circle Y men. Brookhaven grabbed for him, missed, and Malone landed on his back at the base of the stairs. He didn't move.

Brookhaven stared down at the unconscious gunman. He looked up at Ric, blowing on his knuckles. "You must've fought in the ring," Brookhaven said.

"My business," Ric said.

"Malone's knocked cold. Carry him into the Merc and throw water on him."

Two men toted Malone away, Malone bending in the middle. Other stunned Circle Y punchers followed and only Brookhaven stood below.

"You'd best pack a gun from here out," Brookhaven said. "Malone ain't forgettin' this."

Ric said nothing as his eyes met and locked with Brookhaven. Then Brookhaven turned, entering the Merc, and Ric walked slowly back to his office. Once inside, he stood, staring at his father's old gun.

He slouched in his chair, still eyeing the .45, his mind seeking answers. Sagebrush town had no lawman. To date, Circle Y had been Sagebrush law; therefore, he could appeal to nobody in town.

A. U.S. Cavalry unit was stationed thirty miles south at old Fort Union. An appeal for horse soldiers to move in would be useless, for no overt act of lawbreaking had occurred.

He thought of his farmers. He had practised law a year after graduation in St Louis, then hooked up with a company there which consigned farmers west to homesteads.

He remembered the farmers who had moved in on Texas grass. They had come from the slums of Eastern cities and Eastern factories. Many had never ridden a bronc until reaching Texas. They had homesteaded to escape the slavery of sweatshop factories and low-paying handwork.

His consignment of farmers would be of the same ilk. Good people, but not gunmen. They would be like chaff before a wind when Circle Y moved ahead.

He strode to the open window and stared sightlessly out. He would have to alert these farmers, turn them back. He couldn't lead ignorant people into death.

He stared at his father's gun. His mother had unbuckled that gun from his father's dead body. To him, with his legal training, guns were the last resort – the emblem of lawlessness. Still ...

Fingers trembling, he buckled the gun around his waist, adjusted the holster correctly, and tied the dangling buckskin tie-down cords around his thigh. He crouched, reached, and drew – knowing lack of practice had made his movements slow.

He holstered the gun, walked to the open window, and went into a gunfighter's crouch, palm slapping the gun's handle. Six times he fanned the pistol. He got but six clicks. He broke the gun. During his absence, somebody had unloaded it. Another Circle Y dirty trick, he thought sourly.

Four

Sun Prairie's sheriff – a beefy, middle-aged man – was a long-time crony of dead Ike Brookhaven, who had got him this soft county job years before. He was playing whist with his deputy when Ric swung down from his lathered horse in Sun Prairie that same day. Dusk clung to the rangelands.

Sheriff Asa Gosden muttered, "It's that lawyer from Sagebrush, Vern. He's the one that Mack Wilson said was shippin' in farmers. Prob'ly come to bellyache about Circle Y wreckin' his office. Keep your big mouth shut. I'll handle this."

The deputy reddened, but said nothing as Ric entered. Sheriff Gosden noticed Ric packed a pistol, tied low. He had heard Ric didn't pack a gun.

The sheriff decided to put Ric immediately on the defensive. "I oughta jug you, fella, for ridin' a hoss that hard in this heat. Look at the sweat on your cayuse."

Ric's grey breathed hard, flanks rising, falling. Ric's jaw tightened, but he saw immediately through the ruse.

"I'm Richard Nelson," he said, "and I take it you're Sheriff Gosden. You've been pointed out to me a few times on the street. I have an office south in Sagebrush."

The deputy leaned back, dug a toothpick out of a vest pocket, and started cleaning his tobacco-stained teeth.

"I've seen you around, too," Sheriff Gosden said slowly. "Seems to me you was in town this forenoon."

Ric nodded.

"An' you took the stage out to Sagebrush, along with Susie Brookhaven. What's on your mind, lawyer?"

Ric told about Circle Y wrecking his office, that Mack Wilson had picked a fight with him, and that the Sagebrush postmaster had disclosed U.S. government official business.

Ric finished. The deputy looked at his scuffed boots in silence, and the sheriff nodded absently.

Ric's eyes travelled slowly from one man to the other. He would get no help here, just as he had expected. Anger rose, but he controlled it.

Finally, the sheriff said, "Your argument with Postmaster Gabby Jackson is out of my jurisdiction. That's a Federal item, not community."

"Circle Y broke into and entered private property."

The sheriff raised heavy eyebrows. "Did you see that with your own eyes, Nelson?"

"No."

"Have you witnesses to that effect?"

"No."

Pudgy fingers dug a soiled toothpick from a vest pocket. "I can't issue a warrant for anybody's arrest without evidence, Nelson."

"You can't issue a warrant on any evidence," Ric pointed out. "You can only accept a taxpayer's complaint. The county judge has to issue the warrant."

The sheriff idly picked his teeth. "I forgot you was a lawyer," he said. "You're right, Nelson." He glanced at the wall clock. "Only a trifle after seven. Judge O'Neill is prob'ly home. One block west, big white house on the corner. I've got but one question – why'd you come to me first? Why didn't you go direct to Judge O'Neill?"

"I wanted first to make an official complaint where it should be made – in your office."

"There's paper on the desk, Nelson."

The two lawmen resumed their whist game in silence. Ric scrawled rapidly and to the point, then handed the note to the sheriff, who glanced at it and threw it on his desk.

"Sagebrush needs a deputy sheriff," Ric said.

"Why?"

"To keep law and order."

The sheriff bit his toothpick in two. "Nelson, I've been sheriff almost twenty years. We've never needed a deputy at Sagebrush. And we don't need one now."

"Circle Y has always been the law, I take it?"

"Circle Y has always been law-abiding. It was so under Big Ike, and young Pete is a chip off the old block. I'm sendin' out no deputy."

Ric had gained his point. "Then what law Sagebrush owns is in the holster – or rifle – of a Sagebrush resident?"

The sheriff evaded with, "If an' when trouble breaks, my office will step in. Just tell your farmers to step light and easy – and legal, all the time."

"How did you know farmers were coming in?"

The sheriff reddened. His tongue had betrayed him. "Kinda common talk," he said, his voice controlled. "Go down and talk to Judge O'Neill."

"I understand Big Ike Brookhaven put Judge O'Neill in office, just as he put you? That true?"

The sheriff spat out half a toothpick. "This county's voters put us both in office, Nelson. I'm sayin' good evening to you."

"Good evening," Ric said sarcastically.

Grinning tightly, Ric left and rode to the Montana Pacific railroad depot, set on Sun Prairie's north edge, realizing that he had not one friend on this Montana grass except, perhaps, Susie Brookhaven.

The thought held irony. Susie was Big Ike's only daughter. Her allegiance naturally lay with Circle Y. He wished he could get the lovely Susie off his mind.

Montana Pacific hired three operators, each working an eight-hour shift. This one sat in his cubicle, his telegraph key clicking. Ric found blank telegram forms on the counter. Carefully, he wrote a telegram directed to the St Louis company that had recruited his farmers.

The operator read it slowly, "Bucking tough Circle Y outfit. What type of persons are my oncoming farmers? Give full details as to farmers' backgrounds. Need gunmen urgently. Where is train now bearing these farmers?"

"I can answer that last question," the operator grunted. "They're forty miles east of here, at Larb Hill station."

Ric scowled. He hadn't expected them for two more days, at least.

"Got orders over the wire about a hour ago," the operator continued, "sayin' them sodbusters would unload here in the mornin'."

"When I was in here yesterday, you told me you had no idea where they were!" Ric said angrily.

"That was yesterday, lawyer. This wire just come

through a hour ago, like I said. You want to rub out that last sentence?"

"No use sending it." Ric drew a line through the sentence. Resentment against fate stirred him; everything possible seemed to have gone wrong.

Outside, a whirlwind hit suddenly, whistling in the depot's eaves, swirling scrap papers and debris high.

"This wire's goin' to St Louis, huh? This company'll be closed at this hour."

"St Louis delivers messages by bicycles," Ric clipped. "And keep this information to yourself, understand?"

Their eyes locked. "All telegrams are secret," the agent mumbled, and his key began clattering.

Ric then wrote a telegram to the territorial governor asking for the militia to move into Sagebrush to maintain law and order, knowing the governor would pay the wire no attention.

He had heard that the governor and Big Ike Brookhaven had been close friends. Big Ike had been the first president of the Montana Stockman's Association; the present governor was a board member. Pete Brookhaven was now an Association vice-president.

The governor ran thousands of cattle in Montana's Judith Basin. He was cowman – one hundred per cent.

Ric paid for his telegrams and left. He would loaf around town, for he expected St Louis to answer immediately. He entered Sun Prairie's only saloon. The stench of unwashed humans, tobacco smoke, and stale booze assailed his nostrils. After ordering a beer, he took a seat at an empty table.

Four drifting cowboys played a listless game of seven-up at a table. Two more cowboys stood at the bar, chinning with the bartender. Ric immediately recognized one of them as a Circle Y cowboy who had been with Brookhaven and Malone that afternoon in his wrecked office.

The cowboy's eyes met Ric's in the dirty bar mirror. When the cowboy looked away, Ric grinned. This cowboy, acting on Brookhaven's orders, had trailed him into Sun Prairie.

Ric waited, nursing his beer. A small boy entered an hour later, bearing a telegram. "Only one?" Ric asked.

"Only one, mister."

Ric gave the boy a dime. The wire was from St Louis. Brief, pointed, it said only that the farmers were city people; no mention was made of sending in guns.

Disgusted, Ric wadded the telegram and stuck it in his pocket. Each farmer had paid St Louis two hundred dollars. One hundred of this had been mailed on to Ric. St Louis had its money and there interest had died. Ric now carried full responsibilities.

He glanced quickly at the Circle Y rider, who had been watching in the mirror. Suddenly, the man's attention returned to his beer. Ric grinned sourly.

Again, he thought of his farmers. He would lead them into guns. He had the sinking feeling of being a bell-goat leading poor sheep into a slaughterhouse.

He had wired St Louis a hot telegram, collect. He had established credit with a big Minneapolis wholesale house before coming to Montana. He would wire them to send out a carload or two of lumber.

He would also ask the wholesaler to send out grub and fittings for a general store in Sagebrush. He got to his feet and started for the door; then the prairie storm hit.

Rain suddenly smashed against the saloon's dirty windows. He had heard that storms came this suddenly on the prairie. He had a slicker tied behind his saddle, but he would be sopping wet before he reached the raincoat. He stepped into the dark night.

Instantly, he was soaked to the skin. He untied his slicker and hurriedly got into it. At least, it would cut the driving rain.

Jagged chain lightning flashed and showed Sun Prairie in bright relief. Rolling thunder crashed and, within minutes, creeks and gullies – dry but a short time ago – would be rolling with high muddy water.

Sourness churned his belly as he realized that each farmer would come equipped with a wagon, at least four head of workhorses, perhaps a milk cow or two, and much heavy farming equipment. Wagons would be heavily loaded and would sink to the hub in this mud. What other disaster would happen?

Bent against the wind, he hurried toward the depot, its faint lamplight glowing ahead.

They jumped him, then. There were five of them, he counted. They leaped in behind him as he passed the empty space between a store and a saddle shop. Because of darkness, he never got to see their faces clearly.

Their unexpected charge sent him sprawling off the sidewalk. He landed on his belly in the mud. Boots flailed in hard. Somehow, he got to his feet, slugging, legs spread wide.

The loose-hanging slicker hampered him. Before he went down again, he knocked two sprawling. Fists hammered his face, split his bottom lip, and bloodied his nose. Then something, hard and round, whamming down, smashed his hat aside and crashed solidly on his skull.

For the second time in hours, blackness came.

Five

Circle Y left Sagebrush in their usual manner – guns thundering into the air, broncs squealing and bucking. The tough riders headed for the ranch house and fanned across the prairie, dust rising from steelshod hoofs; big Pete Brookhaven, silk shirt billowing in the wind, led his cowpunchers.

Bat Malone grimly rode at Pete's left, his bronc a pace behind the plunging buckskin of his boss. They galloped across Sagebrush Flats; the flung-out ranch was lying ahead, situated at the base of a high hill.

Pete Brookhaven went down in front of the barn, his horse skidding to a lathery stop, scattering chickens. He flung his reins to the ground, Bat Malone following suit, and they clomped up the flagstone walk to the ranch house, chap wings flapping, spurs clanging.

The hostler would unsaddle their horses. Circle Y cowboys had to strip gear from their steaming broncs, for only Circle Y's owner and range boss could demand such privileges.

Pete looked at the sky and saw faint clouds to the west. "This dry spell has to break soon. Cattle are so bony you can hang a Stetson on their hip bones. Water holes are near gone."

"It'll bust loose soon," Malone said.

"Who are you?" Pete snarled. "A weather prophet?"

Malone's thin lips tightened, but he wisely said nothing.

They clomped into the enormous living room, its huge black-faced fireplace occupying the entire west wall.

"Whisky, Many Feathers," Pete said loudly.

Bat Malone slouched into a big chair at the long table, boots stuck out in front. Pete Brookhaven paced to a window, stared out on Circle Y's many buildings. A stallion neighed in a corral.

Malone gently waggled his jaw. That lawyer had really laid one on him. Handy with his dukes, that shyster – but next time, it would not be fists, he thought.

A small, young Cheyenne squaw shuffled in, carrying two whisky bottles and glasses on a silver tray. Wordlessly, she put the tray on the table, poured two tumblers of whisky, and retreated to the kitchen, her long braids joggling.

Pete eyed her thin waist, and Malone smiled wickedly. "You've had her quite a while," he said quietly. "Over six months, and usually a squaw never lasts more than three with you."

Pete grinned, for this compliment pleased him. "I've got my eye on her replacement. The other day I visited the reservation. Ol' Walkin' Eagle's got a pretty sixteen-year-old daughter. Trouble is the old idiot wants five good horses."

"He'll come down to one or two," Malone said. "Where's Susie?"

"She'll be out later. Stayed in town to visit." Pete's eyes pulled down. "Wilson an' you didn't do so good today against that shyster, did you?"

Anger flared in Malone's eyes. "Seems to me you never come out top dog, either – you got no homestead entries."

Pete grinned. "That wasn't the final showdown. Tomorrow mornin' Circle Y squats on water. An' it'll take more than the guns of a lawyer and crazy sodbusters to move Circle Y."

"'Peared to me Susie really took a sudden shine to that lawyer, Pete."

Pete wet his lips. "Look thataway to me, too. Circle Y'll have to get rid of her. Circle Y's got guns to use ahead. A few days here, an' I'll ship her back to California."

"She might not want to go. She's a Brookhaven. She's got Brookhaven stubbornness."

Pete smiled again, again liking. "Susie isn't the point at hand. This shyster is. Kinda thought he was up to somethin', movin' into Sagebrush – where there's no darned need for a lawyer."

"Gabby Jackson ain't happy," Malone said. "This lawyer rubbed Gabby's face in that ink pad. Gabby had to use coal oil to wash off the ink. Took some hide with it, he said."

"Gabby's small spuds."

"Sure, but Uncle Sam ain't. And if this lawyer raises a stink with postal men in Washington ... We can't afford to have Uncle Sam step into this, Pete."

"As of tomorrow, Sagebrush'll have a new postmaster." Pete grinned crookedly. "Maybe you want the job?"

"Lay off, Pete."

"Two hundred bucks cash if you gun down Nelson."

"I'll kill him for nothing!"

"Those farmers come in in the mornin'. Lucky, we've got ears and eyes all over – a thing only money will do. Circle Y's got the sheriff an' the gov'nor in its pocket. The railroad-depot agent was bought off today. Cost me three hundred, but worth it."

Malone threw down two fingers of whisky and wiped his mouth with his sleeve. "And down in Sun Prairie this lawyer gets the hell beat out of him again?"

"Five tough Circle Y boys," Pete Brookhaven said.

Malone shook his lank head. "Nelson's a Texan. He's stubborn and tough. That beatin' won't change his mind. It'll only make him more determined."

"Who you workin' for? Nelson or Circle Y?"

"Don't talk loco, Pete."

"My fists changed Mack Wilson's mind. After I worked him over in Sullivan's, he got on his bronc an' headed out hell bent for some other range. He bungled once, an' he was through."

Malone said nothing.

Many Feathers brought in supper: thick Circle Y steaks, boiled spuds, homemade slabs of bread. She served them in silence, then trekked back to her kitchen domain.

They were finishing supper when Susie entered. "Looks like rain coming," she said.

Pete asked sharply, "How long you goin' stay?"

Her sea-blue eyes hardened. "You forget something, big brother. Our father left half of Circle Y to his only daughter."

"Circle Y shows a profit. More money made than when the Old Man ran the spread. You've got quite a few thousand in that California bank."

"I'll stay as long as I want."

Malone scooped gravy with bread, wisely remaining

silent. Covertly, he occasionally stabbed a glance at Susie's dark-haired loveliness, his blood stirring. He wanted her but he knew he would never get her. She treated him with the cool indifference she treated all other Circle Y hands.

Many Feathers came to the doorway. Unnoticed by Pete or Malone, she sent Circle Y's owner a probing glance that only Susie saw.

Pete said, "My new woman. Many Feathers, my sister, Susie."

The pretty squaw only curtsied and smiled. Susie realized that this was the loveliest squaw her brother had ever had.

"Are you hungry?" Many Feathers asked.

"Thanks, but I ate in town at the March home."

"My kitchen is always yours," Many Feathers said, and disappeared. Susie looked at her brother. "She's just a girl," she said accusingly.

"She's eighteen," Pete said. "And it's none of your business, sister. I'm up to my ears in enough trouble without chaperonin' you."

"You'll never win," Susie said sharply.

Pete, breathing deeply, stared at her, his fork suspended. "They're just bohunk farmers," he said. "Circle Y has guns."

"Guns won't win this, big brother."

Malone glanced at Susie, then at Pete, and again remained silent. Outside, a sudden wind hit, whirling dust in the gathering darkness.

"Talk," Pete ordered brusquely.

Susie sighed. "There's no use. You've got the Old Man's innate stubbornness. But Montana's changing, big brother. The day of the open-range cowman is doomed."

"Continue, if you want."

Susie was close to tears. "The Old Man tore this land from the Sioux and Gros Ventres. He used naked force – guns and tough riders. That system was all right in those days, but it doesn't fit today."

"Where'd you learn this? In that fancy college?"

Susie sank into a big chair. "My words will be wasted, but I'll waste them, anyway. The U.S. is moving West, Pete. When Lincoln signed the Homestead Act, he doomed open range. Farmers are coming into the West in all states and territories."

"You've listened to too many stupid history professors!"

Anger broke in Susie. "You're like dad was – bullheaded, arrogant! No wonder mother left him down in Texas right after I was born!"

Susie fled down the hall to the kitchen. Many Feathers absently stirred something in a kettle with a big spoon. For a long moment, the two young women – one a redskin, the other white – stared at each other. Susie brushed away a tear.

"I love him," Many Feathers said slowly in her best Reservation School English.

"I love him, too," Susie sobbed.

"He can tell me when to go," the Indian girl said, "and I will go, I am Indian, he is white. But what he learned lately – and what he is doing – it is breaking me."

"Don't go," Susie said.

Tears welled in dark eyes. "I cannot stay and see him get killed. He can win against the farmers no more than my people's braves could win against your people."

"Maybe we can do something between us," Susie said desperately.

They went into each other's arms, sobs shaking them. Out in the living room, big Pete Brookhaven paced while Bat Malone sat silently watching.

Much that that lawyer had said was true. Milk River's gigantic Running M had gone down in gunsmoke before oncoming homesteaders. So had Yellowstone River's mighty Pothook S.

Montana Territory cattlemen had seriously discussed the advancing barbwire and windmills and farmers at the Spring meeting last April. Words had been angry and hot and a vote taken. The question had won a positive vote by only three cowmen. Montana cattlemen would fight nester encroachments.

The Territorial Governor had voted against fighting. His plan had been simple. Big cow outfits would have cowpunchers file homestead entries on water holes and choice hay meadows. These cowboys would then sign over homestead rights to their home ranch. This way Montana cowmen would have clear deeds to valuable pices of land. Cattle would graze in rough country unfit for the plough.

Montana cattlemen, the governor said, should import good-blooded Hereford and Shorthorn bulls, animals that were beef to the hocks. Most of the cattle on Montana ranges were bony offspring of original Texas herds. Steers ran to bone, not beef – and Eastern slaughterhouses wanted meat, not gristle. With proper breeding, two steers could be raised that would weigh as much as three present steers.

Pete had voted to fight farmers. At that time, though, Circle Y had not been threatened; now it was.

Suddenly, he stopped pacing, cocked his head, and listened. Rain hammered the shake roof and ran from the eaves.

"This will bring grass," Malone said. "Circle Y will trail in fat beeves this fall."

Pete listened, his heart pounding.

"It'll also raise hell with them farmers," Malone continued. "Wagons will sink to the axles in mud. An' you sent Slim to dynamite Roarin' Crick's only bridge. Roarin' Crick will soon be bank-high. They'll never be able to ford it, Pete."

Brookhaven nodded.

"Them farmers'll be marooned in Sun Prairie," Malone said.

Pete Brookhaven didn't answer. Carefully, he ran over the day's proceedings, finding only one flaw – Ric Nelson. But Malone would take care of the lawyer.

"Hope you're right," Brookhaven said.

Six

That midnight a flash flood washed out Montana Pacific's tracks three miles east of Sun Prairie. Had section hands not been on patrol, the wood-burning locomotive might have toppled into the washout.

Ric heard this while eating breakfast. Were this rain to continue, many days could pass before tracks could be repaired. He had expected to unload farmers' belongings on the railroad platform in Sun Prairie, a plank structure built level with a boxcar's door. Now that was impossible.

"Your farmers are waitin' t'other side of the washout," the depot agent said. "You got a black eye, Nelson."

"Got drunk and fell down."

Ric rode east toward the stalled freight train. Gumbo was slippery, and the shod hoofs of his grey occasionally slipped. The railroad barrow pit ran full of water. To get materials from box cars to the road, this stream would also have to be forded.

Section hands were sandbagging the cut to keep it from washing away further. The train had backed fifty feet from the cut. Farmers walked about wearing yellow and black oilskin slickers.

Ric saw a tall, bony man standing to one side. A

black raincoat hung over his wide shoulders. "I'm Lawyer Richard Nelson," Ric told the man.

Sunken dark eyes studied him sharply. "I'm the Reverend Amos Zachary," the man said. He had a firm handgrip. "We have encountered some ill fortune, Mr Nelson."

"We'll whip it," Ric vowed.

Farmers gathered about them. "Does it rain like this all the time here?" one asked.

Ric told about the terrible drought this rain had broken. He gazed down the train where women and children watched from boxcar doors.

An empty feeling sagged his belly. "Call all your people together in a boxcar, Reverend Zachary," he said. "I want to talk to them, please."

"I shall summon my flock."

Within minutes, the twenty farmers were huddled, wet and cold, into a boxcar. Twelve men had wives and families. Children shivered, babies wailed, women brushed back wet hair. Reverend Zachary introduced Ric, who went straight to the point, for this situation required naked truth, not deceit.

Briefly he sketched the good possibilities of this virgin Montana loam. Dry-land farming would raise head crops such as barley, wheat, and oats. With irrigation, the valley would bloom. But there were, he said bluntly, dangers.

One would be the difficulty in transporting across this sea of mud to Sagebrush, twenty miles away. Coulees that but a few hours ago were dry washes now would have to be forded. And there was, also, the danger of Circle Y's roaring guns.

When he finished, silence held the group, broken only by a baby's thin wail. All eyes, Ric noticed, were now on Reverend Zachary.

"What answer is there rather than trek to Sagebrush?" the reverend asked.

"After this track is repaired, you can continue west. Idaho has no cowmen bucking civilization. I understand Oregon and Washington are the same. Or you can go back."

"But we paid your company in St Louis," the minister informed. "Will our money be refunded if we return?"

"Every cent. I'll see to that."

A stocky man said, "I'm not returnin'. Bessie and me left everything behind. We have nothin' to return to. I rode horse-soldier with General Crook a few years back down in Wyomin'. Wyomin' soil is much like this. This rain will have to stop."

"But when?" a woman asked.

Eyes moved back to Ric. "I've only been here a short time myself," Ric informed. "So I don't know this country well. Some say these rains hang on for weeks. Others say they soon stop."

"God is with the weak and just," Reverend Zachary intoned. "We shall vote on it, my people."

Hostile rumblings stirred the group. Ric noticed more than one person looking at him angrily. "You knew all the time the danger we was gettin' into," a woman accused, "yet you an' your St Louis company let us go on."

Ric spoke honestly. "You have a just cause for complaint there, lady. Frankly, I should have prepared the ground better. I see that now. But I didn't think Circle Y would really move against us."

"We cannot see all things," Reverend Zachary said. "There are certain things that God keeps hidden from us weak mortals."

Ric felt irritation toward the reverend's intonations, but said nothing. Reverend Zachary apparently had firm control over these people. He thus had to make the bony man his friend.

"The reverend is correct," a young girl said.

Ric glanced at her. He had noticed her immediately. She was small – no taller than Susie Brookhaven – and she had Susie's wonderful feminine form. Two braids of thick yellow hair hung down over each shoulder.

Beside her, leaning against the boxcar wall, was a tall young man. Ric judged him to be the girl's husband.

"We shall vote," Reverend Zachary said, "and then pray."

Ric leaped to the ground. He was of no use here. He went to the cut where the section crew toiled.

"These people might want to unload," he told the boss. "If so, could we borrow ties to make an unloading platform?"

The short man grinned. "Take your pick, buster. But you gotta rip them off the rails yourself."

Ric waited for the results of the voting. A buggy drove in from the direction of Sun Prairie, the driver having a note for the conductor, who hurried up to Ric.

"We got orders to back up to Larb Hill," the conductor said. "I'll give you a couple of hours to unload. If you don't unload by then, back goes this train."

Ric told about the voting.

The conductor dug out his watch. "They should be endin' their prayer meetin' soon," he said.

He and Ric walked back to the car holding the farmers. Reverend Zachary was praying. The conductor continued on to the caboose, and Ric waited patiently. Zachary's voice droned on and on. Impatience surged through Ric. Finally, the monotonous voice stopped, and Ric looked into the car.

"Do we or don't we?" he asked.

The minister hesitated, then said, "We unload, Brother Nelson."

"Everybody to work," Ric said. "We got two hours."

Men swarmed out of the car, and women followed. All started loosening rails from ties in the washed-out area. Luckily, there were a few crowbars in the group, for the section foreman would lend them no tools.

Women and older children helped. Men carried cross ties back to boxcars. They piled them up before a boxcar containing work horses. They laboured feverishly; Ric's eyes were on his watch. They hadn't enough ties to make a level unloading platform. Horses would have to step down over a foot. Two horses rebelled, snorting and pawing. Ric put his lasso around each horse's neck and pulled them, protesting and kicking, down to the ground. Milk cows unloaded easily.

Wagons and buggies were dismantled for easier shipping. Wheels and reaches and tongues were handed out of cars. One car contained food supplies. Luckily there were a few canvas tarps. These supplies were unloaded, placed on the gravel roadbed, and covered before they could become saturated.

The conductor said, "You've got six more minutes."

"We can't be unloaded by that time," Ric growled.

"I got to move this train. Orders."

Ric said stoutly, "It's not moving until all is unloaded. If needs be, I'll send some children back to sit between the rails. Their blood will be on your hands." He was bluffing.

"I'll lose my job," the conductor snarled.

Ric grinned. "Then you can come and farm with these people."

"An' buck Circle Y guns? I'm not an idiot."

The engineer lay on his whistle. The blonde girl had overheard the conversation. She gathered two little girls about her.

"We'll stand in the rails behind the caboose," she said.

"What's your name?" Ric asked.

"Trudy Carson. That boy with me is my brother, Bill."

"Your parents here?"

"No, there's just Bill and me, now."

Ric got her aside. "I only bluffed that conductor. I don't want you hurt."

"He doesn't know you ran a sandy," Trudy said.

She had an open, lovely smile that revealed white teeth. Ric looked down at the two little girls who stared up at him.

"This train start to back up – you three jump for safety, understand?"

Trudy nodded. "We'll do that, Mr Nelson."

"Ric," Ric corrected.

"Thank you, Mister – Ric."

The conductor watched the three females leave. "I'll report this to the authorities!"

"Report if you want," Ric said.

"There should be a law against men like you, Nelson. Takin' these poor, ignerant people into this danger. This ain't farmin' country."

"You an agronomist?"

The conductor scowled deeply. Ric felt wry

amusement, for the conductor probably did not know what an agronomist was.

Four hours and fifteen minutes passed before the train finally began reversing. Ric was sopping wet and very hungry. Women had built a stove of rocks under a nearby cottonwood tree. He caught the aromatic scent of frying ham and boiling coffee.

"God bless womanhood," Reverend Zachary stated. "Without a good woman, a good man is not complete."

Ric remembered his bachelor quarters next to his ruined office. He had thought the same many times when cooking his breakfast of bacon and eggs and glancing at the deep lint under his bunk.

He looked at the piled-up wagon parts and other farming equipment. Two boys had the horses under herd along the right-of-way.

"This rain might be of long duration," the minister said. "There's not a clear spot in the entire heavens."

Each farmer's gear contained a dismantled windmill, Ric noticed. Government geologists claimed that a twenty-five-foot well would contain plenty of good water for a house and garden and small pasture.

"We shall eat," Reverend Zachary said. "After a hot meal, things will look better. We still have much work to do before wagons roll."

"These children should be under shelter," Ric said. "There's a small church in Sun Prairie."

"I shall ride in and consult its pastor."

"I forgot to ask," Ric said, "but how did the voting come out?"

"The *ayes* won by three slim votes."

Seven

Next noon found all wagons loaded. Noon also found seven Circle Y riders approaching, headed by Pete Brookhaven and Bat Malone. Women and children had been taken the previous night to the Sun Prairie church where there was warmth and a roof over their heads; only Trudy Carson stayed behind.

"Will there be trouble?" Trudy asked Ric.

"I doubt it, in broad daylight." Ric spoke to the Reverend Zachary. "Please spread word among your people to keep their hands away from weapons. Let me do the talking, please." The minister hurried away.

"One is a woman," Trudy breathed.

All Circle Y riders wore long slickers. As they came closer, Ric saw that Trudy was correct. Susie Brookhaven rode with Circle Y; her buckskin horse pranced and fought his bit.

Slowly, Circle Y rode along the string of loaded wagons, eyeing each's load. Rifles protruded from saddle holsters. Reverend Zachary returned to stand at Ric's right. Finally, Circle Y halted before them, Pete Brookhaven's big sorrel stud pawing muddy soil. Ric introduced the minister.

"Sky pilot, huh?" Brookhaven said scornfully. "We

need a preacher here just as bad as we need more rain!"

Reverend Zachary's face showed no emotion. Ric glanced at Bat Malone, who leaned on his saddle fork, eyes on him. Ric introduced Susie to Trudy.

"The pleasure is mine," Susie said, and Trudy curtsied slightly.

Brookhaven asked brazenly, "When will you get these wagons rollin', lawyer?"

"Our business," Ric said shortly.

"Be rough goin'," Brookhaven sneered. "You'll be blazin' a trail. Stage ain't left Sagebrush since the rain. Too much mud. An' Roarin' Crick bridge has washed out."

"Roaring Creek can be forded."

Brookhaven's cold eyes roamed over the group. Ric tried to read the cowman's big face, and failed. Finally, Brookhaven said, "Windmills an' barbwire. You should be jailed for life, Nelson, for gettin' these ignerant people into this mess."

"Here comes *your* sheriff," Ric said.

Brookhaven angrily eyed Sheriff Asa Gosden, big and beefy in a grey slicker. "What're you doin' here, Asa?" he demanded.

"Just rode out to see what was goin' on."

"Circle Y don't need you here no more than we need these farmers." Brookhaven waved a big arm. "Come on, Circle Y. Nothin' here." Circle Y thundered back toward Sun Prairie, leaving Sheriff Gosden behind.

"And we don't need you, either," Ric told the lawman. "Can't you read the handwriting on the wall? I have many more farmers coming in. Soon they'll control this county by outvoting Circle Y. And you'll be out of your easy office, sheriff."

"I'll wait," Gosden said stiffly. "When do you roll wagons?"

"As I told Circle Y, that's our business – and ours alone," Ric said. "Now do us all a favour and get out of here, will you? We got work to do."

"You talk rough, Nelson!"

"Move," Ric ordered.

Gosden swore, turned his horse, and rode back toward Sun Prairie. Reverend Zachary spoke to Ric. "I would be led to believe the sheriff is a Circle Y man?"

"Completely, Reverend. Well, let's get to work, men."

Horses were harnessed and hooked up. Grudgingly, heavy laden wagons started to roll, running gear creaking, horses braced into collars. Dusk found tired stock and protesting wagons halting before Sun Prairie's small church. It had taken all afternoon to move three miles.

Ric shook his head slowly. "These wagons got too much load for this mud, Reverend. We should store about half this stuff and come back for it later."

"Perhaps we can use the church?"

"I don't know. We can make inquiries, though."

The church's potbellied stove was red with Montana lignite coal; women were cooking. Pots sent out delicious aromas while children played noisily. Teams were unharnessed and put out to graze on the scant grass. These work horses needed grain. The farmers had none, having used their supply on the trek west.

Bill Carson took the first shift as horse herder. Ric broke the work into two-hour shifts, lasting until dawn. He would take the last tour of duty.

He rode toward the depot as a cold wind pounded his slicker. The governor had not answered his wire.

This didn't surprise him. He had expected a telegram from Larb Hill saying his surveyors had arrived, but there was none.

He had one telegram, though, from the Minneapolis wholesale house. That company was shipping out two boxcars of lumber. They were also sending out a boxcar of groceries and other supplies.

After supper, the farmers held a meeting conducted by Reverend Zachary. Wagons were too heavily loaded. Much of the load would have to be stored in the church. They could return for it after the rain had stopped and the trail had dried out.

Just then, the depot agent entered. Ric had learned that Sun Prairie's small congregation could not support a full-time pastor, and the agent acted in the capacity of minister.

The agent spoke abruptly. "I'm sorry, folks, but you can't stay here. An' you can't store things here, either."

"Why?" Ric asked.

"County commissioners just finished a suddenly called session. Sheriff Gosden summoned them into town. They just passed a law saying this church couldn't hold this many people an' nothin' could be stored here."

"Why not?" Ric again asked.

"Commissioners say it would be a fire menace."

Ric snorted. "This building is sopping wet. You couldn't light it on fire with kerosene."

"I'm sorry, folks."

Dismay hit the homesteaders. Angry rumblings passed through them; even children had stopped playing.

"Can we store at your depot?" Ric asked.

"Not a chance, Nelson," the agent said. "Railroad laws are ag'in it. Can't be done."

Reverend Zachary spoke to Ric. "Perhaps we can store some other place? The livery barn, maybe?"

Ric shook his head. "A county commissioner owns the barn, and Pete Brookhaven owns the commissioner. There'll be no place open for us in Sun Prairie."

"Then we move without unloading," the minister said.

After the depot agent left, Ric rode out to where young Bill Carson held the horse herd. The coulee south of Sun Prairie ran bank full; yesterday it had been dusty dry.

"Not much grass," Bill grunted.

Ric circled the grazing horses, saw all was well, and returned to the church. Mothers were putting smaller children to bed in blankets and quilts thrown on the floor. Children were saying prayers. Ric's throat caught, for he was responsible for the safety of these little tykes; this rode heavily on his shoulders.

He slept on a quilt in a corner. Sleep came slowly, then was marked by terrible dreams. One red dream jerked him awake, cold with sweat. Sanity returned.

As rain continued to pound the church's roof, Ric's mind ran ahead. If this rain continued, and if these nester wagons finally reached Sagebrush, where would he house his people?

The Mercantile? Sullivan's Saloon? He decided to face that problem when it arose, and returned to his bad dreams, but not for long.

He sat, back against the wall, smoking a cigarette. In the darkness, he heard men snoring more loudly than the sound of rain on roof. Thunder crackled, and jagged lightning lit the church's interior. During one lightning flash, he looked at his watch.

He would go on horse guard within an hour. He must have dropped to sleep, for Trudy Carson shook him awake. "Time you ride out to guard the horses," she said quietly.

"How do you happen to be awake?"

"I can't sleep, Ric."

He buckled on his spurs and donned his slicker. His saddled grey horse grazed on picket behind the church. Dawn was trying to break through the clouds, but light was very uncertain.

He mounted a cold saddle and rode south toward the herd. He had been in leather only a few minutes when, up ahead, a massive roar crashed through the rain. Jagged flames leaped upward from the steaming soil.

Lightning had hit close to the herd. Sitting stiff in leather, he saw another flaring boom smash across the wilderness. Two lightning bolts would not hit that close together, logic told him. He realized then that the roars and flares had been caused by dynamite.

Circle Y was stampeding the work horses! He jerked his rifle from the saddle, his bronc plunging forward. Up ahead, six-shooters snarled flame. A rider swept in from the west, pounding leather hard. He was a dim, obscure figure wearing a long black raincoat. Automatically, Ric swung his Winchester, toward the man, then held fire. He couldn't tell whether the rider was from Circle Y or one of his farmers. Within seconds, the rider was gone, hidden by slanting rain.

Pounding hoofs jarred the earth. The work horses were stampeding south. Now another rider roared in screaming, "I'm Jiggy Williams, a farmer!"

Ric's rifle sagged. "Them riders – they come from the west, Nelson. From the direction you said Circle Y was located! They threw dynamite, man. I know it was black powder. I was a powder monkey in the Pennsy coal mines! They never shot at me. They just shot into the air!"

"Just a Circle Y nuisance raid," Ric said shortly. "Come on, let's head those horses off!"

They spurred ahead, Ric's mount leaving the farmer's old work nag behind. There was no more firing, no more dynamite roaring. Circle Y had swept in, hit, swept out. He caught the tail end of the running horses just as the last plunged into the creek. Ric followed, his horse kicking spray.

His plan was simple, remembered from cattle stampedes on the Pecos. Get to the lead, swing in, turn the stock, get the horses milling. Swiftly, his tough saddler forged ahead, past work horses running hard, manes flowing, steel-shod hoofs pounding.

At last, he was in the lead. Brandishing his rifle, he turned the lead horse, a big sorrel mare, pounding her bony nose with his rifle barrel. Soon he had the herd turned and milling. The farmer rode up. "Think we lost any?" he asked.

"Can't tell till dawn," Ric grunted.

They commenced hazing the hard-breathing broncs toward town, their run gone. Reverend Zachary's gaunt form materialized, astraddle a roan gelding, two other mounted farmers behind him.

"That was dynamite," the minister said.

Ric nodded. "Have we lost any of them?"

"A grey gelding back yonder," the minister said. "Has a broken foreleg. Plunged off a cliff."

A farmer said, "He'll have to be shot." He rode off into the rain. The wild run had taken more energy from the work stock. And they desperately needed every ounce of pulling horseflesh available.

A rifle cracked in the distance.

"We should notify Sheriff Gosden," the reverend said, and Ric laughed sourly.

Eight

Outside, the Circle Y stallion trumpeted in his corral, hungering for a mare. Sheriff Asa Gosden sat in an easy chair, plump legs extended. "One horse broke his leg," he told Pete Brookhaven. "They shot him. No other damage done."

"We jus' wanted to put the fear of Circle Y in them," Pete Brookhaven said.

Bat Malone, seated at the big table, said nothing.

"You didn't do it," the sheriff said. "They rolled wagons out this morning."

"Roarin' Crick'll stop them," Brookhaven assured him. The three didn't know that Susie and Many Feathers were listening in the hallway.

Sheriff Asa Gosden dug out his pipe from a vest pocket. "I noticed Roarin' had no bridge," he said slyly. "Rain must've washed it out, huh?"

"Flood took it out," Pete Brookhaven said.

Slowly, the lawman loaded his pipe. Brookhaven noticed Gosden's hands shook slightly. Malone, also noticing this, sent Pete Brookhaven a slow smile.

Brookhaven said sharply, "You gettin' cold boots, Asa?"

Gosden looked over his flaring match. "What're you talkin' about, Pete?"

Brookhaven stood in front of the sheriff. He looked down at the heavy-set man. Brookhaven clipped his words. "I'm not a greybeard, Sheriff, but I learned one thing early from my father. A man buys his friends with money. My old man put you into office. Since he died, I've kept you there."

"Don't say nothin' you'll be sorry for, Pete."

Brookhaven laughed cynically. Susie and Many Feathers listened, all ears. Again the stallion neighed. "Circle Y pinned that badge on you!" Brookhaven snarled, "and Circle Y can take it off'n you, Gosden!"

"I know that, Pete."

"I know what eats you, Gosden. You're thinkin' so many farmers'll come in they'll outnumber Circle Y at the polls! Well, them farmers won't stay — unless they're weighted down by six feet of soil!"

"How about the gov'nor, Pete?"

"What about him?"

"He's a cowman, sure," Gosden placated, "but he's also a good politician. An' the *Stockman's Journal* says the territory's fillin' up with sodbusters."

"Go on," Brookhaven said.

"Well, like I said — the gov'nor is a politician. He wouldn't want to lose his job. He's makin' good money in politics — mebbe more than his cattle pay him. He'll go which way the political wind blows, Pete." Gosden cleared his throat and continued: "This country won't be a territory much longer, the way the U.S. is spreadin' west. The gov'nor wants to be a senator. He might swing against you cowmen. Besides, I done heerd thet farmers are movin' in on his range, too."

"He'll run 'em off!"

Gosden climbed to his feet. "I wonder ..."

Brookhaven slapped the sheriff's beefy face. Gosden's pipe slithered to the floor; its stem broke. The slap almost knocked Gosden down, but the sheriff held his feet with difficulty.

Gosden's fists doubled before discretion surged in, making his fists break again into open hands. "I wish you hadn't done that, Pete!"

Brookhaven ripped the badge from Gosden's greasy vest, taking cloth and all. He tossed the star to Malone, who caught it expertly.

"Why'd you do that, Pete?" Gosden whined.

"From this moment on, Malone is sheriff," Pete Brookhaven said.

"Only the county commissioners can boot me out of office!"

"I'll send a man to each commissioner right now and tell them what I did. They know who butters their biscuits."

Gosden said, "Pete, for cripe's sake! I got a wife, kids. I gotta have a job!"

Bat Malone smiled, playing with the star. Brookhaven whirled to face Malone. "You want him for a deputy, Bat?" His voice held cynicism.

Malone took time before answering. "Yeah, I'll have him for a deputy. That is, if he promises to stay in line."

"I'll do everythin' you say," Gosden assured him.

Brookhaven grinned. "We'll make you undersheriff, Asa. Your undersheriff is now a deputy, savvy?"

Gosden looked at his pipe, started to pick it up, then decided it was worthless. He had a spare in his saddlebag. "Any chance of gettin' my badge back?" he asked.

"There might be," Brookhaven assured. "That is, if you work for Circle Y an' forget these sodbusters."

West of the Barbwire

Gosden's deep-set eyes moved from Brookhaven to Malone, but saw nothing. Wordlessly, he turned and left. Soon he rode past the big front window, hunkered in the saddle against the driving rain.

Malone pinned the badge on his vest. "Maybe I should take an oath or somethin'?" he joked dryly.

"Don't act funny!" Unexpectedly, Brookhaven stepped into the hall, catching Susie and Many Feathers flat-footed. "Well, look who's here!"

"We were just going to the kitchen," Susie said.

"Then get movin'!"

"You can't order me around!" Susie said hotly. "Dad left me one-half of this ranch, remember!"

Brookhaven spoke sarcastically. "Okay, baby sister! Right here an' now we divide Circle Y in the middle. You get the west half, me the east. That puts this house on my half!"

"You've gone crazy," Susie said.

"You're leavin' this country, little sister, and soon!"

"You can't run me out!" Susie stormed. "Mr Beeson asked me to teach school here next winter."

"Beeson forgets one thing," Brookhaven stated. "I'm head of the school board. He's only a member. Now get movin!"

The girls went down the hall to Susie's room. Brookhaven rapped out orders to Malone. "Bat, send a rider out to the other four county commissioners. Tell them to say you're sheriff. That makes the appointment legal, for what that is worth."

Malone stood up.

"Then ride out and check those farmers. Tell me where they're located, how much progress they've made."

"What would they do if they got to Sagebrush?

Where would they stay there?"

"I might let them get to Sagebrush. Then again I might not. But they'll find no shelter in Sagebrush. Circle Y owns that town – lock, stock, an' barrel."

"They pack tents," Malone reminded.

"Happy to hear that," Brookhaven said sarcastically.

Malone left, Brookhaven rode for Sagebrush, rain slapping his slicker. Sagebrush was a sea of mud; even town curs had left the street. Sullivan slid out Brookhaven's favourite bottle.

"How goes it?" Sullivan asked.

Brookhaven poured. "Sheriff Gosden handed in his badge. Bat Malone's now the law."

Sullivan's brow rose. "Notice we got a new postmaster, too."

"You don't say."

"Gabby Jackson left town about a hour ago." Sullivan mopped the bar. "Said he was leavin' for good. He said you'd appointed Mrs Slattery postmistress."

"I'll miss the old fool," Brookhaven said.

"Mack Wilson's pulled out, too. Guess he wants no more of the lawyer's fists. You'll need a new stage driver."

"My business."

Sullivan's lips hardened. "This town is sure losin' population fast. But it'll get a big jump when these farmers arrive."

Brookhaven coldly studied the bull-necked saloonman. Sullivan had been somewhat of a rebel, even to Big Ike Brookhaven.

"Understand them homesteaders got a lot of kids," Sullivan said. "Children sure increase a town's business."

Brookhaven merely nodded.

"Them children will need schoolin'. We'll have to build an addition to the school, I reckon. They tell me the lawyer aims to start a lumber yard. He says that if Beeson won't sell him supplies, he'll also start a general store."

"Where'd you learn all this?"

"Smoky Jorgenson rode in a while back from Sun Prairie. Common talk down there, he said. Nelson sent out wires."

"That depot operator talks too much. You hintin' at somethin', Sullivan?"

"Don't use your spurs on me, Pete." Sullivan spoke shortly. The two drifting cowboys watched and listened. "You might own this buildin', but you don't own me."

"Frosty, huh? Go on."

"Nothin' more to say, Pete. For years this town has stood still. These farmers'll bring in new blood – and money. An' a man's in business to make money."

"Doubt if many of them are drinkin' men. An' I have my doubts that there'll be much money in that crowd of bohunks."

"Bound to be some drinkers, Pete."

Pete Brookhaven spoke harshly. "Don't try to jump off Circle Y's boat, Sullivan."

Sullivan's big face reddened, and his hands became fists. Just then Rosie came down the stairway from the upstairs rooms, wearing a very low-cut dress. She hooked her arm into Brookhaven's.

She smiled up at him. "How are you this rainy day, Pete?"

Brookhaven batted her arm aside. Rosie's mascara'd eyes tightened, but rebuff was nothing new to her. A cowpuncher rattled his empty glass, and Sullivan moved to refill it.

"Just remember what I said," Brookhaven told Sullivan, who had no answer.

Nine

Nothing remained of the plank bridge at Roaring Creek but tips of wooden pilings a few inches above the surging, muddy water. Reverend Zachary shook his gaunt head. "We must wait until the flood subsides, Mr Nelson."

Ric studied the water. A dead Circle Y cow floated past, rolling in the current. "We've got to cross, Reverend. We've got to squat farmers on homesteads, even if unsurveyed. They told me back in Sun Prairie that Brookhaven has already sent out Circle Y riders to squat on choice pieces of land. They're living in tents and wickiups made of brush and trees. Brookhaven, they told me, might import more cowboys. And if these men qualify, I have to issue them homestead entries."

"Is such squatting legal?"

"It is if they qualify as homesteaders. Brookhaven will pay them wages. They can squat for a year, make the necessary homestead improvements Uncle Sam demanded, and then they will sell their homesteads to Brookhaven for a few dollars."

Reverend Zachary rubbed his pointed jaw. "We could leave the wagons on this side and somehow ferry my people across. Or we could camp here, Mr Nelson."

"We camp here, Reverend, and it's too late. By that time Brookhaven will have men squatting on the best land and water. And besides, already some of the children are sick from this rain and cold."

Reverend Zachary nodded.

"We've got to get those sick children under shelter. Somehow, we've got to get across this creek."

Ric stood on stirrups and looked at the wagon train behind him. They had left Sun Prairie at sunup; and now it was ten o'clock in the morning, and they'd gone but three miles. Seventeen long, heartbreaking miles lay between them and Sagebrush.

"Maybe we should turn back?" a farmer said.

"You have absolutely nothing in Sun Prairie," Ric reminded.

"We shall vote," Reverend Zachary said.

Ric was growing weary of the endless voting, but he said nothing. The minister and farmer returned to the nesters. Ric studied the leaden Montana sky; it held no clear spot. Nester wagons were tiny ants under the grey bowl. Something akin to despair tugged at him. Was this worth the effort?

He added points mentally. He had already collected two thousand dollars from these families. He would make more when homestead entries were filed, but was he working only for money? He could return the two thousand, surrender his homestead claim on Sagebrush Gulch, and pack what he owned in a suitcase and move on.

He thought of Mack Wilson's sneering face and his insults. Brookhaven had sicked Wilson on him. Bat Malone had slugged him cold from behind, his office had been wrecked, and local law refused him aid. His St Louis office had sent no help, railroad officials had ignored his telegram, even the governor refused to answer his wire. What if the farmers turned back?

Harsh stubbornness welled in him. He would fight Circle Y alone, and go through with his homestead entry. He had taken too much from Brookhaven. The beating Circle Y cowpunchers had handed him in Sun Prairie had clinched the nail. His Texas stubbornness arose.

These sodbusters could turn back, but not he. Circle Y would never run him out. He'd whip Circle Y, or inherit six feet of Montana's virgin sod.

Trudy Carson rode out of the gloom. "They're voting again," she said.

Ric merely nodded, watching Roaring Creek.

"How will we get across, Ric?" she asked.

Ric looked at the exposed tips of piling. "If we had planks, we could stretch them lengthwise from piling to piling, and let wagon wheels roll on them. Be slow, dangerous — but could be done."

"Where are the bridge's original planks?"

"I'm sure Circle Y dynamited this bridge. The blast might have torn all the planks up."

"Maybe some were blown off whole and might be downstream, Ric."

"That's a good idea," Ric said. "Let's ride downstream and do some looking."

"Here comes a rider from Circle Y's direction."

Bat Malone materialized from the southwest. He put his roan into Roaring Creek, boots on his saddle fork, rifle held high. The roan swam like a beaver, parting the current swiftly.

Ric pulled his Winchester from his saddle boot as Malone's roan climbed out of the water. The Circle Y man rode toward Ric and Trudy, stopping ten feet from them.

Malone's hard eyes first surveyed Trudy, then switched to Ric; he offered no greeting.

"Seen Asa Gosden around?" Malone asked.

"Saw a rider in the distance some time back," Ric told him. "Looked like Gosden. He never stopped."

"He ain't sheriff no more," Malone said.

Ric, eyes riveted on Malone, had no reply. Between him and this gunman lay a deadly, writhing area of suspense. If Malone made a move to raise his rifle, Ric's Winchester would also rise.

"Brookhaven stripped the badge from him, huh?" Ric said coldly.

"He did. I'm sheriff now."

Ric heard a pistol hammer click. He looked quickly at Trudy Carson, who had taken from her slicker pocket a small pistol which pointed now at Bat Malone.

Malone studied the pistol momentarily, face bleak as the day. Then he lifted dull eyes to Trudy's lovely face. "You got women fightin' for you now'days, Nelson?"

"I never asked her to do that," Ric said.

Malone looked back at Ric. "Just thought I'd tell you, Attorney."

"You didn't say *shyster*," Ric reminded.

Malone's jaw muscles jerked slightly. "You talk big with a gun on me, an' a half-loco woman holdin' it."

"Maybe you'd rather shoot from ambush in the brush?"

Anger grooved Malone's face. For one moment Ric thought the Circle Y gunman would raise his rifle, pistol or no pistol on him, and his muscles tightened. Then Malone let his Winchester sag.

"You won't get by with nothin' with me as sheriff," Malone intoned, "so you just watch your step – an' the steps of these farmers, too. This female pulled a gun on the law."

Ric spoke cynically. "You arresting her, Malone? Taking her to Sun Prairie and to jail?"

Again, impending violence hung suspended. Then Malone glanced toward the lined-up wagons. Farmers had seen the Circle Y gunman ride up and had hurried toward them, rifles in hands.

"You win this hand, Nelson." Malone spoke flatly. "But I'm a patient man. There'll be others."

"I'll be here," Ric assured.

Malone whirled his horse and loped toward Sun Prairie, his bronc's shod hoofs flinging back mud. Trudy uncocked her gun and returned it to her slicker pocket.

"You never had to do that," Ric said.

She said, quietly, "Without you, Ric, where would us farmers be?"

Their eyes met, but neither spoke. Her yellow braids hung girlishly outside her slicker, and her prairie-blue eyes were serious. Ric reached out and touched her cold hand.

"Thank you, Trudy."

The oncoming farmers had stopped, now that Malone had ridden away. They hesitated, then started back toward the wagons.

"Guess Malone temporarily broke up their voting," Trudy said. "Let's look for planks, Ric?"

"Good idea."

They found the first solid plank within two hundred yards. Flood waters had washed it to shore. Within a mile, they had found a dozen good planks. Ric's heart beat quicker, for this was indeed a stroke of luck.

"How many will we need?" Trudy asked.

"I think there's enough here. We'd better get men to carry them back." Ric took down his lasso, his fingers rough because of the cold. He roped one plank to drag back. "I've got no rope," Trudy said.

They rode back toward the wagons, the plank sliding behind in the mud. Trudy looked at the dismal, wet surroundings.

"I already love this country, Ric."

Ric glanced at her. She was in earnest. "Where are you from?" he asked.

"Cleveland, Ohio. I worked in a bank there. My brother Bill, he has a bit of trouble with his lungs. Doctors told us to go West to the high, dry air."

"Your parents?"

"I'll be honest, Ric. Father was a shoemaker. He drank himself to death about five years ago. Mother was never well. We had a hard time. She died a year ago."

Ric said nothing.

"Bill will get well here. I feel sure of that. Weekends I worked teaching grammar school children – the slow group. Both Bill and I went through high school."

"Maybe you can teach here," Ric said.

"I love working with children. Of course, someday I expect to have a houseful of my own." She looked sidewise at him. "You're from Texas, aren't you?"

Ric began telling her about himself. She was easy to talk to, he realized. She seemed to have a good sense of humour, too – something he was sure Susie Brookhaven lacked, for he had tried to joke with Susie when he first met her, there in that lunging Sagebrush stage. The thought came to him that their meeting, although just a few days ago, seemed years away.

They came to the bridge. Reverend Zachary asked what they intended to do with the plank and Ric told him. The minister rubbed his pointed jaw.

"That will be dangerous, Brother Nelson, but I believe it can be done."

"We'll get women and children across on planks first," Ric said. "Without them in wagons there'll be no lives lost if a wagon does plunge off the planks, or break one."

"I'll dispatch men for other planks immediately."

Ric and Trudy dismounted. "How did the voting go?" Ric asked.

"The *ayes* won by one vote." Ric felt a moment of bitter bleakness.

Ten

Next morning Susie Brookhaven found Many Feathers sitting at the kitchen table. When she greeted her, Many Feathers merely nodded.

Susie boiled two eggs, made toast, and sat down, facing the lovely little squaw.

Finally, Many Feathers said, "I have to leave, Susie. I can't stay here and see him get killed or go to jail."

"Where would you go?"

"Back to my people on the reservation."

"What would you do?"

Many Feathers rubbed away a tear. "Just worry about him. I'd like to tell you what's inside me, but I don't speak your language well enough. I wish you could speak mine."

"I used to speak a little Assiniboin, but I've forgotten what little I knew. Since I was nine, I've been out to school each winter. Where is Pete now?"

"He never came home last night. He might be dead on the prairie. He might have spent the night in town. A thousand things could have happened."

Susie gathered her dishes. She doubted if the Cheyennes would again accept Many Feathers, for she had abandoned her race and tribe for a white man.

"One just cannot run away from one's troubles," she said philosophically.

She washed the dirty dishes, dried them, put them in the cupboard, patted Many Feathers in sisterly fashion on the shoulder, and went into the big living room where she gazed into the drizzling rain, thoughts on the nesters and Roaring Creek. Had they crossed safely?

She breathed deeply, her bosom rising and falling. She had slept little that night, tormented by red, ugly dreams of danger. She faced her problem squarely, as was her habit – was she falling in love with Ric Nelson? Why? She had just come from the University of California. There she had met many handsome and progressive young men. She had planned on staying only a week on the ranch. Then she had met Ric. What did Ric have that appealed to her? She knew that answer immediately. Ric was handsome, Ric joked and laughed easily, and Ric was intelligent. And love was just something that whammed out of the blue and hit two innocent people ...

Many Feathers was right. It was time that she, too, went. Then, this thought was discarded. Pete was, after all, her brother. Could she let Pete go to jail, or get killed?

Pete had lived most of his life on arrogant, powerful Circle Y, one of Montana's biggest cow spreads. He had not seen enough of the outside world, as had she. Circle Y's arrogance had been bred into Pete's bones, and he couldn't read the disastrous handwriting on the wall. She had talked to him, trying to get some sense into him, but he had scorned her. No, she couldn't leave Pete.

Then, what could she do to avert this terrible disaster, this threat of guns, of roaring violence, that hung over Sagebrush range? A dozen thoughts flickered through her brain, but only one seemed plausible, and that was to move in Territorial troops.

She wished the Territorial capital were not so many hundred miles away. Were it closer she would sneak away and visit the governor, and Pete would never know. She knew the governor well, for he had been a long-time friend of her father, having visited Circle Y on hunting and fishing trips.

She would ride to Sun Prairie and wire the governor. She knew Pete had the Sun Prairie depot operators bought off, but she would circumvent that.

She saddled her big buckskin. Occasional bursts of rain – marked by lightning and thunder – rolled across the range, but the rain was mostly a dreary, consistent drizzle. Sometimes these summer rains lasted for weeks. Montana was either blisteringly dry or sopping wet, boiling under the torrid sun or shivering below zero.

She could have forded Roaring Creek directly north of Circle Y's home ranch, where the creek would have been narrower, but she didn't. She realized she wanted to see Ric, so she angled northeast toward Roaring Creek bridge. Again she hoped she wasn't falling in love with Ric. She thought, *I'm just lonesome, nothing more ...*

Was that the reason? She tried to discard this thought, but always it lingered in her mind, bringing a certain warmth. The noon sky hung overhead, a leaden grey, when she reached the bridge.

She was surprised to see the farmers' wagons all on the south side. Heavy planks had been laid from piling tip to piling tip. Ric and Trudy Carson rode up.

Again she noted the beauty of Trudy. She scowled. Trudy and Ric always seemed to be together; circumstances had thrown them together. These same bitter circumstances kept her away from Ric.

She forced a smile. "Hello, Miss Carson. Hello, Ric."

Trudy said, "Hello, Miss Brookhaven."

Trudy seemed rather cold toward her. Was that because she had addressed her as *Miss* and used Ric's given name?

"Hello, Susie," Ric said.

Susie saw Trudy scowl slightly, which made her happy. "I see you got wagons across," she said.

Ric grinned boyishly. "Rather touch and go, though. We lost one wagon. Rocked off the planks, fell over a piling – therefore never tumbled into the creek."

"Anybody hurt?"

"We moved all women and children across on foot on the planks. Then only a driver was on a wagon when it crossed."

"You've got Prickly Gulch five miles ahead," Susie said. "It'll be full of water. And it has a sand bottom, too."

"Cross rivers when you come to them," Ric said.

"And Sagebrush Creek is bank full," she stated. "It's even bigger than Roaring."

Sagebrush Creek had no bridge. It meandered normally through wide meadows, but now these meadows would be under water, Ric knew.

"Sagebrush has heavy timber," Ric said.

She nodded, knowing what he meant. He intended to cut down logs, lace them thoroughly to the hubs of wagons, and float his wagons across. She dimly remembered, when a child, crossing Texas' Red River that way, when her father had trekked Texas longhorns north.

Susie looked at the heavily loaded wagons, some sunk to hubs in mud. The train was getting ready to move. She saw no woman other than Trudy about. No children were in evidence.

"How are the children standing the trip?" she put the question to Ric.

"Some are coming down with colds. If they're not better tomorrow, we'll send somebody in for Doc Smith. That is, if he'll come."

"Why wouldn't he come? He's a doctor."

"Circle Y owns Sagebrush."

"Circle Y doesn't own Doc Smith," Susie said. "He's one man even my father couldn't make toe the line."

"Hope he's still not toeing it," Ric said.

Trudy spoke. "These children should be under a roof and close to heat. They chased us out of the church in Sun Prairie. And there might be no available shelter in Sagebrush, Ric says."

"That is your business, Miss Carson, and not mine," Susie said stiffly.

"Have you no heart?" Trudy asked cynically. "Are you merciless, like Circle Y and your brother?"

"You talk too much!" Susie retorted.

Ric said nothing, finding wry amusement in the women snapping at each other. Susie was white with anger, and Trudy's mouth was hard, her eyes narrowed.

Trudy said, cuttingly, "Maybe the Circle Y ranch would take in the women and children? I understand it's very big, and there should be lots of room there."

"You heard wrong, Miss Carson."

Ric shifted in leather, stirrups creaking, deciding this had gone far enough. "Stop it right now," he ordered.

Susie looked at him. "Your Miss Carson has a very pointed tongue, Ric."

"Thank you for the compliment," Trudy said.

Ric spoke to Trudy. "I said stop it, remember?"

Trudy said shortly, "I'm going back to the wagons."

She whirled her horse and loped away, back straight. Ric noticed Susie's small hand gripped her quirt handle hard. "Why do two women always have to fight?" he asked.

"She started it, but I could have sure finished it!"

Ric leaned forward, his face serious. "Susie, don't get into trouble with your brother because of these farmers. Don't plead the cause of these people, please. I don't want them to move between you and Pete, Susie."

"Are you speaking for yourself, Ric, or for the nesters?"

"For both of us, Susie."

She said suddenly, "I have to go. Solong, Ric."

She slapped her horse with rowels. The bronc reared, neighing in anger, fighting the bit. He whirled on his hind legs, reined toward Roaring Creek.

He plunged into the boiling stream. Within feet, he was swimming. Ric watched Susie cross the torrent, admiration tugging at him. She was a cattleman's daughter, reared in the saddle, and she showed this now.

She kicked her boots out of stirrups. She placed both feet in the saddle's seat, hands braced on the saddle fork. She perched in this precarious position, the buckskin swimming so strongly that the centre of the saddle never even got wet. The buckskin climbed out on the far shore. She whirled him, lifted a hand to Ric, then galloped away and was lost in the rain. Having arrived in Sun Prairie, she went directly to the telegraph office.

"I'm Susie Brookhaven," she told the operator. "I want to send a telegram, and I demand its contents be kept secret."

"All telegram contents are private, Miss Brookhaven."

"Not from this office they aren't. I happen to know my brother has bribed all three of you operators. If the words in this telegram get to my brother, I'm contacting railroad officials."

The operator stared. "This will be kept secret," he promised.

She got a pad and commenced. She described the trouble facing Sagebrush and asked for military help.

She then went to the sheriff's office. Malone was not in, but Undersheriff Gosden held down his old chair. "Bad day to ride about, Miss Brookhaven." Gosden got laboriously afoot.

"Sit down, Asa. Where's Malone?"

"I don't know. I'm not sheriff any more. Maybe that's for the best. I feel a century younger."

"Why?"

"No responsibilities."

Susie laughed shortly. "You've never had to make a decision. Circle Y's always made them for you. Before Pete did your thinking, my father thought for you."

Gosden sat down heavily. "Miss Brookhaven, what is going to happen here?"

"Circle Y is wrong. Circle Y fights to hold land it doesn't own. Circle Y can't hold back western immigration."

Gosden shook his head. "This Lawyer Nelson, he's sure bullheaded. Ain't never seen a man as strongheaded as he is."

"Yes, you have."

"Who?"

"My father. My brother."

She decided to spend the night in Sun Prairie with friends. The governor's return message could thus be easier delivered. She checked the telegraph office at eleven before going to bed. There was no return message.

None arrived the next forenoon, either. Apparently, the governor cared nothing about Circle Y since Big Ike had died. Or he had his hands too full on his ranch trying to turn back the plough and barbed wire.

She rode slowly back to Circle Y.

Eleven

Pete Brookhaven spent the night in Sullivan's. Things had developed fast; he wanted to feel the town's temper. Circle Y owned every building in Sagebrush. Townspeople not backing Circle Y would encounter tough sledding.

Reluctant businessmen would find themselves without housing. Those in residences, who turned against Circle Y, would discover they had no roofs over their heads.

Circle Y hired over a hundred riders during roundups. Between roundups, Brookhaven cut the crew to forty. Those laid off lived in Sagebrush, as a rule. Some had families and lived easily.

Although buffalo were about gone, the range teemed with antelope and deer. Elk ranged back on higher elavations, and lignite coal lay exposed along cut banks. All a man had to do for his winter's supply of fuel was swing a pick.

Straight pine trees were there for the cutting. The town, therefore, consisted mainly of log houses. Its only contact with the outside world was made by stage. Sagebrush was a vast empire sufficient in itself. Whoever bossed Circle Y also ramrodded Sagebrush.

Occasionally, grub-line riding cowboys drifted

through, looking for jobs. Some were hired during roundup, then told to ride on. Circle Y saw that none tarried long around Sagebrush. When they were broke, Circle Y told them to ride on. Down-at-the-heel cowboys, with no money to spend, were not welcome in Sagebrush.

Brookhaven sat in a dealer's-choice poker game with Sullivan, Ira Beeson, the town's barber, and Doc Smith. "You been called out to the nester camp yet?" Brookhaven asked Doc Smith.

"Not yet. But expect to be, sooner or later. Children are with that wagon train. And children catch colds this type of weather."

Brookhaven studied his cards, almost on the point of ordering Doc Smith not to treat nesters, realizing such an order would be useless.

Doc was one man Circle Y couldn't bend; Big Ike had tried and failed.

Nine years ago, Doc had come in on the stage, seedy and bewhiskered. He had carried only a worn satchel and a medical diploma from an Eastern university.

To this day, nobody knew – except Doc Smith – where he had come from. And Doc Smith never mentioned his past. Some claimed he had been booted out of the East because of illegal medical practice. Others said that he had fallen in love and that his love had not been returned.

Brookhaven wondered if the farmers had much money, or were operating on a shoestring. If they had money, Sagebrush's businessmen would prosper. And money was still the root of all evil. It could turn Sagebrush against Circle Y.

Should Circle Y raid farmers? Kill them all off? Strip their bodies of their possessions?

Three years ago, a big Colorado cow outfit had massacred a nester wagon train. The cowman and twenty-two cowpunchers drew life sentences at Canyon City's pen.

Doc said, "I raise five."

"Call and add five," Sullivan said.

Brookhaven threw his cards into discard. His luck was running as muddy as Sagebrush Creek. He leaned back, his eyes narrowing, twisted a cigarette, and dug for a match.

Rosie left the bar to drape a soft arm around his shoulder. "How goes it, darling?" she purred.

When Brookhaven roughly pushed her arm aside, Rosie's red lips twisted. "Circle Y is in a bad, bad mood." As she returned to the bar, hips swaying, Brookhaven didn't look at her.

Players bought rounds of drink. Brookhaven, nursing his whisky, drank little. Outside, rain continued hammering.

Bat Malone swaggered in at four in the morning, pulled up a chair, and sat on it backwards, watching the game. Malone's slicker hung open and clearly showed the sheriff's badge pinned to his greasy vest.

Sullivan glanced at the star, but said nothing, and Pete Brookhaven smiled tightly. "Where are the would-be farmers?" he asked Malone.

"They're waterlogged t'other side of Roarin'. The bridge has done washed out except for the pilin's."

"That's too bad," Brookhaven said.

"But them farmers found some of the old planks off'n the bridge. Them planks was washed in on the banks. They're spikin' them planks lengthwise to the tips of the pilin's. They aim to cross wagons on them."

"Can it be done?" Doc Smith asked.

"Maybe, but it'll be risky," Malone said.

Suddenly, thunder boomed loudly. Lightning followed, dimming the saloon's lamps.

Brookhaven silently cursed the man who had dynamited Roaring Creek bridge. He should have used a bigger charge. He left the game and went to the bar, Malone trailing.

"Where you been, Bat?"

"Scoutin' that nester wagon train, hopin' to get a shot at that shyster, but ain't had a chance so far."

"Where's Susie?"

"I dunno. You reckon she might side with these nesters?"

"If she does, I'll skin her alive."

Malone smiled. "She might be tough to take the pelt off'n, seein' she's a Brookhaven, but it would be a right purty skin."

"Asa Gosden?"

"Sun Prairie. He'll hol' down that end of the range, Pete. We got the country full of eyes, Pete, what with riders staked out on homesteads, watchin' everything."

"They're gettin' paid good," Brookhaven said shortly. "You don't seem to know much, Bat."

"I forgot about them two gover'ment surveyors."

Brookhaven's jaw tightened. "Go on," he said quietly.

"Two gover'ment surveyors got off the train this afternoon at Larb Hill. They had tickets to go on to Sun Prairie, but of course that railroad washout …"

"I know that," Brookhaven said coldly.

"Well, Gosden talked to 'em, Pete. They aim to survey this country. They told Gosden they'd leave Larb Hill this mornin' in a buggy, cuttin' across country for Sagebrush."

"They can't be allowed to reach Sagebrush," Pete Brookhaven said.

"No danger in them, Pete. They can't survey in this weather. An' Circle Y's got cowpunchers located on choice spots. All them surveyors can do is determine property lines where our men are squattin'. An' they can't do that until this rain lets up."

"I don't want them to reach Sagebrush."

"Why?"

Pete Brookhaven's voice hardened. "I don't want them, that's why."

Malone lifted his glass slowly. "They work for Uncle Sam, Pete. They get killed and gover'ment troops could come in to investigate. It'd be risky."

"They're comin' by buggy?"

"So Gosden said. They rented a buggy an' team in Larb Hill, Asa reported."

"That buggy team could have a runaway," Pete Brookhaven said. "Smash up the buggy, throw them to the ground, bruise them up some."

Malone nodded.

"Sanchez is on Wheel Crick. Martin's squattin' at the base of Squaw Butte. You can pick Bern up from the Willow Crick camp."

Malone again nodded.

"Ride with slicker collars up. Mask your mugs with bandanas. Smear your broncs' brands with pitch. Ride horses that have been branded a few times so there'll be more pitch on the broncs. But don't ride a horse with just the Circle Y brand. A smear of tar on only the left shoulder would be like advertisin' Circle Y did it."

Malone laughed quietly.

"What's so funny?" Brookhaven demanded.

"The county sheriff wearin' a mask," Malone said,

"an' stagin' a team runaway."

"Ain't no such thing as an honest lawman," Brookhaven said. "Most of 'em rob the voters without a mask. I'd hate to have the Territorial accountants check Asa Gosden's management of the county road fund."

"Asa crooked?"

"Can the jokin'," Brookhaven growled. "You say you was stalkin' this lawyer fella. You ain't had no chance to ambush him yet, huh?"

"Not a good one, Pete. Always somebody around him, but he usually rides his grey hoss. That cayuse shows up good on a dark night."

"Get him under sod as soon as possible."

Malone drank. "I'll do that, Pete." He made circles on the bar with his glass. "Now, about them surveyors ...?"

"To get from Larb Hill to Sagebrush they'll have to drive through Saddle Butte Canyon. An' the road is mighty narrow there with cliffs on each side."

Malone nodded.

"Get rid of 'em, Malone, an' meet me tomorrow mornin' at the ranch."

"Tomorrow mornin's already here." Malone tugged up his sagging gun belts. He bought a bottle and left.

Brookhaven stood apart at the bar, its only customer. He ran over the plan in his mind, saw no flaws, and grinned.

Rosie, tending bar, saw him smile. She ambled toward him, hips swaying, and stopped.

"Everythin' goin' okay, Pete?"

Brookhaven nodded.

"One on the house," Rosie said.

Pete Brookhaven shook his head. "A quart of Old Crow on my bill." He walked out, stuffing the bottle in his slicker pocket. He mounted and rode fast toward Circle Y.

Twelve

Ric was scouting ahead of the wagon train when Susie Brookhaven rode in from the northeast, the direction of Sun Prairie. He guessed Susie had spent the night in Sun Prairie, but he didn't mention this. Susie Brookhaven's doings were her business only.

"Looks like a day of rain," she said.

Ric merely nodded. Did Susie scout the caravan to report her findings back to Pete Brookhaven? He didn't like that thought.

"How goes it, Ric?" she asked.

They sat broncs on a low, sagebrush-covered hill. A mile north the wagon trail, bound for Prickly Gulch, inched slowly across a prairie. Horses lunged against collars, wheels rolling slowly deep in the mud.

"Slow," Ric said.

"Where's Trudy?"

Ric glanced at her. Raw wind had brought high colour to her cheeks, accentuating her beauty.

"Trudy's not with me all the time."

"She's a lovely girl," Susie said.

"So is Miss Susie Brookhaven."

Susie coloured prettily. "Thank you, Mr Nelson," she said lightly. "I have a chance to teach at Sagebrush school next year. I don't know whether or not I'll do it, though."

"With these farmer kids the school'll need more than one teacher. Miss Carson told me she taught back East."

"We teach together, and we'd sure fight."

Ric smiled, and his eyes met hers. She looked away, fingers nervously playing with her lasso's tie-down strap. "Have you seen my brother around?" she asked.

"No," Ric said.

"I just came from Sun Prairie. I spent the night there. The depot man said your two surveyors reached Larb Hill day before yesterday."

Ric hoped the government men would remain there until the rain stopped. "Are you going to file on a homestead?" he asked.

"I might. To help Circle Y."

"I hear that your brother has a cowboy squatting on the end of Sagebrush Canyon. Your brother is wasting his time and money."

"Why do you say that?"

"I personally filed a week ago on that area. My entry was in Washington when your brother raided my office, and he therefore didn't see the papers."

"I don't understand. You wouldn't let Circle Y file on homesteads because you said the land would first have to be surveyed. Now you tell me you filed on one without having a survey."

"I surveyed it myself. Land Commissioners have that right. Years ago, government surveyors made a preliminary survey of this area."

"Yes?"

"The southwest corner of my homestead abuts a government geodetic concrete marker. I measured off accurately each direction."

"I'll tell Pete." She looked north at the wagons. "Here comes a rider this direction. With him wearing that slicker he looks a lot like you do. He even rides much as you do. And he also rides a grey horse."

Ric looked at the approaching Reverend Zachary. Susie was right. The minister was about Ric's height and rode much as he rode, high in stirrups, body angling forward.

"The Reverend Zachary," he said. "He shipped in five grey saddle horses from Ohio. He had a small farm back there in addition to his parish. He has a yen for grey horses."

"I'd best head for the ranch. Good-bye, Ric."

"Good-bye, Susie."

Ric spurred downhill to meet the reverend, noticing that the wagons had stopped moving.

"Trouble," Reverend Zachary said shortly. "Myers' wagon broke an axle, Ric."

Discouragement hit Ric. All of the farmers with the exception of Mike Myers had brought out new wagons. He had hoped they would make Sagebrush without a breakdown. Now that hope went flying.

He and the minister returned to the wagon train. Ric told Reverend Zachary about the two surveyors arriving in Larb Hill.

"How will they get to Sagebrush?" the reverend asked.

"They'll undoubtedly hire saddle horses in Larb Hill to make the ride, or maybe go by buggy. There's a wagon road between Larb Hill and Sagebrush, and a light buggy – with only two men – can make it easily."

"Maybe somebody should ride ahead to Sagebrush and meet them? Perchance they might run into Circle Y trouble there?"

Ric doubted there'd be trouble in Sagebrush. "They're Uncle Sam's employees. Uncle Sam is still bigger than Circle Y."

"Pete Brookhaven might think otherwise, Ric."

"I might ride to Sagebrush after we get these wagons rolling again. We'll be lucky if we make Prickly Gulch by sundown."

"Gulch?" the minister asked. "Do we have to cross a canyon?"

Ric explained. They would cross on the level land above the point where the gully entered Prickly Gulch, a deep canyon angling northeast across Circle Y range.

"The Haskins baby has a severe cough," the minister said. "I have used what little medicants I have in my possession, but they seem of little avail."

"I'll send a boy in for Doc Smith."

Ric heard the infant crying and coughing as he rode up to the Haskins' wagon. Trudy Carson stuck her head from under the wagon's canvas cover; behind her came her brother.

"How is the baby?" Ric asked.

"He needs a doctor," Trudy said. "Other children are ill, too. And Mrs Watson has a pain in her chest."

"We'd better get the doctor," Bill said.

Ric spoke to Bill. "Will you go to Sagebrush for him? All you have to do is follow this wagon road south."

"What if he doesn't come out?" Bill asked.

Ric spoke shortly. "We'll have to chance that." He and Reverend Zachary rode to where farmers were grouped around Myers' wagon. The right front wheel was off, the wagon slanting, its box resting on the soaked soil. The axle had sheared off completely.

Alex Hanson said, "We need a whole new axle, Ric. An' no wagon carries a spare." Alex had been a wheelwright back east for Studebaker Wagons.

"Can you make one?" Ric asked.

"We could cut down a cottonwood tree."

"Would a cottonwood axle be strong? And have you the tools to make one?" Ric asked.

"I've got all my tools in my wagon," Alex said. "My crosscut saws, my ordinary saws, my axes, my adze and my spokeshave. I've turned out lots of axles in my time."

"We make camp here," Ric said. "All wagons stop. None moves ahead alone. We'll lose some time, but not too much, thanks to Alex here."

Alex hurried toward his wagon, two men following him. One man returned with a heavy screw jack. Somebody brought a piece of wood to set the jack on. They placed the jack under the broken axle and started to raise the wagon.

Bill Carson rode by. "I'll be back as soon as possible, Ric," he said.

Ric said, "Wait a minute, Bill." He spoke to Reverend Zachary. "There might be trouble for Bill in Sagebrush. I'd better ride with him. You can handle this. I'm no good here."

"I shall guard my flock," the minister said.

Ric mounted, turned his horse, and looked down at the caravan. Men were unharnessing weary horses preparatory to putting them on pasture. Rain washed miserably over the scene, running off the wagons' canvas tops. Ric and Bill rode toward Sagebrush.

Sagebrush's short main street glistened with mud. No children played, curs were hidden and dry, and not a single horse was tied at hitch racks. But no horses on the street didn't mean that Circle Y was not in town, for it could have its horses in the livery barn.

The door of Doc Smith's office, where he also lived, was locked. When knocking brought no response, Ric peered in a dirty window. His bunk was unmade, and dirty pots and skillets crowded the Kalamazoo cooking stove.

Ric straightened. "He might be in Sullivan's."

Doc was in the saloon, playing a boring game of whist with Casey Sullivan. Rosie tended bar. Doc, Sullivan, and Rosie were the saloon's only occupants. Sullivan leaned back, listening to Ric ask Doc ro ride to the wagon train.

Doc got to his feet. "I'll drive out right now in my buggy."

"I don't want to get you in trouble with Brookhaven," Ric informed, "but those kids have to have a doctor."

Doc pulled on his slicker. "Let's get melodramatic," he said cynically. "Let's expound about the sanctity of the Hippocratic oath and other similar nothings."

"Well," Ric said hesitantly.

"Brookhaven can't do any more than kill me," Doc said. "And if he tries, I might rebel a little, you know." He pulled on his rain helmet. "You two riding out with me?"

Ric shook his head. "We got to get a few supplies at the Merc, if Beeson will sell them to us. I'd check for mail, but no stage has come and gone, they tell me, during this storm."

Doc winked at Sullivan. "You could gossip with the new postmistress," he told Ric.

"Gabby Jackson has the post office no longer?" Ric asked.

"Gabby found it convenient to leave Sagebrush," Doc Smith said, and left.

Sullivan said, "Pete ran Mack Wilson out of town, after you whipped him so easy, but he came back yesterday."

Ric nodded. Sullivan was discreetly warning him. He unbuckled his gun and rebuckled it outside his slicker. "Thanks," he said. He started away, stopped, again faced Sullivan. "These women and children in my wagons should be brought to town. Would you house them, Sullivan?"

Rosie listened from behind the bar. Sullivan looked at the wall, wet his lips, said slowly, "I'll give it some thought, Lawyer."

"No answer right now?"

"No answer," Sullivan murmured.

Ric and Bill Carson went out into the rain. "That man has no heart," Bill said.

"Maybe and maybe not," Ric replied. "Walk twenty feet behind me, Bill."

"Walk behind you? Why?"

"Because I said so."

The thin youth sent Ric an inquiring look, then dropped behind. They went toward Ira Beeson's Mercantile, Ric's eyes missing nothing on the street, a tense feeling inside him. Ira Beeson played solitaire, alone in his store. Ric took out his list.

"Your money's no good here," Beeson said, getting to his feet. Suddenly, his fat body froze. His eyes bulged as he stared into Ric's drawn .45. "Is this kind of *money* any good?" Ric asked coldly.

"Brookhaven ordered me to sell farmers nothing," Beeson sputtered, still eyeing the pistol. "You sure can drag that thing out fast, Nelson," he blurted.

"I'm good at pistol-whipping, too," Ric assured.

"This will be the same as robbery," Beeson said, lips

quivering. "Takin' my stock under duress. I'll notify Bat Malone. Malone's sheriff now, Nelson."

"So I already know."

Beeson spoke to Bill Carson. "You'll witness for me that Nelson held a gun on me?"

"That'd clear you with Brookhaven, huh?" Bill's thin face sported a smile. "Yes, fat man, I'll swear Nelson had a gun on you."

Beeson sat down. "Get what you want," he said.

Ric handed the grocery list to Bill. "Get to work, storekeeper," he said. Bill went around the corner of the counter as Ric kept watching the main street through the dirty front window. Bill stored necessary items in a gunny sack, and Beeson kept track of their costs.

"I got all the list says," Bill finally said.

Ric nodded. "How much, Beeson?"

Beeson's fat fingers trembled as he added. Ric paid him the sum he demanded. "Anybody else raid my office upstairs?" he asked cynically, and Beeson shook his head.

"Unless I'm wrong," Ric said quietly, "I rented the whole upstairs from you. That means I can move in anybody I want, doesn't it?"

Beeson pleaded, "Nelson, don't move in your women and kids. Brookhaven'll kill me!" He got to his feet. "Brookhaven's fightin' mad, Nelson. He might even burn this buildin' down!"

"It's his building," Ric reminded. He spoke to Bill Carson. "I'm leaving now for our horses. You come behind me – twenty feet, at the least, savvy?"

"I don't understand why, Ric?"

"You might later, but I hope not."

He stepped into the rain. Doc Smith's buggy wheeled past, pulled by a span of snappy sorrels, thin wheels splashing water and lifting mud. Ric went to their saddle horses, eyes missing nothing. When he was opposite the livery barn, Mack Wilson stepped out, hand over his holstered gun.

"I'm comin' after you shyster!" Wilson hollered.

Wilson moved into the street, assuming a gunman's crouch, eyes riveted on Ric, who had stopped in his tracks, swung to face Wilson, his fingers also hovering over his holstered .45.

Tingling sensations played along Ric's spine. His belly roiled, and his breathing was deep. Wilson, he had heard, was a fast, competent hand with a gun. He realized Bill Carson had stopped, petrified in his boots. The youth was out of gun range, Ric figured.

"Don't be an idiot, Wilson," Ric called. His voice sounded distant. "Don't die for Circle Y. Circle Y isn't worth that to you, man!"

Wilson's harsh laugh cut the rain. "Circle Y ain't in this, shyster. This is between you an' me! You hammered me down, knocked me cold. You got me run outa town. Me, I don't forget, Nelson!"

Ric felt hopelessness, for Wilson's mind was made up. There'd be no evasion. Twenty feet lay between him and Wilson. Was he drunk? Ric peered, his blood settling, and decided Wilson was sober.

Suddenly, Wilson made his draw. Ric threw himself hurriedly on his belly, his gun rising from leather as he hurled himself forward. Wilson, he saw, was forked lightning. Already his gun was rising – a blur of fast action.

Ric hardly knew he drew. His gun, suddenly, was in his hand, the butt smashing back angrily, roaring and hot. Ric only shot once, but once was enough.

His gun's roar pounded Ric's ears. Wilson's pistol

had been clearing leather when Ric had started his draw, yet Ric shot first. His bullet ploughed through Wilson's heart.

Wilson shot once. A reflex action made his forefinger pull the trigger, and the bullet harmlessly slapped mud. For one long second, Wilson stood on tiptoe, dead in his boots. He landed face down in the mud and didn't move.

Heart hammering, Ric got slowly afoot. Sagebrush had come to life as citizens emerged from the surrounding buildings.

Beeson, his face the colour of a white sheet, hurried from his store, saw Wilson prone, and stopped.

Bill Carson moved close to Ric. "Now I understand, Ric."

"I've never killed a man before," Ric said. "I often wondered how a killer would feel. Now I know."

"He pulled first," Bill said.

Casey Sullivan and Rosie hurried from the saloon, Rosie's high heels punching mud. Sullivan rolled Wilson onto his back.

"Smack through the heart," Sullivan said.

"Help us get him off the street," Rosie said.

Beeson left the sidewalk, his big feet sloshing mud, a bit of colour returning to his jowls.

"This'll have to be reported to Sheriff Malone," Sullivan said loudly. He grinned, looked at Ric.

"You report it," Ric said.

Ric and Bill went to their horses. Sullivan and Beeson carried Wilson off the street, Wilson a broken sack between them. Ric and Bill rode out of Sagebrush.

"You still carry your gun," Bill reminded gently.

Ric holstered his pistol. He would replace the spent shell later, after his fingers stopped trembling.

Thirteen

Pete Brookhaven stood looking out the ranch house's big window when Rosie loped madly into the Circle Y yard, a black slicker hiding her curvaceous form. Brookhaven frowned. What brought this saloon girl to Circle Y?

Brookhaven was not the only one on Circle Y to see Rosie thunder in. Susie and Many Feathers also saw her through the window in Many Feather's room and hurried into the livingroom.

"One of your saloon floozies," Susie told her brother. "And openly riding out to visit you in broad daylight."

Many Feathers said nothing, staring at the approaching Rosie, now hurrying up the flagstone walk. The little Cheyenne, her jaw set hard, knotted her fists.

"Somethin's gone wrong," Brookhaven said.

"Maybe we've had a stroke of luck?" Susie asked. "Maybe our great new sheriff has drunk himself to death?"

Brookhaven glared at his sister, who retreated not an inch. Many Feathers longed for her boning knife in the kitchen. She would take Rosie apart, bone by bone.

"Lay a hand on me, Pete, and I'll hit back," Susie said coldly.

Brookhaven studied her cynically. "I believe you would, at that!" He flung open the door. "What is it, Rosie?"

Rosie's breath came in pants. She told about Ric Nelson gunning down Mack Wilson while Brookhaven listened in tough silence. "I happened to be standing by the saloon window," Rosie panted, "an' I had a good view of the whole thing."

"Another pest gone." Susie winked at dead-pan Many Feathers.

Brookhaven disregarded his sister's caustic remark. "Then what happened?" he asked Rosie.

"Wilson came out of the livery barn. He called this lawyer's hand. Wilson drew first, but the lawyer went to the sidewalk on his belly. Wilson had his gun cleared — he drew first."

"An' then?" snarled Brookhaven.

"Wilson got in one shot. It went into the mud when he was dead in his boots. Wilson drew first, but the lawyer got him with one bullet — right through the heart. I've seen gunfights in my life, but I never seen a man as fast as this lawyer."

"Sagebrush range's got other fast gunmen," Brookhaven said slowly. He spoke to his sister and Many Feathers. "Get her some dry clothes. Pour a few shots of my best liquor into her."

"Anything to please an old friend of my brother's," Susie said.

Brookhaven strode to the clothes rack, hurriedly slipped into his yellow slicker, then ran to the barn, his head down against the rain. When he reached Sagebrush, sweat steamed from his sopping-wet bay gelding. He flung reins into the mud before Sullivan's Saloon and strode inside. He wore his six-shooter strapped outside his slicker.

Every idle man in Sagebrush was in the saloon, discussing Wilson's death and drinking. Sullivan tended bar. Brookhaven strode up to him, asked harshly, "Where's Sheriff Malone?"

"How would I know?" Sullivan countered surlily.

"Git off'n your high horse!" Brookhaven growled, "or I'll knock you off it. Anybody here know where Malone is?"

"Seen him headin' for Squaw Butte some time back," a cowboy said.

Brookhaven understood. Malone was gathering Circle Y men to turn back the surveyors. "Go after him," he ordered the cowboy, who left hurriedly. Then, to Sullivan, "A bottle, Casey."

Sullivan spun out Brookhaven's private bottle, a glass following it. He looked up and down his filled bar.

"Biggest bunch of customers I've had for a long, long time," the saloonman said dryly. "Maybe somebody else should get killed, huh?"

"You might get that wish," Brookhaven prophesied.

Ira Beeson moved close to Brookhaven. "You didn't treat Mack Wilson right, Pete. You sicked him on the lawyer an' he got beat up. You run Wilson outa town. Yet Wilson came back to fight and die for Circle Y."

Brookhaven studied the storekeeper. Was this monkey joking? He was in no mood for horseplay. Then he realized that Beeson's wide face was serious, and his right fist landed under his jaw.

Beeson flew backwards, crashed into a card table, and went down. He sat stupidly on the floor, waggling his jaw; then he started to his feet, his eyes glazed, and he fell down again. Somebody laughed. Brookhaven sent the man who laughed a hard glance, and the laugh choked off short.

"You'll pay for this," Beeson finally choked.

"Don't make me laugh. Get back to your store. And make it fast!"

As Beeson staggered out the door, Brookhaven drank from his bottle, ignoring his glass.

Brookhaven lowered the bottle. "Idiot! What this burg needs is a new storekeeper."

Sullivan mopped the bar. "You fire Ira an' Sagebrush might have two new storekeepers, one tendin' the farmers' store."

"Those sodbusters'll never reach Sagebrush. Where's Wilson's carcass? Over to Doc Smith's office?"

"We toted him in there. Doc ain't in town."

"Where's he at?"

"He left right before the shootin' for the nesters' wagons to tend to the sick kids an' women out there."

Brookhaven's eyes tightened dangerously. "This town might get a new doctor, too."

Sullivan moved down the bar to tend to a grumpy customer banging a beer stein on the bar. Nursing his bottle, Pete Brookhaven studied the townspeople in the bar mirror.

He knew each and every soul, and each and every soul was indebted to Circle Y for food on his table. Yet, for some reason, a strange premonition lurked in his mind – a feeling of impending doom, but that was only logical.

A sudden harsh wind rushed in, hammering rain wildly against the windows. Brookhaven liked that sound. Beside making much grass for Circle Y cattle, it also made it harder for the farmers to advance. Even nature worked in his behalf, he thought sourly.

When Malone arrived, he would swear out a warrant, charging Ric Nelson with murder. He would send out a handful of tough Circle Y riders to back Malone up.

Would nesters fight to protect Nelson? Would there be a pitched gun battle? He thought of the Colorado cowpunchers now serving sentences.

But this case, he reasoned, was different. The Colorado cowman had raided and killed without an arrest warrant. Malone would be a sheriff, merely doing his sworn duty. And Nelson, if it turned to a gunfight, would be resisting the law.

One point, though, bothered him. Everybody claimed Wilson had drawn first. Therefore, Nelson had killed in self-defence. He brushed this aside. Eye-witnesses could be made to testify otherwise.

Carefully, he studied faces in the mirror. Circle Y still bossed these people. Yes, he would have Malone arrest Nelson.

Malone, wet and tired from the saddle, rode in an hour later with six Circle Y riders. They clomped into the saloon, spurs jangling, and trekked back to Sullivan's office to confer behind the closed door.

Malone grinned. "Them gover'ment surveyors really had a buggy runaway. We dynamited the gulch with black powder ahead of their buggy."

Brookhaven nodded.

"When that powder flared, them harness broncs just turned, runnin' back toward Larb Hill almighty fast. They tore that buggy apart, threw both surveyors out."

"How bad were they hurt?"

"We watched through field glasses. One could've had a busted leg. He couldn't walk. T'other could hobble, but not much."

"You left them there?"

Malone nodded. "Done seen a rider comin' toward us from Sun Prairie, prob'ly somebody headin' for Sagebrush. He was bound to run into them."

"Then you never rode at all into the gulch?"

"Never showed a horse or face." Bat Malone grinned. "Now how about this lawyer gunnin' down Mack Wilson?"

Brookhaven told of his plan to arrest Ric Nelson. Cowboys exchanged anxious glances. Malone played with his bottom lip.

"There might be gunsmoke, Pete," Malone said.

"I doubt that," Brookhaven said. "Them people is just ignorant Easterners, not gunhands."

"You're the boss," Malone said.

When the eight Circle Y men rode in, Ric was ready for them, having stationed farmers out in the sagebrush with rifles. Brookhaven scowled at Doc Smith's buggy, then halted his big gelding in front of Ric, Malone at his right.

"Sheriff Malone here's got a warrant for your arrest," Brookhaven told Ric. "The charge is murder of Mack Wilson."

A tall youth standing close by said, "I saw the gunfight. Wilson challenged Ric and Wilson drew first."

"Tell that to Judge O'Neill down in Sun Prairie," Brookhaven said tonelessly. "You comin' peaceful Nelson?"

Ric grinned tightly. "I could change this into a gun battle," he said. "I've got my farmers surrounding you men. I'll deal with you, Brookhaven. For each one of you there'll be one of us ridin' into Sun Prairie."

Brookhaven stood on stirrups, looking at the farmers, now moving into the wagon train, rifles alert. He hesitated, and for one long second Ric thought guns would leap. Brookhaven's eyes returned to Ric. "You're the one I want," Brookhaven said softly. "I get you outa the way an' the rest of these are only sheep. Pick out seven sodbusters."

Ric spoke to Reverend Zachary. "You stay with the wagons, sir. I'll select the men I want." He spoke to the tall youth. "You're one, Bill."

"I'll ride with you," Bill said.

Ric selected six more farmers. Soon sixteen men rode northeast. Circle Y men rode in a body around Ric, but the farmers spread out, riding through the sagebrush with rifles across saddle forks.

"You don't know much about Montana law," Ric told Brookhaven.

"What'd you mean?"

"Your warrant is no good. A Montana sheriff cannot issue a murder warrant. It has to come from a grand jury."

"You don't know Judge O'Neill."

"I see through your plan. You want me behind bars — to hold me there until the Circuit Judge comes through this fall to hold court. Well, you can't do it, Brookhaven."

"Why not?"

"I have with me a witness who saw me kill Wilson. He will testify that Wilson drew first, that I shot in defence of my life. The most Judge O'Neill can charge me with is manslaughter, an offence that offers bail."

"Tell that to the judge."

Judge O'Neill immediately held Ric's hearing in Sun Prairie's log court, Ric acting as his own attorney. The gaunt, grey-haired jurist seemed rather ill at ease. Ric pressed the point that Malone's warrant was worthless because a grand jury had not issued it.

"This county has no grand jury," the judge said, "and never has had one."

"Then this court is not legally convened," Ric pointed out. He stepped to the row of law books lining the wall, found the one he wanted, pulled it out, found the right page, then laid the heavy volume on the judge's desk. "Please read this, your Honour."

Judge O'Neill read aloud. Brookhaven, his eyes narrowed slits, listened, and Malone stood to one side, studying Ric. The judge closed the book. "Mr Nelson is right," he said nervously.

Brookhaven's huge hands were hard fists. Malone dropped his hands to his two holstered guns. This was open defiance of Circle Y. Ric mentioned he had a witness, saying he had killed Wilson in self-defence. Judge O'Neill asked who the witness was.

"I am the witness," Bill Carson said. "I was with Mr Nelson at the time Wilson called for him to go for his gun. Mr Wilson drew his weapon first."

Ric started toward the law books again. Judge O'Neill said, "I am very well acquainted with that section, Mr Nelson. How many farmers are in your party?"

"Twenty families in this group. I have about fifty more coming in within a month or so."

Judge O'Neill leaned back, eyes closed. Brookhaven saw Ric wink at Bill Carson. Malone saw it, too, and his knuckles grew white against black gun grips.

Judge O'Neill, Ric knew, was mentally counting votes. Finally, the jurist opened his eyes. "You have no case here, Sheriff Malone. The defendant is dismissed."

Brookhaven stepped forward, then stopped. Ric and his men left, leaving Circle Y with the judge. The door behind them slammed shut; Ric heard a key turn. He also heard another sound – a hard, resounding slap.

"They might kill him," Bill Carson said.

Ric grinned. "I doubt that. They'll just work him over good. Actually, he's been crooked law here for years. He'll have earned what he's getting. Possibly many an innocent man has been sent to prison through his and Circle Y's double-crossing."

"It pays to know the law," Bill said. "You cleared yourself in no time. You need a partner? I'll study hard."

"That's one way to get admitted to the bar," Ric said. He saw a man whom he didn't know approaching hurriedly. The man was headed for him. "Wonder what's wrong now?"

"You Lawyer Nelson?" the man asked.

Ric nodded.

"Them two surveyors – they was goin' to Sagebrush today in a buggy. Team got scared, run away with 'em. They're down the hotel now, both in bed. An' one's bad hurt."

Ric winced.

Fourteen

The next morning, skies were leaden with gusts of rain. Wagons moved slowly through deep mud toward Prickly Gulch. Ric, rubbing a whiskered jaw, and Reverend Zachary were checking the wagons.

The wheelwright had done a good job on the axle for Myers' rig. Work horses, tired and stumbling, were in terrible shape.

Reverend Zachary said, "Well, you finally won a round last night in Judge O'Neill's court."

"The round I want to win is the last one, Reverend."

He had talked to the injured surveyors last night in Sun Prairie. One had a broken leg, the other had a twisted ankle and bad bruises. After the runaway, a stray cowboy, headed across country, had found them. Somehow, he had repaired their buggy and gotten the team back into harness. Instead of directing them to Larb Hill, he had taken them to Sun Prairie, which was closer.

The surveyors had little to relate. The canyon floor ahead of their buggy had suddenly erupted, blasting boulders skyward. "I know dynamite when I hear it," one said. "Now who would want to dynamite us?"

Ric told about the trouble with Circle Y. He remembered the planks he had dragged out of wild

Roaring Creek, some of which bore flash marks. Circle Y had dynamited that bridge.

"See anybody around?" he asked.

The surveyors had seen no men or riders. They had sent a wire back to Washington telling of their trouble. Ric grinned tightly.

Washington bigwigs would file the telegram and forget it. He had won a round in Judge O'Neill's court. Brookhaven had won another ... with black powder.

Now he spoke to the minister. "How is the Haskins child this morning?"

"Much better, Mr Nelson. But a few other children are coughing badly, not to mention Mrs Myers and Mrs Garcia."

"But Doc Smith said he'd be out today, too."

"After we cross Prickly Gulch, he said. He had difficulty crossing the stream yesterday with his buggy."

"Reverend, I don't know what we'd do without you." Ric spoke the truth.

"Man was made to aid other men, not to fight them."

Ric grinned. "Wish you could make Brookhaven understand that."

Reverend Zachary's gaunt face broke into a small smile. Ric found himself admiring this strong man more each day. He had first catalogued the minister as a sin-shouting, rabid reformist, but daily contact with the man of God had changed his mind. Reverend Zachary was a true friend of mankind.

The few milk cows moved with the herd of extra horses, Bill Carson hazing them. Despite the mud, children ran and played in the sagebrush, pacing the slow-moving wagons. Dogs yipped as they chased a jackrabbit.

Wagons moved for fifteen minutes, then rested five. The lead wagon had the best team, for it broke trail. When its horses tired, the wagon moved to one side, the next wagon coming up as trailbreaker, the former lead wagon dropping to the rear.

Trudy Carson rode up, her face flushed with cold. "I'm going to spell Bill off with the horses," she told Ric.

She loped away, riding a good saddle. Ric wondered which girl was the most beautiful – Susie or Trudy. He decided Susie's was a more sophisticated, worldly beauty, and let it go at that.

"Nobody talks about going back?" Ric asked.

"That talk has entirely disappeared," the minister said. "These people are all solidly behind you."

Ric had a lump in his throat. He waited until it left before he said, "And I thank them for that. The life of a land-locator at times is not easy. And there have been many unscrupulous land-locators working the West. They settle people on worthless land and let them starve, just for their fees."

"This is wonderful soil, Mr Nelson. Look how this grass has shot up since this rain."

The minister was correct. Montana prairies were rapidly becoming a billowing sea of tall bluejoint grass. Ric's thoughts swung to Circle Y. He could see Pete Brookhaven's reasons for fighting to hold this virgin land.

"Time changes all things," the minister said. "Once buffalo, by the thousands, roamed here, stragglers followed by prairie wolves. Then came Texas cattle; the buffalo had to go, but now will come fences and farmhouses, and cattle will have to move back to land not fit for the plough."

"Wish you could convince Brookhaven of that, also," Ric said. "I'm going to lope ahead, Reverend, and study Prickly Gulch for a crossing."

"I'll keep things moving here," the minister said.

Prickly's banks were dirty with the high-water mark of twigs and debris. Water had fallen about three feet, Ric judged. Downstream a dead Circle Y steer had become lodged against the bole of a box elder tree. Despite the drizzle, flies buzzed around its bloated carcass.

Ric rode into the stream, his horse snorting in displeasure. He rode up and down, seeking a gravel bottom. He decided that the point where the stagecoach road crossed had the hardest bottom. He would move wagons across on that area.

He forced his horse to traverse the stream at that point. The horse didn't have to swim, and this pleased him. Steel-shod hoofs ground on a firm, gravel bottom.

He would transport women and children across ahead of the wagons on horseback. Only drivers, perched on high spring seats, would be with the rigs when crossing. Therefore, if the current swept a wagon downstream, only the driver's life would be imperiled.

He rode back to the wagon train. At noon, the farmers reached Prickly's north bank. Ric held his bronc, watching the teams take to the water, which was muddy and reached above the bottoms of wagon boxes. He hoped each wagon's contents did not get too wet.

Sitting a weary, wet saddle, he looked about him. From here to Sagebrush Creek, five miles south, the road ambled through rougher country. Raw flat-topped mesas towered, kings of the land. Foothills rolled, became steeper, their sides marked by raw coulees.

Trudy rose in stirrups, pointing. "That wagon got off the trail a little. It's having a hard time."

Roiling water smashed into the wagon, swinging its tail-end downstream, the horses pawing for footage frantically, the driver standing and pounding their wet rumps with his lines.

Ric spurred into the stream, water splashing, but drew rein, for the farmer had righted his wagon, his team's hoofs finding firm footing. Slowly, horses straining, the wagon swung into line, wide steel wheel rims again grinding gravel.

Ric rode across the stream, Trudy following. He dismounted among the grouped women and children.

"Here comes a buggy," a woman said excitedly. "From the direction of Sagebrush!"

"Doc Smith," Ric said soothingly.

The woman's voice had held fear. Ric realized these people were on edge, some women almost at the breaking point. Doc Smith circled his buggy, stopped, and walked to the group. He glanced at the wagons crossing the stream. "One more Rubicon behind, Ric?"

"Only one more to cross, Doc. Sagebrush Creek."

"And it's full," Doc said. "I just crossed it."

"How are things in Sagebrush?"

"Quiet."

Ric noticed that the doctor's cheek had a dark bruise. "Get drunk and fall down?" he joked. Doc's limit was one whisky, he knew.

"Circle Y cowpuncher came into my office last night. Big, rawboned man – I forget his name. Had a boil on his neck. I went to lance it. He got mad and swung on me."

Ric said nothing, watching the medico.

"We had quite a tussle," Doc Smith said. "For a while it looked like he'd beat me up. I broke a chair over his head, knocked him out, kicked him into the street."

"Brookhaven sent him?"

Doc Smith shrugged heavy shoulders. "Who else?" he countered.

"I don't want to cause you trouble, Doc," Ric said.

"Why go into that? Line these people up and let me examine them. Heard Circle Y tried to book you on a murder charge?"

"Brookhaven tried," Ric said.

"Law has its compensations, Ric. You plead your own case and got free. Medicine lacks that compensation. My liver ails me occasionally, but I'll be darned if I can take it out and look at it."

"I feel sorry for you, Doc," Ric joked. "What's hard-boiled Pete Brookhaven doing?"

Doc examined a woman's throat. "Heard in town he's riding around, checking Circle Y squatters. Malone's somewhere in the rough country, too."

Ric rode along his wagons, checking them, thinking about Bat Malone. Malone was somewhere in the hills. He didn't like that idea, but there was nothing he could do about it.

All wagons had now crossed the stream. They stood in a line waiting for wives and children. The Haskins baby cried monotonously. Mrs Garcia crawled painfully into her wagon after Doc's examination. When all passengers were aboard, Ric waved the wagons on.

"That Haskins infant still has some lung congestion," Doc Smith told Ric, "but it's clearing. It needs warm blankets and protection and some of that medicine I gave the mother to administer. Mrs Garcia – she's got me puzzled."

"Think it's serious, Doc?"

"I don't know, Ric. Honestly, I don't. She might just have an upset stomach – bouncing in that wagon, drinking creek water. I hope everybody boils their water, as I ordered."

"Reverend Zachary sees that they do," Ric said.

"By nightfall you should be on Sagebrush Creek, or very close to it. If anything comes up – anybody really sick – send to town for me. Any time of the night, Ric."

"Thanks a million, Doc."

"How are you going to cross Sagebrush?"

"Cut down cottonwoods, trim them. Truss cottonwood logs on each side of a wagon, float the wagons across."

"It has been done, Ric."

Doc Smith's buggy rolled toward Sagebrush. Nesters made noon camp. Women cooked over open fires, the sweet aroma of boiling coffee permeating the rain. Antelope steaks sizzled.

Ric ate with Reverend Zachary and Mrs Zachary. Usually he dined with the Carsons, but he decided not to be too much around the lovely Trudy. Her beautiful presence disturbed him.

Reverend Zachary possessed a dry wit that many times had Ric laughing, but always the thought of danger lurked in the back of his mind, and he thought of the farmers.

When they had first hit the muddy trail, he knew some farmers had been distrustful of him, thinking he would get them into Montana just for their money. The first few days out had seen slight conflict among the homesteaders, a few hot and angry words flung, but this was now gone. Seemingly they completely accepted him, put full faith in him. And this thought was comforting.

His meal finished, he thanked Mrs Zachary and sat in the mud, back against a wagon wheel, and rolled a Durham cigarette. Women were washing and stowing away dishes while men dozed on the sopping wet ground. Horses had been unharnessed; fresh teams would take up the afternoon struggle. Weariness seeped into Ric's cold bones. When and if this was ever solved, he decided he would sleep for at least two days running.

He dug out his watch: one-ten. Wearily, he got afoot. "Time to roll wheels," he hollered.

Grumbling, the camp came to life.

Once again wide-rimmed wheels ground into mud. Ric rode ahead to scout. Doc Smith had been right. Sagebrush Creek ran very high. Flood waters swirled around cottonwood trees that normally were many feet above the stream.

He glanced west at the gaping mouth of Sagebrush Creek Canyon, thinking of the cowboy Brookhaven had squatting there. Had Brookhaven moved the man? He doubted it.

Anger roiled his belly, souring his thoughts. Each morning he had sent a rider back to the telegraph station at Sun Prairie. He had received no reply from Montana Pacific Railroad, nor from the governor – not to mention no word from Washington.

He had hardly expected to hear from the governor, who was a cattleman, but he had expected a wire from the railroad officials and from Washington.

He drew rein, squinting through the falling rain. A rider was approaching from Sagebrush. He waited, cold inside, hand on his holstered gun.

The rider hit the flood waters, horse swimming gamely. Soon he drew up on the bank below Ric. Ric had never seen him before.

He was a tall man – as tall as Ric. A black oilskin slicker graced his wide shoulders. He grinned good-naturedly, sitting sidewise in saddle, emptying water from his boots.

"Just a grub-line riding cowboy," he said with a grin. "Headin' for Sun Prairie."

Ric nodded. The stranger stood on stirrups. He looked at Ric's wagons coming into view a half-mile away. "You're herding in a flock of sodbusters, I take it?"

Ric liked the man's square, sun-tanned face. "Riding pilot," he said jokingly.

"Well, gotta get movin'," the man said.

He rode on. Ric had seen a Bar T S Brand on the horse's left shoulder. He didn't know where the Bar T S was located. Anyway, the rider hadn't been astraddle a Circle Y cayuse.

The stranger swung off trail, rode around the wagons, and headed north toward Sun Prairie. Ric returned to the caravan. They made camp at dusk a hundred yards north of roaring Sagebrush Creek. Trudy invited him to eat supper with her and her brother. Ric couldn't turn her down, nor did he wish to.

Bill Carson chewed antelope steak. Trudy worked over a dutch oven and didn't hear her brother say quietly to Ric, "You remember that stranger that rode north this afternoon?"

Ric nodded.

"Somethin' about him got me curious, Ric. I trailed him a coupla miles. When he got out of sight of the wagons, he swung west into the foothills."

West was Circle Y's home ranch.

"I hung onto his trail, watchin' him from a butte. He never saw me, but he never went to Circle Y."

Ric's brows rose.

"I could see Circle Y headquarters an' Sagebrush town clear. He never rode into Sagebrush. He swung west of town, headed south an' out of sight."

"What do you read in it?"

Bill scowled. "Danged if I'd know, Ric. All I can figger is that he wanted to scout these wagons. But if he'd scouted for Brookhaven, he'd have gone to Circle Y. Or at least stopped in town and talked to Brookhaven, if Brookhaven is in Sagebrush."

"You sure you saw right, Bill?"

"I've got good eyes, Ric."

Why would a stranger scout ... unless for Brookhaven? Ric could see no logic in what Bill had told him. After supper, men cut down cottonwoods with the wheelwright's crosscut saw. By darkness ten trees had been cut to proper length, their branches trimmed.

Two guards rode out. One would ride west side, the other east. They would meet along Sagebrush Creek, then circle back, meeting again at a point north of the caravan.

Ric borrowed a black horse from Bill to ride his shift from ten until midnight. His grey was leg-weary. No danger lurked; the shift passed without incident.

He was relieved by Reverend Zachary astraddle the minister's top grey saddler.

"You should ride a dark horse," Ric said. "That grey can be seen too easily."

"Yes, I guess I should have borrowed a darker horse, but I'm here now."

Both Ric and the preacher wore dark oilskins. Ric turned his horse toward the wagons, dots in the sagebrush.

"Sleep good, Ric."

"Thanks, parson," Ric replied, and the minister rode away.

Fifteen

That night when Circle Y rode from Sun Prairie, it left a battered, bloody Judge O'Neill behind. Brookhaven, anger churning his belly, headed his riders.

Was Circle Y's power slipping? Judge O'Neill had turned against Circle Y. O'Neill had counted future votes and aligned himself with the farmers. And O'Neill had paid. Pete Brookhaven blew on a skinned knuckle.

Nelson had won one round, but would not win another. Brookhaven had long considered Doc Smith a weak link, but the doctor had no legal powers. He had never figured Judge O'Neill to break away.

Bat Malone, taciturn and silent, rode against the rainy wind, a deadly aura about him. One by one the Circle Y men left the group, drifting toward homesteads; finally, Brookhaven and Malone rode alone, heading across the prairie for Circle Y's home ranch.

They swam Sagebrush Creek and plunged on, two ghostly shadows moving through sagebrush, the night lighted by the faint moon occasionally shining through breaks in the clouds.

Circle Y's guard flung a challenge; Brookhaven flung back an angry retort. Brookhaven and Malone thundered into Circle Y, halting before the barn. Bunkhouses and cook shack held no lights. The only light on the immense ranch was a lamp, turned low, in the ranch house's livingroom.

"Not even Many Feathers waitin' up," Malone said. He meant it as a wry joke, nothing more.

"Watch your tongue!" Brookhaven said shortly.

Malone stabbed his boss a hard glance, which Brookhaven didn't see, for he was dismounting. Malone started to leave his wet saddle.

Brookhaven's sharp voice stopped him. "Stay up there! You've got a job to do, so get at it!"

"This lawyer?" Malone asked, settling back into saddle.

"You've bragged, but did nothin'!"

Malone's voice pleaded. "I'm bone-tired, Pete. Like a wolf-tired buffaloer, ready to go down. I've did nothin' but pound leather from here to Sun Prairie, then to Sagebrush, then here again."

Brookhaven studied him narrowly.

"Them nester wagons is on open prairie tonight, too," Malone said. "Tomorrow night they'll be t'other side of Prickly, in the hills. Them hills will give a man a better chance."

Brookhaven saw logic in this. "Tomorrow night, Bat."

"Tomorrow night," Malone promised.

Brookhaven stalked to the house. Malone could unsaddle horses. Brookhaven entered the dimly lit living room. Somebody turned up the Rochester kerosene lamp.

"I'm hungry," Brookhaven said roughly, and then stared at Many Feathers. She was a redskin no longer. Her black hair no longer hung in braids. Her hair was done in the latest mode, bun on her neck. A stylish housedress hugged her small waist. No moccasins now; high heeled shoes. "What happened to you?" Brookhaven demanded.

"What do you mean?"

"Your hair's been cut." Brookhaven sat down at the table. "Susie?" he asked, and she smiled, dark eyes glowing.

She had changed entirely. Very beautiful now, she looked like an olive-skinned Mexican girl.

"Susie said it was time I stopped being Indian. Your supper is ready. I hope it isn't too cold."

Brookhaven hung up his hat and slicker. He sat down again, thinking this over. He wondered why the change in Many Feathers bothered him. The thought that any man would be proud to go anywhere with this beautiful woman on his arm disturbed him slightly. He tried to put it from his mind, but it lingered.

Many Feathers returned with a platter containing a thick Circle Y steak, French-fried potatoes, and a vegetable salad. "Did the laywer get killed?" she quietly asked.

Brookhaven cut tender steak. He had never had a squaw who could cook as well as Many Feathers, nor one as lovely.

"The lawyer isn't dead," he said. "Why did you ask?"

Her small shoulders shrugged. She sat opposite him, elbows on the table, dark eyes on him. "How is the steak?"

"Wonderful, as usual. Where did you learn to cook?"

"Reservation school. I love to cook and keep house."

Lamplight touched her beautiful features, glistened on her smooth black hair, became lost in her dark eyes. Brookhaven decided to change the subject. "My sister?" he asked.

"She is in bed. She is worried."

"About what?" he asked gruffly.

"I think you know, Pete."

"Things will come out all right."

"You cannot defeat those farmers, Pete!"

He rose suddenly, his face bleak, and hammered the table. "I'll whip every last one of them!" he shouted.

She got to her feet, said, "I am sorry," and walked out. Brookhaven sat down slowly.

Soon Susie entered sleepily. A red bathrobe hugged her slim waist and her small feet were bare.

"I was sleeping. The hollering woke me up. What are you yelling about?"

"That fool, Many Feathers. There are times she drives me loco."

"What did she say?"

"That's atween me an' her," Brookhaven said shortly.

"Maybe you get angry at her because you love her," Susie said.

Brookhaven glared at her. "You're also crazy," he growled. "I think you'd better head back for the hay."

Susie yawned. "You're like Father. Truth always hurt him, too. Just don't do any more hollering, please?"

"Get out!"

Brookhaven finished his meal, carried his dirty dishes to the kitchen, and yawned. Unrest held him; he slept little that night. Dawn found him in the cook shack, rousing the cook, who was invariably the first human stirring on the spread. He glanced into Bat

Malone's cabin. Malone slept, mouth open, snoring loudly. Disgustedly, Brookhaven went to the barn, selected a sorrel from the stall, saddled and bridled him, and rode slowly toward Sagebrush.

What if the nester wagon train reached Sagebrush? What if Malone bungled killing Ric Nelson? And if Nelson were murdered, would the nesters turn back? He had heard that this preacher – this Amos Zachary – held much influence over the farmers. With Nelson dead, would Zachary assume farmer leadership, take the role of Nelson in settling families on homesteads?

The answer to that was simplicity itself. He would either kill the preacher himself or get a Circle Y man to do it.

Deciding to check on the farmers, he rode east. clouds swirled thickly, but occasionally sunlight broke through. Rain came now in savage bursts.

An hour later he sat saddle on a high rim-rock ledge, tumbling wildernesses sprawling below as far as the eye could see. Below him, nester wagons moved slowly toward Sagebrush Creek.

An odd thought came. Twenty years ago – when he was a mere boy – his father had trailed wild Texas longhorns along the toe of this mesa. Had an Assiniboin brave, gaudy and hideous with war paint, wearing only moccasins and breechcloth, then sat his pinto pony on this butte, watching leg-weary Circle Y longhorns trek in on this new grass?

Had dark, glittering eyes, savage with hate, glared down on the longhorns, just as his own satanic eyes now studied the nester wagons moving south?

He pushed this thought aside. Time was running out. Tomorrow the nesters would be moving into Sagebrush town. Malone had been right – tonight farmers would camp north of Sagebrush Creek in the rough country.

He told the wind, "Shyster, this is your last day on earth."

Strange unrest pulled him. For some reason he remembered the warning of Many Feathers. He felt self-anger. Why should the words of a stupid — but lovely and good — Cheyenne squaw haunt him?

He swung off the butte to check some cowboys squatting for Circle Y. They were all wet, miserable, and touchy. How true to Circle Y was their allegiance?

He headed for Sagebrush. He forded Sagebrush Creek in the high western reaches where water was not so deep. Sagebrush huddled under the rain. Only Doc Smith and Casey Sullivan were in the saloon. Doc cradled a cup of hot tea.

"Heard Circle Y hammered the hell out of Judge O'Neill night before last," Doc said.

"News travels fast on this grass," Brookhaven growled. "Too fast, I reckon."

Doc's lips tightened. "That Circle Y cowpuncher who came in the other night with the boil. He and I had a set-to. I had to break a chair over his thick skull."

Brookhaven's eyes pulled down. "What Circle Y cowboy?"

"I don't know his name. That fellow from Nevada, I believe. He happened to have a boil at just the right time, didn't he?"

Brookhaven glanced at Sullivan. Sullivan had a wide, dead face. "I don't follow you, Doc," Brookhaven said.

"Well, that boil gave him an excuse to come to my office."

Brookhaven said, "Are you tryin' to say I sent a Circle Y man in to beat you up, Doc?"

"That's what I'm saying, Pete."

"Maybe I did. Maybe I didn't. Where's the fellow now?"

Sullivan spoke for the first time. "After Doc worked him over, he come in here. He bought a bottle and said he was pullin' out for Nevada."

Brookhaven remembered looking into the bunkhouse early this morning. Sim Winters had been missing.

"Said he was afraid to ride back to Circle Y," Sullivan said. "Claimed you might kill him."

Brookhaven spoke to Doc Smith. "What're you goin' to do about it?"

"Not a thing," Doc Smith said. "I won, didn't I?"

"Hear you been doctorin' them nesters?"

"You heard right. And I'm driving out there again around noon."

Brookhaven unexpectedly backhanded Doc Smith across the face. The medico went backwards, tripped, sat down. Blood spurted from his nose, colouring his beard. Eyes slitted, he grabbed a chair, advanced. Brookhaven's .45 leaped from holster, bore unwinkingly on the doctor.

"I'd just as soon kill you now as later," Brookhaven growled.

Despite his bulk, Sullivan leaped the bar, got between them. "Doc, go out," he pleaded. "For ol' time's sake, Doc, listen to me!"

Doc glared at Brookhaven, who grinned back. The medico dropped the chair and left. Brookhaven laughed loudly. "Any Circle Y men come in, Sullivan, I'll be in your office."

Sullivan merely nodded.

Once in the office, the door closed, Pete Brookhaven paced, pounding a fist into his palm, going over details carefully, building, adding, looking for defects – but finding none.

Circle Y was alerted, ready to hit. Within an hour, all Circle Y hands could be in Sagebrush. What if Malone bungled and didn't kill the lawyer? Malone wouldn't, he felt sure; still, a man had to prepare for all emergencies.

He heard the door slowly open. He whirled automatically, hand on his gun. Then, his hand fell away, for Rosie's pretty head stuck in. "Hello, Pete," she said.

"Don't you ever knock?" Brookhaven rapped.

"We're friends, ain't we?"

"Not today. Get out!"

Rosie stuck out her tongue and left. Brookhaven slammed himself into the swivel chair, raised his bottle, drank deeply, hot whisky burning down his gullet.

At noon, Sullivan knocked. "There's a drifter who jus' rode in, Pete. He's at the bar. Said he was lookin' for a ridin' job. You want to talk to him?"

"Gunman?"

"Never asked."

"Send him in. Where's Doc?"

"He just passed, drivin' out to the nester wagons."

"Send the man in," Brookhaven said.

The man was tall. He wore a black slicker. He had a sun-tanned lined face and didn't give his name or where he was from; he wanted a job punching cows.

"Can you sling a fast gun?" Brookhaven asked.

The man smiled. "I'm fair, but not good. You got trouble here on Sagebrush range?"

"A little. I'm hirin' guns."

The man shook his head. "Thanks, but I'm not interested." He closed the door.

Ten minutes later, Brookhaven looked into the saloon. A few patrons, mostly town loafers, inhabited the place while Sullivan washed glasses at the end of the bar.

"That tall varmint that talked to me," Brookhaven said to Sullivan. "He's left, huh?"

"He rode north right after talkin' to you."

"What brand did his horse pack?"

"Bar T S, left shoulder."

"I don't know that iron," Brookhaven said. "Must be from out of the Territory. Send Rosie in with some grub for me?"

"Sure thing, Pete."

Circle Y riders entered and left. Bat Malone came in at three, his slicker dripping rain.

"Where are the farmers now?" Brookhaven snapped.

Malone saw that Brookhaven was rather drunk as he reached for the bottle. "By night they should be on Sagebrush Crick's north bank. They should get there about dark an' camp there tonight."

"You know your job?"

"I know it." Malone drank. "After I kill this lawyer, where do I go?"

"Report back here. I'll bunk here tonight. Sent Jack Cooners out to the ranch to bring in the boys from there."

"Heard you laid one on Doc?"

"He had it comin'. Doctorin' them nesters. Doc's small spuds, though. This lawyer is the one what counts."

"Tomorrow mornin' he won't be around," Malone said thickly.

"How's the weather out?"

"Rain bustin' in, now an' then. But she's clearin' in the west. Should be some moon tonight. Hope there's plenty to fin' a Winchester's sights."

"Don't bungle it, Malone."

"I won't. I'm dog-tired, Pete. Mind if I catnap on the bunk a spell? Nothin' I can do until dark, anyway?"

"You're always tired."

Malone left at nightfall, two quarts of whisky stowed in his slicker pockets, riding a midnight-black gelding. First, he left Sagebrush heading south to throw off suspicion. Once clear of town, he swung far west, then headed north toward Sagebrush Creek.

Occasional sheets of rain burst across the prairie, followed by intervals of slow drizzle and dim moonlight. His mind ran over his task: he could recognize Ric Nelson by his long black slicker, the way he rode a saddle, and his grey horse.

Within a mile, rough country reached out and enfolded him. Coulees made dangerous riding; the soil was wet and slippery. In this realm, he rode the side hills and higher reaches.

Nesters, he noticed, had out two guards, each riding a half-circle on west and east sides of wagons. They met a quarter-mile below the wagons, circled back, met south of the wagons, then turned to repeat the process. No grey horse travelled the first shift from eight to ten.

From ten to midnight there was quite a bit of rain. He stationed himself on a high rise opposite the point where guards met before riding north again. The riders met about a hundred yards below him. Usually they talked a short while, then continued their shift.

No grey horse travelled the second shift, either. Malone raised his bottle, but it was empty. He started to throw it away, caught his arm in time, and laid the bottle gently to the mud. It might have broken against a boulder and made a sharp, warning sound.

He lay on his belly, his Winchester .30-30 lying over a sandstone rock. He was miserably cold and wondered if he were drunk. Lately, the invisible line between sobriety and drunkenness could be crossed without his being aware of it.

He laid his whiskery face against the rifle's wet stock and searched for the weapon's sights.

Satisfied, he lowered the carbine, and pulled the cork from his second bottle.

Finally, midnight came. The moon had moments of brilliance now, washing sagebrush with soft mystic yellowness. Nesters changed guards close to the wagons. Within minutes, the new guards rode toward him. His blood leaped, pounding arteries. The west guard rode a grey horse; a black slicker draped his frame. The shyster at last, Malone thought.

The guards met below him, talked a while, then rode back south, and Malone again lowered his rifle. His hands shook slightly; he was angry with them. He had noticed sometimes one guard would reach the meeting point ahead of the other and then wait.

He wanted the lawyer to be alone below when he killed him, the other guard some distance away, for he would have to get out fast; he wanted no rider behind him. Or, if the other guard chased him, he wanted a good distance between them.

He raised his bottle again and waited. His patience was rewarded. The grey horse again appeared. He licked his lips. The lawyer would reach the turning spot quite a distance ahead of his fellow guard.

Now the grey bronc was below him, rider waiting for the other guard. Carefully, slowly, Bat Malone took aim. Thankfully, no clouds obscured the moon. The basin below lay in brightness.

The rider faced him. Malone could not see his face, for the rider's rain helmet was pulled low. Malone let his sights fall into line, aiming for the rider's chest.

Slowly, he squeezed the trigger. The heavy Winchester jumped against his shoulder. The report snarled in his ears. Below him, the grey horse suddenly reared, whinnying in fear, and the rider sagged in his saddle.

Malone leaped to his feet, slapped the rifle to his shoulder, and pumped down another hasty shot, but the horse was down, rider on the bronc's other side, and he knew he had hit the horse, for the animal immediately stopped threshing. He glanced at the other guard.

The guard came on the gallop, screaming to awaken the wagons' occupants, his rifle brandished. Suddenly, his bronc skidded to a stop. The rider threw his rifle to his shoulder. A bullet whammed screamingly from a boulder in front of Malone.

Malone wheeled and ran for his horse. Ten minutes later, sitting a hard-breathing bronc, he was on a mesa, searching the tumbling wilderness below. No black dots followed, and he smiled to himself.

He was sure he had killed the lawyer. After falling from his bronc, the man hadn't moved. He wished he had had time to ride down and check for sure, but the other guard had roared in too fast.

He raised his bottle, killed it, and threw it into the night. He heard it crash against a boulder.

West of the Barbwire

Suddenly, he trembled, fingers jerking violently. He had killed, from ambush, the West's most deadly sin. Self-preservation screamed that he whirl his horse and flee Sagebrush grass. Logic stormed in, killing this wild idea. What if he suddenly disappeared? Sagebrush farmers would add two and two ... and not get five.

Words reeled through his brain: Lawyer Ric Nelson murdered from ambush. Circle Y had to kill Nelson. Malone is missing. Malone ambushed Nelson. Malone is a killer.

Montana Pacific's wires would buzz; Reward dodgers would go up; somewhere the law would arrest him. No safety lay in Sagebrush.

He reloaded his rifle as he spurred south. He wished he had had time to pick up his fired cartridge cases. But that would have been needless; Montana held hundreds of similar Winchesters.

He swayed drunkenly in his saddle upon reaching Sagebrush. He didn't ride into the livery barn. The hostler would see him enter, and word would spread that Nelson had been killed.

"Malone rode into the barn right after this lawyer got ambushed," the hostler would think. "An' Malone's bronc was plumb tuckered out from a hard ride."

Behind Sullivan's was a small barn, which was seldom used and held no horses. He rode in and dismounted. Finally, he got his saddle over the rack, laying his wet saddle blanket across it. He fumbled putting a halter on the horse. The manger held some hay, and the bronc had watered back at a creek.

He left the barn, standing in the alley. He carefully shut the barn door. Unless his cayuse neighed, nobody would know he had been in the barn. He bolted the door behind him.

Carefully, his gaze ran up and down the alley. Nothing stirred on its wet surface. Nobody had seen him ride in. His eyes swung ahead, and he studied the rear of Sullivan's, across the alley.

Blinds were pulled low on the three windows in the office. Around each blind showed a rim of yellow lamplight. Was Pete Brookhaven in that office?

He didn't know and didn't care. He didn't want to see Pete. He just wanted to sleep, but where?

His gaze fell on the wooden stairway leading up the Merc's second story. The lawyer had his office on that second floor. There was a bunk there. He remembered it from the day Circle Y raided Nelson's office. He would sleep there.

He slipped once climbing the wooden stairs and skinned a knee, cursing under his breath. The upstairs door was locked. He backed off, rammed a husky shoulder hard against it, and the door swung open. He entered, carefully closed the door behind him, then lurched down the hall, passing the stairway leading down to the Merc's first floor.

Nelson had knocked him cold down that stairway but Nelson had paid. Soon he slept on Nelson's bed.

Sixteen

A rifle roar woke Ric Nelson instantly. He leaped from his blankets, fully clothed except for boots and spurs. Somebody yelled from inside a wagon: "That was a rifle!"

Ric tensed, listening. Another report smashed the still night air. The shooting came from the north. He heard a man holler for help, then another rifle spoke. Then, there was deadly silence before the wagon train came awake, men spilling to the ground, some almost undressed, but all holding weapons.

Bill Carson gripped Ric's arm. "Circle Y's jumped the guards!" he yelled in Ric's ear.

"Up north," Ric said shortly. He started for his horse, standing a few feet away, saddled and with trailing reins. He stepped on a prickly pear cactus, sharp barbs instantly penetrating. He paid the pain no heed and slammed into the saddle, jerking his Winchester from his saddle holster as he mounted.

His bronc reared, wanting to buck. Ric curbed him savagely, his stockinged feet deep in the stirrups.

"You men spread out!" he ordered. "Don't get beyond a hundred feet from the wagons! Women, to your rifles and short guns. I'll see what happened." His bronc lunged north.

A rider looked out of the moonlight, heading back for the caravan. Ric instantly recognized the guard. "What happened?" he rapped.

"The preacher – He's shot down, Ric. Ambusher on the butte ... I got in one shot ..."

"He dead?"

"I haven't checked. I thought maybe Circle Y would hit the wagons. My woman – my two babies ..."

"Circle Y would hit with riders and guns if they wanted the wagons," Ric rapped. "Circle Y has ambushed only to try to kill one man –"

He spurred ahead, truth smashing in. He had not ridden his horse on his night guard, but Reverend Zachary had ridden a grey.

The minister sat on his dead horse, holding his left shoulder, pain grooving his seamed face. Ric went down, knelt beside him.

"How are you, Reverend?"

"I think my shoulder's not broken. I have control of my arm, although it pains much to move it."

Blood showed on the black slicker. "That ambusher never meant to shoot you," Ric said slowly. "He was after me, but I never rode my grey tonight."

"Better he shot me, than you."

"What do you mean by that?"

"You're more important to these farmers than I."

"There'll be somebody from the wagons soon. We'll take you back and then send a man in for Doc Smith."

"I might be able to ride into Sagebrush."

"No, you don't."

Ric stood up, nerves pounding. Reverend Zachary's grey horse was dead, a splotch of blood on his head behind his ears. "I should hunt down Brookhaven and kill him," Ric said hotly.

"Ric, let caution – not anger – hold sway, please. We are all in one group. We must talk this over carefully before acting, perhaps imprudently."

Ric said slowly, "You're right, Reverend."

Two farmers ran toward them, carrying a makeshift stretcher between them. One was young Bill Carson.

"I feel sure I can walk," the minister said.

Ric shook his head. "Get on that stretcher."

They got the minister in his wagon, Mrs Zachary and Ric carefully removing the preacher's slicker and shirt. Flickering lamplight showed a small but clean wound high on the left shoulder.

Ric climbed out of the wagon. "You go to town and get Doc Smith," he told Bill Carson, "but don't ride in openly. Sneak in from the back so nobody will see you."

"Okay, Ric."

Bill returned with Doc Smith within an hour. Doc rode horseback, his valise tied to the saddle fork. Only Ric and Mrs Zachary were with Doc when he treated the minister's wound. His task finished, Doc crawled outside, where he and Ric had a brief consultation.

"The bullet apparently went a little wide," Doc said. "I got a hunch the ambusher shot for the chest."

"How bad is it?"

"Not too bad, Ric. The reverend had the celestial angels on his side tonight. The bullet nicked the top of the clavicle slightly, then tore flesh as you saw. What I have to watch out for is infection."

"Should we take him to your office?"

Doc shook his heavy head. "He's just as well off here, Ric. My office has but one bed and that high table. I'm not a praying man, but if I were, I would pray for a small hospital."

"You'll probably get one, Doc, if Brookhaven doesn't kill off these farmers. There'll be babies coming and sick people, naturally."

Doc spoke quietly. "Pete Brookhaven's in Sullivan's office. Circle Y uses that for its town office, you know."

Ric nodded, for he had known that.

"Brookhaven and Malone got pretty drunk this afternoon in that office. But I don't know if Malone is there now."

"Malone could have ridden out to do some ambushing," Ric said.

Doc spread pudgy hands. "It could have been other Circle Y men – maybe even Pete Brookhaven himself."

"That bullet was meant for me, Doc."

Doc shrugged. "I'd say so, but you have no proof. Circle Y riders are drifting into town, Ric."

"They're waiting for us to roll in wagons tomorrow," Ric said slowly. "We'll ride into a reception, I'd guess."

"You got women and children here, Ric," Doc pointed out.

"We've talked that over, too," Ric said quietly. "The women won't turn back, Doc. They took a vote among themselves. When wagons roll down Sagebrush's main street, the women and kids will be on them."

Doc frowned and shook his head. He went to his horse, mounted, and plunged his bronc into Sagebrush Creek. Ric watched him leave. Doc's horse never had to swim, for Sagebrush Creek had gone down much in the last few hours. Results of flash floods back in the high reaches had subsided, and the stream was receding.

Doc dropped into Sullivan's for a beer. Circle Y cowboys loafed at the bar, slept in chairs propped against the walls. Three played a lazy game of draw-poker, penny a chip. Rosie tended bar.

"Sullivan?" Doc asked Rosie.

"Upstairs sleepin'. Man has to have some rest, you know. What brings you out this hour?"

The office door opened and Pete Brookhaven came out, hair tousled, eyes bloodshot. He settled at Doc's right, one boot on the brass rail, and ordered whisky, then looked at the medico.

Doc moved discreetly beyond Brookhaven's reach.

"What brings you out this hour of the night, Doc?"

"Was out to the nester wagons. Been an ambush shooting out there. Reverend Zachary stopped a bullet."

Brookhaven's brows rose. "The sky pilot get killed, maybe?"

"Just wounded. Shoulder wound. Few days and he'll be good as new."

Brookhaven looked at his glass of whisky. "Ambush, you say?"

Doc gave particulars. Silence now held the big saloon, men craning necks to hear the doctor's low words. Circle Y men lined the bar, listening. Rosie leaned against the bar, missing nothing.

"The lawyer had the ten-to-midnight guard shift," Doc finished, "but he didn't ride his grey horse. Reverend Zachary rode a grey. The ambusher, I'd guess, made a mistake in identity."

Brookhaven considered that, eyes still on his whisky. "Who do they reckon did it, Doc?"

Doc shrugged. "Not my business, Pete. My job is to cure people. This is a job for the sheriff." Doc looked around the saloon, and noticed Bat Malone was missing. "Where is our new sheriff?"

"Prob'ly down in Sun Prairie, the county seat," Brookhaven said. "The sheriff's office is there."

Doc Smith killed his beer. "Maybe somebody should notify him," he said, and left.

Circle Y men moved back to chairs and the poker game. Brookhaven strode into the office, bottle in hand. He slammed the door hard and paced, lips a tight line. Malone had erred, the idiot! Where was Bat Malone? He was supposed to report here after the ambushing.

Brookhaven raised his bottle. Raw liquor tumbled down his leathery throat. Suddenly the office was lonely, walls seeming to press in, and he returned to the bar.

His gaze ran over his riders, moving from man to man. Should they ride out, rifles raised, and smash into those nester wagons – kill and massacre and burn? Temptation pulled hard, but memory won. Then he remembered that Colorado cowman, now behind bars.

Rosie put a filled glass of whisky before him. He realized he was pretty drunk and that the situation required a sober head. He smashed the whisky to the floor.

"Cook me some bacon and eggs, woman," he snarled.

Circle Y men watched, jerked alert by his hard voice. Rosie said, "Pete, I'm not your squaw."

"Cook, woman," he ordered.

Rosie shrugged, eyes slanted. "Okay, Circle Y," she said.

He turned, found his knees unsteady, and went to the office, saying, 'I'll eat in here, squaw."

He slouched in the chair. Grub would kill the whisky's effect. He would get a few hours' good sleep, too, here on the bunk. He would let the nesters roll wagons into Sagebrush, then personally kill the lawyer. He would stake out Circle Y riders along the street with rifles. With the lawyer dead in the mud, the farmers would be without a leader. They would stare into hostile rifles, a tough cowboy behind each Winchester. Their boots would tremble, their knees turn to water.

Then Circle Y would herd the farmers out of town on foot, making them hike back to the railroad, and Circle Y would own everything the farmers possessed.

Rosie came in with a tray and coffee pot. "You going to knock off your drunk?" she asked cynically.

Brookhaven studied her. "You don't sound happy."

Rosie laughed. "Why should I be? Why should anybody in Sagebrush be happy?"

"It isn't rainin' much. Sometimes the moon even shines."

"You're drunk, Pete."

Brookhaven wolfed down fried ham, six eggs, five pieces of toast, and three fast cups of coffee, feeling drunkenness leave. A good meal always sobered him. He leaned back in his chair, remembering that Malone had not reported in, and he scowled.

Had Malone got cold boots and fled Sagebrush range? He could see no danger to Circle Y if Malone were arrested. It would be his word against Malone's, nothing more. And Malone had plenty of personal reasons for attempting to ambush the lawyer. Hadn't the lawyer knocked him cold, sent him tumbling down the Mercantile back stairs?

Malone would show up later, he felt sure.

He emptied the coffee pot, steadily growing stone sober. Crossing the alley to see if Malone's horse was in the barn never occurred to him, but another thought did.

Tomorrow Circle Y would gunfight the nesters, here on Sagebrush's muddy main drag. How would Susie take it?

Susie could do what she wanted; she didn't count. He thought of Many Feathers, wondering why he was concerned with a Cheyenne squaw's reactions. Susie and Many Feathers were out at the ranch, sleeping, he thought, but here he erred. The girls were at Circle Y, yes, but they were not asleep.

There in the massive living room, the Rochester lamp casting a yellow glow, Susie and Many Feathers sat across the table from old Happy Jimson, an ancient cowboy who had come up the Montana Trail herding Circle Y longhorns with Big Ike Brookhaven.

Happy told them about Reverend Zachary's ambushing. Susie's face paled as she rose, her dressing gown tight around her small waist.

"My poor father," she said slowly. "He's rolling in his grave. Circle Y has sunk so low as ambushing!"

Many Feathers also wore a dressing gown. "Where is Bat Malone?" she asked.

"Malone ain't in Sagebrush," Happy said. "Anyway, he weren't there when I left, an' I left in a hurry. Pete never seen me sneak outa Sullivan's. He know I rode out here, he'd skin me alive."

"He'd have to take my hide first," Susie said.

"I had to tell you, Susie. I dangled you on my knee when you was a baby."

"Please, Happy," Susie said.

"And Pete intends to let the farmers roll their wagons into Sagebrush tomorrow?" Many Feathers asked. "Then he aims to gun down Lawyer Nelson?"

"That's the plan right now," Happy said. "An' Pete might bite off more'n he can chaw. I seen this lawyer match guns with Mack Wilson. Nelson is greased lightnin' with a side arm."

"Please, Happy," Susie repeated.

Happy got up. "I'd best head back fer town. Don't want Pete to miss me."

Susie looked at Many Feathers, whose eyes held tears.

"I can't let him get killed," Many Feathers said chokingly. "I love him, Susie. And I'm sure he loves me."

"And he's my brother," Susie said quietly.

Seventeen

Dawn seeped in through heavy clouds as farmers harnessed wet horses. Ric sat saddle and studied wild Sagebrush Creek, Trudy Carson mounted beside him. Bill Carson would drive the Carson wagon across the stream, which had risen somewhat since Doc Smith had crossed.

"Will it make a horse swim, Ric?"

"Only one way to find out," Ric said. He put his grey bronc into the water. "Here goes."

Water soon came high on the animal's shoulders, but he had to swim only a few feet. Ric crossed back and pulled in beside the girl. He poured water out of his boots. "Seems like I've been pouring water out of boots for years," he said, grinning.

"You've had company."

"Sagebrush can be crossed if each wagon hits the water on a hard run," he said, "and lets momentum carry it across the place where horses have to swim."

"And take women and children across first on horseback?"

"That's the way to do it, Trudy."

"Unless we have wagon trouble, we'll roll into Sagebrush about noon, I would judge. Ric, what waits there for us?"

Ric glanced at her girlish face. She had made her question light, but he detected anxiety in it. This, though, was nothing new; each roll of slow, muddy wheels increased the wagon train's tension.

"Maybe nothing serious, Trudy. Brookhaven might back down."

"Doc said Circle Y has the town full of cowboys. Please promise me, Ric, you won't ride in ahead alone and meet Pete Brookhaven."

Ric breathed deeply, considered. "That ambusher never meant to shoot Reverend Zachary. The preacher took lead intended for me. I'm responsible for his wound."

"Reverend Zachary begged you not to ride in alone, Ric. Your responsibility goes much further than to the minister."

"I see what you mean. In one measure, I'm responsible to all people in this wagon train?"

Tears rimmed her blue eyes. "Ric, let us have hope, please. We are twenty men strong, not including bigger boys and us women. Perhaps when Circle Y sees us roll into town, Circle Y will back down?"

"Brookhaven is a transplanted Texan," Ric said, "and many of his riders came from the Lone Star State punching Texas longhorns onto Montana grass. Texans are a proud, stern people, Trudy."

"Ric, promise you won't ride in alone? Promise, Ric?"

Her voice was rather high-pitched. Ric looked at her lovely face, her red lips, the tears in her prairie-blue eyes. His fingers squeezed hers. "I promise, Trudy."

Relief flooded her face. "Thank you, Ric."

As she turned her horse and rode back to the wagons, Ric admired her pretty back and trim waist.

He thought fleetingly of black-haired Susie Brookhaven, realizing that she was in his thoughts less and less each hour. That was only natural, he rationalized; he had been very busy since his farmers had arrived.

He rode back to the wagons, dismounted, and crawled into Reverend Zachary's wagon. The preacher sat on the wagon's floor, his left arm in a sling, a scowl on his face.

"Ric, I can walk without much pain. I feel so helpless."

Ric glanced at Mrs Zachary. "Doctor Smith didn't say he couldn't walk about," Mrs Zachary said. "The doctor told him just not to overexert himself."

"I'll drive your wagon across," Ric told the preacher. "Okay, I'll help you down to the ground, Reverend."

The minister used his rifle to help balance himself. Soon he was on wet ground, studying the skies. "Looks like we might have some sun today, Mr Nelson."

"Let's hope so. We've had enough rain. You need any help to get on your horse?"

"I can navigate best alone, Mr Nelson. Then I can take my own sweet time."

Soon the minister was in the saddle, his rifle in the saddle scabbard. Farmers were taking their women and children across Sagebrush Creek on horseback, some horses carrying three or four children. When all were on the north side, the farmers climbed on the high spring seats. Ric told the lead wagon: "Use your whip and hit hard and keep on going."

"Hi ya, Flip! Get movin', Dan!"

A night's rest grazing on greening grass had put more life into the horses. The team surged into collars, snapping the wagon ahead. By the time the heavily laden Studebaker smashed into Sagebrush Creek the rig was moving very rapidly. Ric sat saddle, watched, and hoped.

Water splashed in all directions as steel-shod horse hoofs dug gravel. The swift current bashed against the wagon wheels. Now was the spot where Ric's horse had to swim. Momentum carried the wagon across, the horses swimming hard. Within seconds, hoofs again dug into firm gravel footing.

"He made it," Reverend Zachary said happily.

Neither mentioned the trouble waiting in Sagebrush. Another wagon lumbered toward the creek, team running, driver's whip popping. Ric climbed up on Reverend Zachary's wagon. The minister would lead Ric's horse across with Mrs Zachary in the saddle.

Although Ric pounded the horses, the minister's team didn't hit the stream fast enough. The strong current swung the wagon dangerously. Ric thought, at one time, it would overturn, but then hoofs dug firm gravel, pulling the wagon into line. The crossing had been made.

Ric helped Mrs Zachary onto the wagon seat. She would drive the team into Sagebrush. Reverend Zachary looked across the mad stream at the cottonwood logs they had cut.

"They'll be bone dry by fall," he said, "and they'll make excellent firewood. Our work was not wasted."

All wagons crossed without mishap, Ric piloted them south, Trudy riding beside him, Reverend Zachary taking up the rear.

Ric's mind ran ahead to Sagebrush. What awaited him and his farmers there? Gunsmoke and death?

Rain now came in savage, chilly bursts. He saw two riders pushing through the rain, heading for Sagebrush. They were to the west, half a mile away, coming from Circle Y.

Rain made for poor visibility, but he recognized Susie Brookhaven's big buckskin. He didn't know who the other rider was, but it was a small person. Both riders wore rain helmets and slickers. They rode fast, and soon distance and rain hid them.

Wagons moved slowly forward, wheels deep in mud. Ric waved the lead wagon off the trail. The second wagon moved up to break the road. The former lead wagon's team stood panting, tugs slack.

"How many miles to town?" the driver asked Ric.

"About three, Williams."

The driver said nothing, team breathing hard, resting in tugs. Slowly, the wagons inched past until the last one was ahead. Then the driver swung his wagon into the rear of the caravan.

Ric saw a rider coming toward them from town. He spurred forward and met Doc Smith.

Reverend Zachary rode in to make it a trio. Doc Smith said, "Ric, you pull those wagons into Sagebrush, and there'll be trouble. Brookhaven's got Circle Y cowboys lining the main street. Some are hiding in stores to shoot out through windows."

"I expected that," Ric said tonelessly.

"You should send a man south to Fort Union for the U.S. Cavalry. Get horse soldiers in, patrol the town."

"How far is it to Fort Union?" Reverend Zachary asked.

"Thirty miles," Ric said. "We'd be camped here three days before cavalry could come. And I doubt if the commander there would send troops to Sagebrush. He'd have to have orders from Washington."

Reverend Zachary's lips were rigid. Doc Smith's face

was heavy. Ric told about the wires he had sent out from Sun Prairie. A farmer boy had ridden to Sun Prairie last night to check to see if the telegrams had brought answers. None had.

Reverend Zachary finally spoke. "We have in this train a few sick women and many ill children. We have taken a vote, Doctor Smith, and all – men, women, older children – are in favour of driving boldly into Sagebrush."

Doc nodded.

Ric asked, "Did Brookhaven see you ride to warn us, Doc?"

"When I left he stood looking out the window of Sullivan's saloon. He couldn't miss seeing me."

"Is he sober?"

"They tell me he was pretty drunk last night. But he ate heavy and slept in Sullivan's office. I saw him clearly in the window. He looked sober, Ric."

"And where is Malone?"

"I don't know, Ric. I talked to a few Circle Y riders, too. They were pretty tight-lipped, but I got the impression our sheriff had disappeared."

Ric and Reverend Zachary exchanged knowing glances. All weight now lay on the minister's bony shoulders. They were his people. His was the decision.

"We drive into town," the reverend said.

"I'll get everything ready in my office," Doc Smith said. "This will be a busy day for me. I wish you all well, gentlemen."

Ric grinned. "We'll need your wishes, Doc."

Doc turned his horse, rode back under the overcast skies. Wagons ground on, rifles now closer at hand. Trudy Carson now carried her rifle over her saddle.

Ric's feet were wet and miserable from having driven

Reverend Zachary's Studebaker across Sagebrush Creek. He stood on stirrups, looking back at his caravan. Everybody was wet and on edge. He settled in the saddle again, seeing that Sagebrush's buildings loomed ahead, squat, rain-washed, and ugly.

Within thirty minutes, the lead wagon was on Sagebrush's outskirts. Ric, the minister, and Trudy rode in the lead. Ric spoke sharply to Trudy: "Go back to your wagon. This is no place for a woman."

"I'm of age, Ric."

"I dispute that," Ric said. "You're only twenty. Legal age is twenty-one."

"Not for women. Legal age is eighteen."

Ric noticed Reverend Zachary, eyes straight ahead, smiling wryly. Appealing to the minister would be useless.

"All right," Ric said, "but be careful."

"You're the one I hope is careful," Trudy said.

Women and children watched the caravan through rain-streaked windows. Nobody stood in front of the log houses. No dogs barked at the teams; the curs were somewhere, wet and cold, hiding from the rain.

"So this is Sagebrush," a driver said.

Ric said, "This is it."

The rain had momentarily stopped, and the sun was trying to break through. Wagon wheels sucked loudly through mud and water. Now the wagons moved slowly into the block holding Sullivan's saloon, and Circle Y riders lined the two sides of the street.

Ric noticed that the Circle Y men had their gun belts buckled outside slickers, some with pistols riding ahead on hips for easy draws. Each man had a rifle.

The plan was to stop in front of Ira Beeson' Mercantile, for the nesters would take the store over by force, if necessary – and turn it into a temporary camp and hospital.

Reverend Zachary said, "I don't see Pete Brookhaven."

"Nor Malone, either," Ric returned.

The minister's face was inscrutable. He might just as well have been on a pleasure ride. Ric glanced at Trudy, whose face was rather pale, her lips compressed; she stared straight ahead.

Now Ric and the other two riders were opposite the Merc. They pulled their horses to one side.

Ric spoke to the driver of the lead wagon. "Keep moving down the street. Stop when the middle of the train is opposite the store."

"Okay, Ric."

When the train stopped, the last wagon would be even with Sullivan's saloon. Ric guessed that Pete Brookhaven was in Sullivan's. Town women and children had discreetly followed the wagons. They stood at the street's far end, huddled against buildings, watching in silence, women clutching children close to them. Except for the noise of the wagons, Sagebrush lay in tense silence. So far not a Circle Y man had called or hooted.

Ric studied his drivers as they passed. Each man had his rifle close; each had a stern, unrelenting face. Children lay flat inside wagons, where bullets would have less chance of hitting them. Ric knew fear clutched the children.

Some women rode on the high seats with their husbands, rifles across their laps; others peered out rear flaps, rifles in hand. Within a few minutes, this muddy street might hold blazing guns; men and women and children might die.

Ric's throat was bone-dry. His nerves wanted to jump, but he held them under stern control. Now the wagons halted, their wheels stopping instantly. Now too, Pete Brookhaven strode from Sullivan's, circling the rear wagon.

Ric said, "He wants me, Reverend."

He dismounted, boots sinking in the mud, and walked toward Brookhaven. His gun was belted outside his slicker, the dark handle moist with rain. Now Brookhaven cleared the last wagon and stood wide-legged, watching Ric advance.

Pete Brookhaven wore no slicker. Rain pelted against his red silk shirt. His calfskin Justin boots were solid in Montana mud, his .45 riding slightly forward on his hip, holster tied down tightly to his thigh.

Ric's boots slopped mud. Ric kept his eyes locked with Brookhaven's. Brookhaven was stone-sober, although his eyes were slightly bloodshot. He said nothing, nor did Ric.

Ric stopped twenty feet from Brookhaven, standing firmly, his hand close to his gun. He worked his fingers slightly, for they were stiff from the cold.

Circle Y cowboys watched from the sidewalk and hiding places. Farmers watched from high wagon seats. A woman screeched from a wagon, her highpitched squeal cutting the still air.

Brookhaven's lips moved. His words slithered across space. "I'm goin' to kill you, shyster. And if a nester lifts a short gun or rifle, he's dead in his wagon seat."

Ric felt sagging hopelessness. He had prayed this could be settled without gunsmoke. Now he realized his prayers had been wasted.

"Come at me, Brookhaven," he coldly invited.

For one tense second time stood still. The sun

stopped, and the clouds remained motionless. Hearts stopped beating.

Ric found himself in a gunman's crouch, his body pulled sidewise and down, to offer a smaller target. Brookhaven, too, had assumed this pose, eyes locked with Ric's.

Ric fastened his gaze on Brookhaven's right shoulder. When it dipped, the Circle Y man would be going for his gun.

Nervousness had passed, and his muscles were under control. Pete Brookhaven's right shoulder dipped. Ric's palm slapped down, then froze, gun half-drawn. Pete Brookhaven never finished his draw. The woman's harsh voice had stopped him:

"Pull that gun, Brother, and I'll shoot it from your hand!"

Brookhaven was a statue, gun drawn slightly. He turned slowly to look at his sister, who had barged from between two buildings. Susie's lips quivered, but her Winchester was steady.

Now another woman said sharply, "And that goes for you, too, Nelson!"

Ric looked left. Another young woman had come out from between two wagons. He had never seen her before. She was small and dark-skinned. At first, he judged her to be Spanish, then realized she was an Indian. Her rifle covered him unwaveringly.

The Indian girl kept her dark eyes on Ric, but she spoke to Pete Brookhaven. "I love you, Pete. You're my life. I don't know if you love me or don't. But I do know this – you're not dying in this mud because of an unrelenting pride!"

Pete Brookhaven tore his eyes from his beautiful sister and looked at the dark-skinned girl. Ric saw tears well into the girl's eyes. Now, lips quivering slightly, she looked at Pete Brookhaven.

Brookhaven looked at her, then took his eyes from her. He noted the Circle Y cowpunchers – lined, armed, and ready. He looked at the nesters' wagons, then back at the girl.

Ric watched Brookhaven's handsome face. The man's grey eyes were filled with conflicting emotions. For one raw moment, Ric thought that Brookhaven would complete his draw, despite the rifles.

Suddenly, Brookhaven sighed. He said quietly, "Many Feathers."

"I love you, Pete," the girl repeated. "You can beat me, Pete, you can drive me back to my reservation. But if you beat me – and make me go – I'll be happy, for you'll still be alive."

Ric looked at Susie. Her eyes held tears, but her rifle was unwavering. He let his gun hand fall.

From behind Ric came Reverend Zachary's deep voice. "I thank you, God, for the good of womanhood."

Pete Brookhaven took his eyes from Many Feathers. He looked at his gunmen lining the street. His grey eyes fastened on Ric.

His lips moved slowly. "I can't lift my gun, Nelson. You were right all the time. I can't fight progress. Circle Y cattle will move back into the hills where a plough can't take over."

Ric felt his muscles loosen.

"Circle Y pulls back. Your farmers will not be disturbed."

The bullet smashed into Ric, then. He went sidewise as though slugged with a sledge and landed on one knee in the mud. He thought at first he had been hammered from behind. Then he heard the roar of the rifle and realized he had been shot high in the left thigh. Excruciating pain surged through him.

Then he saw the rifle. The barrel jutted from the window of his office over the Merc. He could not identify the man behind the Winchester. He shot by pure instinct, fanning the hammer. He put six shots into the window.

He heard the man's high-pitched scream over the roar of his gun. Ric's .45 was empty. Blood ran down his leg. He stared at the window.

First, the rifle fell and clattered on the plank walk. Then the man bent in the middle and fell through the open window. Ric recognized Bat Malone.

"So that's where he hid," Brookhaven said.

Malone crashed to the sidewalk and never moved. Ric tried to get to his feet, but daylight swam before his eyes; the faces of Susie and Trudy wavered.

Suddenly the street was filled with mounted men. Horses reared and whinnied. Circle Y was hitting! No, that was not logical. All Circle Y men had been on foot. They could never have got horses in this short time.

Then he saw that the riders wore U.S. Cavalry uniforms. A roan horse stopped, and a man knelt beside him. Ric looked into the face of the stranger he had talked to yesterday – the one Bill Carson said had doubled back.

"Colonel J. V. Henderson reporting, Mr Nelson. From Fort Union, sir. We got here a bit too late, I would judge."

Ric stared, not comprehending.

"Your telegram to Washington was heeded, Mr Nelson. Your St Louis company and Montana Pacific Railroad also put pressure on Washington."

Ric nodded through his pain.

"The Territorial governor also acted."

Ric said, "Uncle Sam brands his horses on the hoof. Your horse bore a Bar T S iron."

"I borrowed that horse, sir, to throw off suspicions, just as I was out of uniform. I wanted to scout this trouble thoroughly first."

"I see," Ric said.

"I have warrants here for the arrests of Mr Bat Malone and Mr Peter Brookhaven. Shall I serve them, sir?"

The faces of Reverend Zachary and Doc Smith swam before Ric. He heard Doc Smith say, "Malone is dead. You'll not arrest him. But Ric is wounded, you idiots, an' he needs ..."

Ric heard no more.

He came to in Doc Smith's office on the high table. He and Doc Smith were alone.

"How long have I been out?" Ric asked.

Doc Smith grinned. "Almost an hour. I helped with a little ether. You'll be laid up for a week or so. You're young; you heal fast. No bones broken, but Malone's lead really gouged a hunk out of your thigh."

Ric looked down. His thigh was heavily bandaged. Doc Smith covered him with a sheet.

"There are three lovely girls outside who want to see you," Doc Smith said, adding, "you lucky young dog!"

Ric grinned. "One at a time."

First came tear-stained Many Feathers. "I keep house for Pete Brookhaven," she said slowly. "I love Pete, and Pete now loves me."

Ric touched her hand. "I thank you, Many Feathers. You possibly saved my life. Pete might have killed me."

"The Cavalry is taking Pete to Fort Union. Colonel Henderson will keep Pete there some time. Pete admits sending out Malone to ambush. Reverend Zachary dropped that charge against Pete."

"The reverend is a forgiving man."

She smiled and kissed his cheek lightly. "I go now to Fort Union with Pete. But I shall see you when I return."

Susie Brookhaven entered and took his hand. "I am not teaching here," she said simply. "I am returning to California."

"I shall miss you."

"Good-bye, Ric."

She kissed him full on the lips and left hurriedly.

Trudy Carson came in next. "Doc, is he hurt bad?"

"He'll live," Doc Smith said, grinning.

Trudy stood uncertain, looking down on Ric. Her red lips quivered, her prairie-blue eyes held tears. Ric had a sudden crazy thought. When she became a grandmother, she would be as beautiful as she was today.

His arm went around her waist and pulled her close. Neither saw a smiling Doc Smith slip out into the hall and silently close the door. Reverend Zachary stood there.

"May I see him soon?" the reverend asked.

Doc Smith shook his head. "You won't see him for quite a while, Reverend," he said.

REAL WEST
The true life adventures of America's greatest frontiersmen.

THE LIFE OF KIT CARSON by John S.C. Abbott. Christopher "Kit" Carson could shoot a man at twenty paces, trap and hunt better than the most skilled Indian, and follow any trail — even in the dead of winter. His courage and strength as an Indian fighter earned him the rank of brigadier general of the U.S. Army. This is the true story of his remarkable life.
_2968-5 $2.95

THE LIFE OF BUFFALO BILL by William Cody. Strong, proud and courageous, Buffalo Bill Cody helped shape the history of the United States. Told in his own words, the real story of his life and adventures on the untamed frontier is as wild and unforgettable as any tall tale ever written about him.
_2981-2 $2.95

LEISURE BOOKS
ATTN: Customer Service Dept.
276 5th Avenue, New York, NY 10001

Please add $1.25 for shipping and handling of the first book and $.30 for each book thereafter. All orders shipped within 6 weeks via postal service book rate.

Canadian orders must reflect Canadian price, when indicated, and must be paid in U.S. dollars through a U.S. banking facility.

Name _____
Address _____
City _____State _____ Zip _____

I have enclosed $ _____in payment for the books checked above.

Payment <u>must</u> accompany all orders.   ❑Please send a free catalogue.

Get more for your money with special Double Editions of the wildest Adult Series around!

SPUR

More gunslinging gangs, more wild women, more non-stop Western action!

SPUR DOUBLE EDITION: ROCKY MOUNTAIN VAMP / CATHOUSE KITTEN by Dirk Fletcher. In Rocky Mountain Vamp, while on the trail of a gang of counterfeiters, Spur McCoy helped a woman find the men who brutally murdered her husband. In Cathouse Kitten, Spur went to Abiline, Kansas, to search for a missing Secret Service agent. Instead he found himself accused of rustling cattle and murdering cowhands.
__2740-2 $3.95

SPUR DOUBLE EDITION: INDIAN MAID / MONTANA MINX by Dirk Fletcher. In Indian Maid, someone was determined to stop McCoy from learning who was selling contraband weapons to the Sioux, and his only hope for survival was an Indian beauty, who asked for nothing in return but Spur's love. In Montana Minx, Spur was sent to Montana to investigate the massacre of a stagecoach full of people, and soon he was caught in the middle of an all-out range war.
__2856-5 $3.95

LEISURE BOOKS
ATTN: Customer Service Dept.
276 5th Avenue, New York, NY 10001
Please add $1.25 for shipping and handling of the first book and $.30 for each book thereafter. All orders shipped within 6 weeks via postal service book rate.
Canadian orders must reflect Canadian price, when indicated, and must be paid in U.S. dollars through a U.S. banking facility.

Name _____
Address _____
City _____ State _____ Zip _____
I have enclosed $ _____ in payment for the books checked above.
Payment <u>must</u> accompany all orders.   ❑Please send a free catalogue.

SPEND YOUR LEISURE MOMENTS WITH US.

Hundreds of exciting titles to choose from—something for everyone's taste in fine books: breathtaking historical romance, chilling horror, spine-tingling suspense, taut medical thrillers, involving mysteries, action-packed men's adventure and wild Westerns.

SEND FOR A FREE CATALOGUE TODAY!

Leisure Books
Attn: Customer Service Department
276 5th Avenue, New York, NY 10001